DEFENSELESS

"What are you afraid of, Sonya? Love? Companionship? I assure you these things are nothing to fear."

Sonya attempted to laugh at his observation but failed. Her voice cracked, and she knew then she was caught. She turned around to face him, knowing he could see the tears gathering in her eyes. "It's been my experience, Mr. Hamilton, that a woman's love is something very fragile. Unfortunately it's also something too many women give away carelessly. I don't plan to make that same mistake. I fought for too long to prove that I define my happiness. I don't need or want to depend on anyone else to give me what I am capable of doing myself."

Dwayne's face softened under the tranquil glow cascading through the window. "I know you've been hurt, Sonya." He reached up and gently began to caress her cheek. "Don't let the ignorance of a couple of men rule your heart against the rest of us."

"Are you considering yourself in a different class than Curtis, Mr. Hamilton?" Sonya wanted to pull away but couldn't.

Dwayne smiled. "I think you already know the answer to that question."

SENSUAL AND HEARTWARMING
ARABESQUE ROMANCES FEATURE
AFRICAN-AMERICAN CHARACTERS!

BEGUILED (0046, $4.99)
by Eboni Snoe
After Raquel agrees to impersonate a missing heiress for just one night, a daring abduction makes her the captive of seductive Nate Bowman. Across the exotic Caribbean seas to the perilous wilds of Central America . . . and into the savage heart of desire, Nate and Raquel play a dangerous game. But soon the masquerade will be over. And will they then lose the one thing that matters most . . . their love?

WHISPERS OF LOVE (0055, $4.99)
by Shirley Hailstock
Robyn Richards had to fake her own death, change her identity, and forever forsake her husband, Grant, after testifying against a crime syndicate. But, five years later, the daughter born after her disappearance is in need of help only Grant can give. Can Robyn maintain her disguise from the ever present threat of the syndicate—and can she keep herself from falling in love all over again?

HAPPILY EVER AFTER (0064, $4.99)
by Rochelle Alers
In a week's time, Lauren Taylor fell madly in love with famed author Cal Samuels and impulsively agreed to be his wife. But when she abruptly left him, it was for reasons she dared not express. Five years later, Cal is back, and the flames of desire are as hot as ever, but, can they start over again and make it work this time?

DEFENSELESS

Adrianne Byrd

Pinnacle Books
Kensington Publishing Corp.
http://www.pinnaclebooks.com

I wish to dedicate this book to Lenny Vaccaro, always remember the Nile.
To Howard Jackson, for a new friendship I will always cherish. And to Kathy and Charles Alba and Tina and William Gainey, for being my best friends and loving me no matter what.

PINNACLE BOOKS are published by

Kensington Publishing Corp.
850 Third Avenue
New York, NY 10022

First Printing: November, 1997
10 9 8 7 6 5 4 3 2 1

Printed in the United States of America

Chapter One

"Why can't I see my sister?" Sonya looked past Curtis's towering frame.

"Because she's busy," he answered, irritated.

"Move out of my way, Curtis."

Curtis grinned. "Perhaps you should go home, Sonya. I'll have Laura call you later."

Sonya's gaze locked with that of her demented brother-in-law. She matched his eye-warning with one of her own. She hated this man. What her sister saw in him, she'd never know. True he had good looks, but he also had the devil's eyes and personality. She felt sure his midnight complexion and flashy white teeth sent plenty of hearts fluttering, including her sister's.

"Let me pass, Curtis. Or do you prefer I call the police?"

Curtis only smiled at her weak threat. "And what will you tell them? That your brother-in-law refuses to let you talk to your sister? That ought to send them flying over here. Take my advice and go home, Sonya."

Sonya ignored his warning and threw her entire weight into him, knocking him off guard and enabling her to get past. As she passed the overturned furniture leading the way into the

living room, she feared what she might find. The tiny hairs on
the back of her neck stood at attention. Her breathing became
shallow as she saw small drops of blood throughout the hallway.

"Laura . . . Laura?" Sonya's voice trembled with fear. When
she finally saw her sister crouched on the floor, her heart broke.
"My God, Laura, what did he do to you?"

Laura continued picking up the broken furniture from the
floor, ignoring her sister. Sonya stood there. No words came.
Laura looked as if she had been in a war, with the many cuts
and bruises across her arms and legs. Her shirt was ripped so
bad that it seemed to stay on by a thin thread.

Sonya couldn't make out her sister's face, so she called to
her weakly. "Laura . . . Laura, honey, please look at me."

Laura's hands stopped. She hesitated for a moment, then
looked up at Sonya with tear-soaked eyes.

Sonya gasped at Laura's bruised face and swollen lips. She
ran to comfort her sister.

Curtis entered the room to see the two sisters huddled together
in the middle of the floor. He made an undistinguishable sound,
then left them alone, slamming the front door.

Sonya gently eased Laura out of her arms, then searched her
face for answers to the questions she feared to ask.

"Please . . . Please don't, Sonya. I already know what you're
going to say," Laura whispered.

Sonya let out a frustrated sigh, then the room grew loud with
the silence.

Laura pushed herself up, a painful expression crossed her
features.

This was all Sonya needed to witness before she exploded
with built-up emotions. "When are you going to learn? He's
going to seriously hurt you one of these days. Pretty soon
you're not going to be able to hide your black eyes and broken
noses. What are you going to do then?"

"Sonya, please."

"Don't 'Sonya, please,' me. This is serious. No man should
ever raise his hand to a woman. You were not put on this earth
to be his punching bag!"

"Look, Curtis is just . . . going through some things, that's all. He doesn't know who he can trust anymore."

Sonya threw her hands up. But she couldn't let it end like this. "Laura, I love you. You know that. But I'll be damned if I'm going to let that man continue to pound on you to vent out his frustrations. All the trouble that he's in right now is his fault. Not yours. And if there's any justice in this world, the judge will put him away and throw away the damn key!"

"Stop it, Sonya! You just don't understand. He's trying really hard to . . . to make this marriage work. He just needs some time to get his head together, and everything will be fine. I just know it."

"That's bull, and you damn well know it. You've only been married eight months, and before all his troubles started he was pounding on you. What was his excuse then?"

"That's a lie!"

"Come on, Laura. This is me you're talking to. I knew what was going on. Everybody knew what was going on. Mama used to pull these same excuses you are. She had an accident, or she fell down the stairs. Didn't you learn from her that this behavior is unacceptable?"

"You don't know about men, Sonya. They don't hit you unless you've done something to provoke them. All men are that way."

"The more you talk, the more nauseated I get. Who told you that? Curtis?"

"I knew you wouldn't understand. Curtis loves me. Can't you at least see things from his point of view?"

"You're serious, aren't you? He has you completely brainwashed. Love, true love, shouldn't hurt. Not physically anyway. And a man should respect you enough to never raise his fist to you. He should—"

"Oh, please, Sonya. You're spinning Cinderella tales. People don't live happily ever after anymore. This is the real world with real problems, and I have to stand by my man through thick and thin. I know that this looks bad. But trust me, all this will blow over. I know Curtis."

"Are you asking me to stand by and watch him kill you? I know you love Curtis. That's not the question. The question is, does Curtis love you? I can't continue to save you."

Laura turned angry eyes toward Sonya. "I don't remember anyone asking you to save me, Sonya. You stand there casting judgment on the world. You—with your Harvard degree. You—with your own advertising company." Laura's voice thickened with bitterness.

"No one ever passes inspection with you. Well, I might not have your education and fancy job, but at least I have a man. When you leave your big office at night, who do you go home to? Who's there to share your so-called success? No one! You go home to that big empty house with no one to love. I married Curtis for richer or poorer, in sickness and in health."

"Till death do you part? Laura, you need help. Take a good look around you. I might not have a man right now, but that's because I refuse to take whatever is just handed to me. When I settle down, it will be with someone who wants to be with me for me. Someone that respects my mind as well as my body. That doesn't make this a fairy tale. It's just common sense. This whole relationship revolves around Curtis's needs. What about your needs. Don't you count?"

Laura began to cry again. "Oh, Sonya. I just don't know what to do. I mean ... I'm scared. He'll never let me leave him."

"Finally, the truth. Did Curtis threaten you if you left him?"

Laura nodded. "He said that he'll kill me if I ever leave him."

"Then we'll go to the police. We can have some kind of restraining order filed against him. I won't let him harm you, Laura. Come home with me. I'll protect you."

"He'll come after me, Sonya. I know it. He'll never let me go."

"Don't you trust me?"

Laura nodded.

"Then come with me. I've always taken care of you before, haven't I?"

She nodded again.

"Then come with me."

"She's not going anywhere!" Curtis bellowed from behind them.

Both Laura and Sonya jumped at the sound of Curtis's thundering voice.

Sonya turned to confront Curtis, who stood at the entrance of the living room with a bouquet of flowers in his hands.

"Laura, baby. I came back to apologize. You know I didn't mean to hurt you. You know this, right?" Curtis began his routine excuse.

Sonya opened her mouth to say something, but her sister immediately flew into her husband's outstretched arms, forgiving him once again. Sonya watched helplessly as husband and wife hugged each other. She held Curtis's look of triumph and knew she had lost another round to him.

Snatching up her purse, Sonya stormed out of the house. She could hear her sister apologizing profusely to her husband. In her heart she knew Curtis would continue what he started before the night was through.

Sonya stepped out of the house and into the rain, grateful that it would hide the tears that flowed down her cheeks. *Why can't I get her to see reason? What kind of hold does Curtis have over her?*

Sonya walked to her car slowly. She didn't care about her jade silk suit plastering against her body. She didn't care about her matching pumps filling with water. She opened the door to her black Lexus and slipped into the firm leather seat.

Hurt and confused, she continued to stare at the house while huge pellets of rain drummed against the windshield. Only when she felt her bottom lip tremble from the cold and wet clothes that clung to her body, did she start up the car and head for home.

She fought against a series of emotions during the long drive. She swore never to speak to her sister again, then began planning ways to kidnap Laura from her husband. *There has to be some way I can help her.*

Sonya entered through the gate and drove up the long, curving driveway to her eight-bedroom estate that sat in the middle of ten acres.

She parked the car right in front. It would save her time in the morning from going all the way to the east wing of the house to the garage. Right now, she wanted to get out of her wet clothes.

She pushed open the bronze-and-glass framed door, relieved to be home. She rushed across the granite-marbled floor, stripping out of her clothes as she climbed the long spiral staircase. Her sister's words seemed to echo loudly throughout the house: *Who do you go home to?* The words hurt her more than she cared to admit. It didn't matter that she owned this large home. Her family meant the world to her, though all she had left was her sister and mother.

She opened her bedroom door to see her three walls of ceiling-high windows dark and cloud filled. She watched as the rain poured down over her bedroom windows.

A flash of lightning brightened her room for a moment, then it fell dark again.

Stripping the rest of her wet clothes from her body, Sonya threw them on her cold floor. She felt drained. She needed to relax and then think over the situation with Laura.

She walked naked to her accompanying dual granite and marble bath. She ran a hot bath and poured in more than a generous amount of scented oils to soothe her tired body. When she finally stepped into the hot caressing water, the anxieties of the day drained out of her.

She refused to think about all the discouraging reports lying on her desk at work. She absently twirled the gold coin necklace. It was a gift from Laura on her birthday. An extraordinary mint, she mused. *I wonder where she found such a beautiful coin.* She closed her eyes and refused to think about the chaotic scene she had just left at her sister's house. She tried to concentrate on relaxing.

* * *

Sonya woke up shivering. The bubbles had vanished from the tub and the water was cold. *I must have dozed off.* She heard it again. *The phone's ringing.* Splashing her way out of the tub, Sonya hurried to the phone.

"Hello?" Sonya answered, trying to get her towel wrapped around herself.

"Son—Sonya?" came the trembling voice from the other end.

"Laura? Laura, honey, is this you?" Sonya felt a strong sense of dread creep through her bones.

"Oh, Sonya . . . I . . ."

"Laura, what's wrong? Why are you crying?"

"Sonya, I need you to come over. Please, I need you." Laura's voice cracked.

"Why, what's wrong?"

"It's Curtis. I . . . I think I killed him."

Chapter Two

Sonya hung up from Laura after she promised to get there as fast as she could. Her hands shook uncontrollably while she searched through her dresser for something to put on. She jerked on the first pair of pants and shirt she came across. There was no time to do anything to her frizzy hair. It really didn't matter since she was about to run back into the rain, she reasoned. She grabbed her purse from the floor as she ran out of the room. Halfway down the staircase, she realized she didn't have any shoes on and ran back, taking the stairs two at a time.

She flew through her bedroom door and into her walk-in closet where she frantically tore through massive pairs of shoes. She picked a pair of tennis shoes and wiggled her feet into them. She wore no socks but didn't care. Again she ran out of her room and down the stairs.

Sonya dashed to her car, cursing at the hard pelting rain that drenched her instantly. "Damn, where are my keys?" Sonya muttered, fumbling through her small purse. She went through her purse twice before she found them. She jumped into her car and started the engine almost in the same motion. "Calm down, Sonya," she told herself. But it was easier said than done. *Laura killed Curtis? This has to be some kind of cruel joke. Laura couldn't have hurt anyone.*

Sonya sped out of the long driveway and onto the dark road. Laura said that she was too terrified to call the police and begged Sonya to hurry. Her thoughts were being pulled in a hundred different directions as various scenarios played across her mind—each one worse than the last.

Sonya turned on her high beams. The rain made it impossible to see. However, her foot continued to nail the accelerator to the floor.

Sonya's headlights shadowed something lying in the middle of the road. She swerved to her left, then screamed at seeing an approaching car. She tried to swing back into the right lane. Yet it was too late, her car began to hydroplane across the wet asphalt.

Dwayne watched in horror as the sleek Lexus spun out of control, then stopped without flipping over the side of the small road. The Lexus's horn blared as Dwayne saw the passenger's body slump over the steering wheel. *Was he dead?*

Dwayne hastily turned to park his car in front of the Lexus. He jumped out of his vehicle and ran to the driver's door and tried to open it. It was locked. He tried the other doors. They were all locked, too. *I have to break the glass.* Running back to his car, he scrambled to find his crowbar in the trunk. He smashed the backseat window of the Lexus and reached his hand around to open the driver's door. He then heard moaning sounds coming from the driver. *Good, he wasn't dead.*

He jerked open the door just as the driver was coming to. The driver lifted his body off the car's horn, and Dwayne was momentarily shocked to discover the driver was a woman. Even with her wet hair plastered to her head, and the outrageous green and orange attire, Dwayne was spell-bound.

"Ma'am, are you all right?" he asked, leaning into the car to see if there were any bruises. When her eyelids fluttered open, Dwayne swore he was staring at the closest thing to a black Venus. He found himself fascinated by the sandy brown hair, drooping a few inches past her shoulders. Her caramel skin looked soft enough to touch. He glanced at her small nose and inviting lips and felt a surging heat wash over him.

Dwayne looked back into the driver's eyes and took a retreating step at the anger that was reflected there.

"What in the hell did you do to my window?" Sonya demanded as she turned to see the rain soak the back carpet and form tiny puddles in the leather seats.

"I was only trying to help, ma'am," Dwayne answered, his irritation evident in his voice.

"Help? How? By destroying my car?"

"Now, look here! You were the one that was driving like a bat out of hell. You could've killed us!" Dwayne watched the woman pale even from the dim light given off from his car.

"I have to go." She said, dully and turned back to start her car. It wouldn't start. She pumped the accelerator hoping the engine would kick in. It didn't work. She tried again.

"Ma'am, you're flooding your engine."

Sonya stopped and cast angry eyes at him.

"I suppose you're going to blame me for that also," He accused, his own hostility mounting.

Sonya clenched her mouth shut and reached over to slam her car door.

Dwayne stared at the driver. Her ungratefulness agitated him. *I have better things to do than to stand here in the pouring rain and let this woman treat me like this.*

Dwayne stormed back to his car but didn't bother to start it. His conscience wouldn't allow him to leave a woman stranded no matter how upset he got.

Sonya watched as the stranger departed. Was his leaving suppose to scare her? She could care less if he left. She continued to watch him open the door to a beautiful golden luxury car. She wasn't sure what type of car it was from this angle, but it resembled a Lincoln. When he didn't attempt to start his car, Sonya intended on giving him a look of indifference. Yet when their eyes met, they were both held prisoners by something powerful. Sonya felt the intensity of his dark gray eyes. Handsome, she thought. His mature features appeared to have been created by an artist's skilled hands. There was a sense of familiarity about him.

Sonya realized she was gawking at the stranger and jerked her head away, chastising herself for her bold behavior. She reached and turned the ignition. It started. She gave a quick prayer of thanks, and then without a backward glance, drove away from the parked Lincoln.

Thirty minutes later, Sonya arrived at her sister's house. She was blinded by the flashing blue lights that lit up the small subdivision. She parked behind an Atlanta police car and jumped out and ran toward the house. But she was quickly grabbed by one of the officers at the scene.

"Sorry, ma'am. This a restricted area."

"This is my sister's house. I have to see my sister!"

"I'm sorry, ma'am. But I can't let you through."

"Like hell, you can't!" Sonya pushed past the officer only to find herself jerked back.

"I understand your situation, ma'am—but if you try to go on this property, I will have to arrest you."

"Arrest me? You can't arrest me—"

"What seems to be the problem, ma'am?" another officer cut in.

"I want to see my sister," Sonya answered, lowering her voice.

"Your sister? Are you Sonya Walters, ma'am?"

"Yes, I am."

"I'm Sergeant Freeman. Do you mind if I ask you a few questions?"

"Where is my sister?" Sonya ignored the sergeant's question.

"We've already taken her downtown for questioning."

Sonya turned to run back to her car when Sergeant Freeman grabbed her arm. Sonya turned back and flashed him an angry glare. He released her arm.

"Sorry, ma'am. But I was hoping to ask you a few questions."

"Are you arresting me?" she asked coldly.

"Well, no, ma'am," he answered.

"Then I have nothing to say to you."

Sonya left the crime scene and focused on getting down Peachtree Street where the Atlanta Police Department was located. It was nearly 3 A.M. when she arrived. She entered the station and found her way to the front desk, where she rudely interrupted the officer talking on the phone. "I'm here to see my sister, Laura Durden."

The heavy officer ignored Sonya's interference and continued his conversation.

"Excuse me! I want to see Laura Durden!"

The officer held his hand over the phone and looked at her for the first time. "I'll be with you in just a moment, ma'am."

Sonya straighten her shoulders and tapped her foot impatiently. By the time the officer hung the phone she was entertaining thoughts of strangling him.

"Now, may I help you?" The officer rolled his eyes up to her.

Sonya clenched her hands into tight fists, trying to control her anger. "Yes, I want to see Laura Durden, please."

The officer scrolled his plump finger down a list in front of him, then shook his head. "I'm sorry, ma'am. She is being questioned and arraigned in the morning. You won't be able to see her until tomorrow."

"Tomorrow!" Sonya asked astonished.

"Yes, ma'am. I'm sorry."

She turned away disappointed but immediately began thinking of different avenues to help her sister. She needed to find a good lawyer. And she knew just the person to see.

Sonya arrived at the Valley Apartments at 4 A.M. and found her way to Sharon Ellis's apartment. She knew she was asking a lot, showing up her friend's apartment at this time of night.

She pounded on the door and waited a moment. When no answer came, she rang the doorbell a few times. *This will wake her up*. Still there was no answer and Sonya feared that she wasn't home. She banged on the door again.

"I'm coming!" came the irritated voice on the other side.

The door swung open, and Sharon stood glaring at Sonya. "Please say that you drove all the way over here to tell me I have tomorrow off. Or shall I say today?"

"May I come in? I need to talk to you."

Sharon sighed and stepped back, allowing Sonya entrance.

"I need your help," Sonya began. "It's Laura."

Sharon's eyes widened at the sight of water tracking across her Asian rug. "Oh no, Miss Thang. Twitch back over here and take off those wet shoes before you ruin my expensive rug. Let me get you a towel." Sharon ran down her narrow hallway and returned with a pink towel for Sonya to dry off with.

Sonya quickly dried off and returned the towel. "Now may I talk to you?"

"If it's about your hardheaded sister, I don't think I want to hear it."

"She's in trouble, Sharon."

"You woke me for that? What happened now? Did Curtis break her nose or black both her eyes again." she asked sarcastically.

"She killed Curtis."

Sharon's honey-colored face paled. "You're joking."

"No. She called me at my home and told me she thought she had killed Curtis. By the time I made it to her house, the police had arrived and arrested her."

"My God, Sonya. What are you going to do?"

"I don't know. I need to find her a good lawyer. I remember you said that your brother was a criminal lawyer. Is he any good?"

"He's very good. I'll call him first thing in the morning for you."

"Can't you call him now?"

"Sonya, it's four in the morning."

"I'm aware of what time it is, Sharon. Please, will you call him?"

Sharon gave an exasperated sigh. "You're lucky my husband is out of town because I would've had your rude butt thrown out of here by now."

"Just call, Sharon."

"I'm calling. I'm calling."

Sonya rewarded her with a grateful smile as Sharon walked into the kitchen and dialed her brother's number.

"Hello, brother dear, it's me Sharon. Yes, I know what time it is. I need a favor."

Sonya turned and walked away, giving Sharon privacy to talk to her brother. She entered Sharon's pearl and peach living room. She twirled her golden coin absently as she studied the various pictures of Sharon and her husband, James.

The pictures reflected a charming couple hopelessly in love, Sonya thought. She picked up one of the many silver picture frames and studied the beautiful couple's wedding pose. Looking at the happy couple didn't calm her any, so she placed the small frame back among the others.

"Okay, kiddo. My brother may never speak to me again, but I got him to hear your case first thing this morning at seven. That was the best I could do."

Sonya smiled. "Thank you."

Sharon walked over and hugged her depressed friend. "You want to talk? I can make a us a fresh pot of coffee," she offered.

"No, I don't want to trouble you any more than I have," Sonya answered with a fading smile.

"It's no trouble. In fact, I don't want you driving back in that rain."

"Sharon, I—"

Sharon held up her hand silencing Sonya. "I don't want to hear it. You will sleep in the spare bedroom, and I'll get you something to put on. Anything will be better than what you got on."

Sonya looked down and noticed her attire for the first time.

She wore a pair of forest-green sweatpants, brown sneakers, and an orange T-shirt. "I guess I won't be posing for the cover of *Essence* anytime soon."

"I guess not. Let me get you something to wear and turn the bed down for you." Sharon exited the room, and Sonya slumped down on the peach leather sofa. Despair swept through her body, leaving her feeling drained.

She reflected on the night's events and wished that she could have done things differently. She should have forced Laura to come home with her or called the police herself. Then she thought of her careless actions tonight. She didn't remember locking her front door or turning on her security system. She placed herself in danger by speeding down the narrow street, then scolding that handsome man who was only trying to help her. Sonya sat up at that thought. *Why did I use the word "handsome"?* She remembered the man's short-cropped hair, neatly groomed, while sparkling drops of water caressed his black Adonis features.

"Here we go!" Sharon swept into the room holding a long pink nightshirt with a large fuzzy teddy bear decorating the front.

Sonya jumped up from the sofa, blushing from the vivid picture her mind had painted.

"What's wrong?" Sharon asked.

"Nothing."

"So why are you blushing?"

"Forget it."

"Okay," Sharon said, shaking her head.

Sonya dressed quickly. After she was settled, she went on to tell Sharon of the night's events—except for the near car collision. Sharon listened with wide, disbelieving eyes.

Sonya finished and began to massage the temples of her head. Sharon sat beside her, looking as if she was trying to absorb everything. "This is serious, Sonya," she said, shaking her head.

"I know. But I have to do something to get Laura out of

this mess. I already don't like the fact that she was taken downtown without a lawyer representing her."

"Don't you have your own team of lawyers?"

"Yes, but they're experienced in tax cases and lawsuits. None of them is experienced in murder cases."

"Then let me assure you that my brother is good. I know that you've never met him. I wish I knew where I boxed up those pictures at. Anyway, I'm sure you'll like him. And if he takes your case, you can rest easy."

"If?" Sonya asked, frowning.

"He does have to decide if he feels right about this case. Trust me, he'll do this—if for no other reason than as a favor for me."

Sonya started massaging her temples again.

"Do you want some aspirin?"

"Please," she whispered.

Sharon disappeared, then returned with the two aspirins and a small glass of water.

Sonya swallowed the tiny pills and washed them down with the water. "I think I'm ready to go to bed." She stood up from the sofa. "I remember where the guest room is. You don't have to show me." Sonya glanced down at her watch. It was 5 A.M. She had about one hour to sleep before getting up to meet Sharon's brother. "Oh, by the way." Sonya stopped halfway down the hallway. "Where is your brother's office and what's his name?"

Sharon smiled, shaking her head. "I forgot to tell you. His office in Buckhead, not too far from the Lindbergh Station. The building is called Hamilton, Locke, and Associates. When you get there, look for the name Dwayne Hamilton.

Chapter Three

Dwayne shifted the stacks of paper on his desk, searching for the notes on the Graham *vs.* Georgia case. He had waited for his seven o'clock appointment for more than an hour. Now he was running late for the courthouse. Obviously the woman didn't want him to handle her case. Normally, he didn't give his potential clients such leniency on his time, but he was doing this as a favor to his sister. He pressed the intercom button to his secretary. "Miss Deaton, could you please come in here?"

"Yes, sir," came the syrupy voice through the small speaker. Carmen Deaton entered the room. "You called?"

"Uh, yes. The Graham case. I can't find my notes."

"That's because you gave them to me last night to type up." Carmen left the room, then quickly returned, holding his lost notes.

"You're an angel. Did you ask Byran to meet Mrs—" He searched for his small notepad.

"Mrs. Durden?"

"Yes, Mrs. Durden."

"Yes. He said that you'll owe him for this one."

"Good. Just have him leave everything with you until I get

back. I don't know what the story is on why Miss Walters hasn't shown up, but at least the sister will have someone to represent her this morning,'' Dwayne said as he grabbed his jacket, briefcase, and the notes, then ran out of the office.

He had ten minutes to get to the courthouse, which was twenty minutes away. He scolded himself for waiting so long for Miss Walters. Still running, he glanced down at his watch. It would be a miracle if he made it.

Sonya half ran, half walked while looking at the different names on passing doors. The building was huge, she thought. She hoped she could still see Mr. Hamilton. She was already over an hour late. Both she and Sharon had overslept. Turning another corner, she collided into a massive chest that caused her to land on the floor with a thud.

''Oh, excuse me, ma'am,'' a deep baritone voice said. A strong hand appeared to help her to her feet.

Sonya accepted the hand angrily. She pushed her hair from her face as she started to give the assailant a piece of her mind. Yet when her eyes crashed with those familiar gray ones, an electrical charge surged throughout her body. She was suddenly aware of how warm her hand felt. Her hand was still enclosed with his. Her eyes studied his neatly manicured nails. She noticed the gold Rolex and gray Armani suit that enhanced his muscular frame. Gorgeous. There was no other word to describe him. Sonya realized that she was staring again and jerked her hand from his.

''Are you all right?'' he probed.

Even his voice was perfect, she thought; rich and seductive.

''Yes, I'm fine. Nothing broken this time,'' she said, annoyed.

''Well, I see that your manners haven't improved much since our last meeting.''

The sharp rejoinder hurt. ''And I see that you're just as boorish!'' She watched his thick brows gather close together.

''I assume you didn't track me down to hurl insults at me!''

Sonya dusted off her borrowed navy suit with hard vicious strokes. "I didn't track you down, your highness. I have an appointment here. But while I'm at it, maybe I should see about pressing charges against a certain someone who demolished my back window."

"I'll be happy to pay for your window. Had I known how ungrateful your reckless-driving butt would be, I wouldn't have bothered."

Sonya's cheeks colored deep red. "I don't need your damn money!" she exploded. "In fact, I'd prefer that I never see you again!"

Dwayne tipped his head and said, "Your wish is my command."

Sonya watched the stiff back of the most arrogant man she had ever met. She turned down the opposite hallway, still angry that she allowed him to upset her so much.

"Ma'am, may I help you?" asked the secretary.

"Yes, I'm here to see a Dwayne Hamilton," Sonya said in her best professional voice.

The secretary gave a beautiful smile, which sparked a little envy in Sonya's eyes—even though she knew the secretary's long, silky, straight hair was a weave, and the flashy red fingernails were pure acrylic.

"I'm sorry. You just missed him. May I take your name?"

Sonya dispensed a frustrated sigh. Because she was busy arguing with that no-account cad, she'd missed Mr. Hamilton. "Do you know when he'll be back? It's urgent that I speak with him."

Carmen smiled and glanced down at a copy of Mr. Hamilton's schedule. "He's busy most of the day, Miss . . ."

"Walters."

"Oh, Miss Walters." The secretary perked up, recognizing the name. "Mr. Hamilton waited for you. Would you like to set another appointment?"

Sonya cursed herself again for oversleeping. "When's the next available appointment?"

Carmen flipped through the tightly scheduled book. "The next available date I have is Wednesday at nine o'clock."

"Wednesday? That's almost a week away!" Sonya's voice thundered.

"I'm sorry, Miss Walters, but Mr. Hamilton is a very busy man."

Sonya rolled her eyes, annoyed with the pretty woman. "Are you absolutely sure there are no earlier appointments? This matter can't wait a week."

Carmen checked her schedule book again. "I'm sorry, but I don't have anything available."

Before Sonya could say anything else, the secretary's phone rang. She promptly held up a slender finger and answered the phone.

"Hamilton, Locke, and Associates—Dwayne Hamilton's office. Yes, Mr. Hernandez. Okay, I'll let him know. Thank you. Goodbye." She hung up the phone and smiled at Sonya. "You're in luck. Mr. Hernandez canceled his four o'clock meeting. Do you want me to pencil you in?"

Sonya squared her shoulders and gave a tight smile. "Yes."

"All right, Miss Walters, we'll see you at four."

Sonya nodded and walked away. She knew she'd behaved rudely. After all, she was just doing her job. By the time Sonya reached the elevator, she was ashamed of her behavior. Right now she wanted to go down to the police station and talk with Laura. Maybe she would get some answers as to what really happened last night. She stepped out into the scorching Georgia sun and put on her sunglasses. Georgia in the summertime was a very peculiar thing. There was no trace of the record rainfall from last night. It was just hot, humid weather.

She walked to her car and frowned at the missing window as she got in. He thought she was tracking him down. Of all the conceited things she had ever heard. It didn't matter. With a little hope, she wouldn't have to see him again.

Sonya arrived at the Atlanta police station in record time. She had no problem getting to the visitation room, where she sat in a small wooden chair, listening to the sobbing families around her.

When Laura walked in, dressed in a dingy blue gown, Sonya stood. Their eyes locked, and a lone tear trailed down Sonya's face. Obviously Laura hadn't slept the previous night. Her dark brown hair looked dry and matted. Her eyes, circled by puffy bags, told she had been crying. Her soft brown eyes sat in a backdrop of crimson red.

Sonya sat in her chair and waited for Laura to take her seat. Both reached for the phone simultaneously.

"How are you feeling?" Sonya's voice cracked. A sense of helplessness overwhelmed her. Never in her life did she imagine having to see her baby sister this way. After years of scolding Laura over her many abusive relationships, she could never get her to see things differently. Laura would accuse Sonya constantly of being jealous of her. Curtis wasn't the only man who had abused her sister. There were scores of men that dated back to when they were in high school. Sonya had nursed plenty of broken noses and busted lips in her lifetime.

Sonya placed her hand against the plastic shield that divided them, and Laura mimicked her actions. What she wouldn't give to be able to pull Laura into her arms and comfort her.

"I'm doing all right, considering," Laura answered with a raspy voice.

More tears flowed down Sonya's face. "Laura, honey. What happened?"

Laura shook her head as if she didn't have an answer to give. "I only remember bits and pieces. After you left, Curtis turned cold toward me again. He demanded that I finish cleaning up the house. So I did. Then he was upset that it was after ten o'clock, and he hadn't had his supper yet. So I threw on some instant mashed potatoes and fried him a steak." Laura paused and wiped the tears streaming down her face.

"I put his plate on the table and went to clean up the kitchen. The next thing I knew, I was being whacked against the back of my head." Laura covered her mouth with her trembling hand.

"Go on," Sonya urged.

"He said that his steak was too rare and that I knew better . . ."

"What do I have to do to get you to do things right around here? You know I can't eat this garbage," Curtis shouted.

Laura crawled away, still holding the back of her head. She watched in terror as her husband stormed toward her again. "I'll cook it some more," she replied weakly.

"Forget it. I'll starve waiting for you to do anything right! I don't know why I keep putting up with you!"

"I'm sorry—"

"You're sorry. Is that all you can say?"

He was going to hit her again. She could tell by the tiny muscles that twitched along his jawline. She tried to run away, but a blow landed on her right cheek. Laura flew onto the small kitchen table, where the utensils and butcher knives were kept. When he came toward her again, her hands fell on a knife lying beside her. When he reached to haul her up, she plunged a ten-inch blade into his right shoulder.

A powerful roar erupted from Curtis as he dropped her back onto the floor. He looked at his wounded shoulder. Disbelief replaced the rage on his face. "You bitch!"

Laura knew that she had gone too far and tried again to get up from the floor. But Curtis recovered quickly and jerked her back to him. The next thing Laura felt was Curtis's rock hard fist slamming against her jaw . . .

"Then everything went black," Laura finished, looking into Sonya's eyes, which were as red as her own.

"So you don't actually remember killing him?" Sonya asked, confused.

"No, but I do remember stabbing him. When I came to, Curtis was lying beside me in a pool of blood. The knife I used still pierced through his chest." Laura broke down and let her tears flood her face.

Sonya watched her sister's body tremble from the heart-wrenching sobs. Her feeling of helplessness returned.

"Laura, honey, I'm going to try my best to get you out of here. I'm looking for a good lawyer to represent you. I have an appointment today with Sharon's brother at four. Meanwhile I don't want you answering any more questions, understand?"

Laura nodded her head in acknowledgment. "Isn't Mr. Locke going to represent me?"

"Who?"

"Mr. Locke. He works for . . . Hamilton, Locke, and Associates."

Sonya's shoulders slumped in relief. At least someone was sent this morning.

Sonya watched the uncertainty in Laura's eyes. She feared that her sister would see the same emotion reflected in her own, so she smiled weakly. "I'll get you out of here, I promise."

Laura forced a smile and stood to leave when an officer approached her, signaling that their time was up.

Sonya stood and waved at her sister's retreating back.

When Laura was gone, she dropped her face into the palms of her hands and wept. At the sound of heavy footsteps stopping behind her, she tried to dry her eyes.

"Miss Walters," a familiar husky voice said.

Sonya slipped her sunglasses back on. Turning around, she faced Sergeant Freeman.

"Sergeant," Sonya said, showing no evidence of her troubled emotions.

"I see you remember me," he said, unsmiling.

"I remember you."

"Good, I was hoping we could have that talk now."

"I'm sorry, but I'm not in the mood for talking," she answered, stepping past his rigid figure.

"I thought that you wanted to help your sister," he patronized.

Sonya turned abruptly on her heels and glared at the annoying officer. She was sure that he could feel her heated gaze when she witnessed him shifting nervously on his feet. "Don't you dare cast judgment on me," she half shouted. "My sister doesn't deserve to be in this damn jail, and you know it. Just look at her face. Surely you're not blind to those bruises plastered there. That man was an animal and—"

The officer's lips curved into a small smile. "And?"

Sonya squared her shoulders. "Very clever, Sergeant Freeman. I guess this is the part where I crucify my sister. Nice try. If there's anything else you want to ask me, I'm sure you know the proper procedure to get me in here for questioning." Sonya spun around and hurried out of the crowded police station. She made it to her car before her tears resurfaced. After a long moment, she calmed down. *I have to be strong.* Glancing down at her watch, she realized that she had just enough time to make it to Mick's, where she was to have a late lunch with Sharon.

Mick's at Underground Atlanta was crowded as usual, but she didn't mind. She didn't realize how hungry she was until the various aromas assaulted her senses. She spotted Sharon seated in their favorite booth toward the back.

"There you are." Sharon stood and gave Sonya a much needed hug. "There wasn't much to do at the office, so I came early."

"So everything is all right?" Sonya asked but wasn't really interested. Walters Intercorp was a solid company that she had built from the ground up. Yet today she didn't want to deal with business. Today she wanted to take care of what was most important: her sister.

"Dwayne said that you missed your appointment this morning, but I took the blame."

"So you've talked to him?"

"Yeah, I think he's very interested in your case. I let him in on what little I know and—"

"And what did he say?"

"He just said that it sounded interesting."

Sonya's hopes were lifted. The women ate their lunch as

Sonya related what happened at the jail. When they finished their meal, Sharon headed back to the office. Sonya handled a few personal errands, then flew back to Hamilton, Locke, and Associates. She was a few minutes early, so Carmen let her wait in Mr. Hamilton's office until he arrived. She sat in a jade leather chair. At least that was something she could tell that brother and sister had in common: a fetish for leather chairs.

At four ten, she grew nervous that he wasn't going to show, but when she heard the door crack open, her fears subsided.

"Okay, Miss Walters, sorry to keep you waiting," came the familiar baritone.

Sonya's eyes widened as she jumped to her feet, swirling around to her black Adonis, who stopped in midstride. "Please say that you're not Dwayne Hamilton," Sonya whispered.

A crooked grin covered his lips as he replied, "The one and only."

Chapter Four

The room grew hot. Sonya's palms felt slick with moisture as a piercing headache stabbed her temples.

"Are you all right?" Dwayne asked with concern.

Sonya snatched her purse from the chair. "This is a mistake," she said angrily.

Dwayne crossed over to his desk and plopped his briefcase down. "If that's the way you feel . . . You came to me, asking for help."

"You are the last person I would ask for help!"

"Suit yourself," he said, just as Sonya turned to leave. "But shouldn't you be thinking about your sister, Miss Walters?"

Sonya stopped at the door.

"I mean, let's face it—you're not hurting me by storming out of here. Business couldn't be better. You need me."

Sonya turned to face him. "You are the most arrogant man I ever had the displeasure to meet. You are not the only lawyer in Atlanta, you know."

"No, but I am the best," he answered seriously.

Sonya watched him sit behind his desk. "I expected you to say nothing else," Sonya smirked.

"Believe what you want, Miss Walters. You're more than welcome to find yourself a dime-a-dozen lawyer. It makes no difference to me. Just remember, you get what you pay for."

Sonya held his gaze, trying to think of a good retort.

"Perhaps, Miss Walters, we should start again." Dwayne stood and offered his hand. "I'm Dwayne Hamilton."

Sonya never knew swallowing her pride would hurt so much. She stared at his outstretched hand for what seemed like eternity. She walked slowly to his desk and shook his hand. "Sonya Walters."

Dwayne flashed her a smile that showed his pearl-white teeth. Sonya's cheeks flushed as she snatched back her hand.

"That didn't hurt, did it?"

Sonya squared her shoulders.

"Won't you have a seat?"

She returned to the leather chair. She crossed her legs, then cleared her throat when she noticed the direction of Dwayne's eyes.

A sly grin caressed his lips. "Now, Miss Walters, do you want to take it from the top?"

Sonya dropped her eyes to study her braided fingers. "I hardly know where to begin."

"Begin with the murder."

"Laura, my sister, called me at my home late last night. She said that she thought she killed Curtis, her husband."

"Why did she think that?"

"We didn't talk about that last night. She was too distraught to talk about it. I told her that I would get to her house as fast as I could."

"Did she call the police?"

"She said that she was too scared, but they were there by the time I arrived—"

"That explains why you nearly ran me off the road," Dwayne interrupted.

Sonya glanced up.

"Sorry, please continue."

Sonya took a deep breath and told him everything that she

knew. She never looked back at him. When she finished, she waited patiently through his silence. After a while, she wondered if he was still in the room. She lift her head slowly to look at him. Their eyes locked. Sonya felt butterflies fluttering madly in the pit of her stomach. She didn't know how long they'd remained that way before Dwayne lowered his gaze to a notepad before him.

Sonya released a rush of air she'd been holding.

"Your sister doesn't remember killing her husband?" Dwayne asked thoughtfully.

Sonya cleared her throat before answering. "She said she had a blackout."

"Do you believe her?"

Sonya jumped to her feet. "Of course I believe her! What kind of question is that?"

"Calm down, Miss Walters. These are questions I have to ask. I don't know your sister. I don't know her character."

"Her character? You're making her sound like—"

"Like someone I don't know. Now, please, sit down."

Sonya held his eyes for a brief moment then complied. "Laura was an abused housewife. If anything, this is a cut-and-dried case of self-defense."

"The prosecution won't see it that way. It's their job to make your sister out to be a cold, calculating murderer. And that won't be hard to do."

Fire sparked in Sonya's eyes. "How can you say that? Laura could never hurt anyone!"

"Yet we have one dead man."

"That does it!" Sonya jumped up and raced to the door, but Dwayne made it there to block it.

"This is going to be a hard and painful experience for you and your family, Miss Walters. I wish that I could make it easy for you, but I can't. It's going to get worse. Every facet of your life will be up for grabs. That's what the prosecutor on this case will do. If you can't handle these questions, then your sister is in more trouble than you think."

"I'm not going to sit here while you condemn her, Mr. Hamilton."

"I'm not condemning her. If I take this case, it's imperative that I know everything there is to know about Laura."

What he said made sense. Sonya silently took her seat. *What was it about him that put her on the defensive?* She watched him return to his desk with long confident strides.

"Perhaps you should tell me how long your sister was in this abusive relationship."

"I guess you could say that it's been going on since the beginning. She wouldn't admit it, though. She would always come up with some silly explanation about how she broke her nose."

"Did she report these beatings?" Dwayne asked with a concerned voice.

"There were a few times when she called the police. But she refused to press charges."

"That will cause a problem. Was she ever admitted into the hospital?"

Sonya fought her tears. "A few times."

Dwayne continued writing down her responses. "How long were they married?"

"Eight months."

"How about life insurance?" Dwayne asked, leaning back in his chair to study her.

Sonya shrugged her shoulders. "What about it?"

"It's a possible motive."

Sonya clenched her jaws shut.

"I'm going to take this case, Miss Walters. It's going to be a tough one to win, though."

Sonya remained silent. She didn't know whether or not to be happy.

"Miss Walters?"

Sonya flushed. He caught her staring again.

"Miss Walters, I was saying that I'll stop down at the jail tomorrow morning to talk with your sister. Meanwhile I suggest you get prepared for the police department to drag you in for questioning. You can put them off only for so long. They also won't be as gentle as I was, so get that chip off your shoulder."

Sonya's cheeks heated, but before she could say anything he cut her off.

"And make sure you call me before they drag you in." Dwayne pressed the intercom button. "Carmen, could you please come in here?"

In a flash Carmen appeared with pen and paper.

"Carmen, I need you to get me a copy of any criminal records on" Dwayne flipped through his notes—"on a Curtis and Laura Durden. I want the works. I want to know about any traffic violations, civil suits. I even want to know if they have ever been picked up for jaywalking."

Sonya tensed but was impressed by his take-charge attitude.

"I want copies of any medical info you can get your hands on. See who's handling this case downtown."

Carmen kept nodding her head as she took notes.

Dwayne glanced over to Sonya. "Also get me any criminal record on Sonya Walters."

Sonya's eyes widened. "Why me?"

"I don't like surprises. And conspiracy isn't too far-fetched for the prosecution to conjure up."

"Conspiracy? That's absurd," Sonya shouted.

Dwayne hid a smile. "That may be true, but I know how our wonderful judicial system is. It's now the battle of wits. Guilt or innocence has very little to do with it."

"That's a bitter pill to swallow," Sonya answered sarcastically.

"Then I suggest you find some water," Dwayne retaliated.

"Is there anything else?" Carmen jumped in.

"I want a copy of last night's police report on my desk by morning. We've already lost a day's worth of work."

"Yes, sir," Carmen said, leaving the room.

"As for you, Miss Walters, I suggest you go home and get some much needed rest. There isn't much more we can do today," he said, picking up the phone.

Gathering herself together, she headed for the door. The sound of his voice halted her exit.

"May I ask you a question?"

Sonya turned to face him.

"Did you try to get Laura help?"

Sonya's shoulders slumped in defeat. "Often," she said softly. "I've taken her to group meetings and to different counselors. Nothing worked. Whenever I thought something was working, Curtis would come back into the picture. He promised her the moon, and she believed him. He told her how much he would change, or how very sorry he was for hurting her. And every time she would take him back." Sonya's eyes brimmed with tears. "But the beatings got worse." Her lips trembled. "I tried. Oh, how I tried to help. But she . . . wouldn't listen." Her vision blurred as tears flowed freely down her face. Before she knew it, she was encased between two powerful arms.

"It's going to be all right," he whispered against her hair.

Sonya remained enclosed in his arms. His strength comforted her. It made her feel safe. She didn't know how long she stayed that way, but it was well after the tears subsided.

"Are you all right?" he asked tenderly.

Sonya pushed away from his chest and smiled meekly at him. "I'm sorry."

"Don't be." His eyes caressed her face.

"Maybe I should go."

Dwayne nodded. "I'll call you tomorrow."

Sonya turned and walked out the door. She started walking down the hallway when she heard Carmen call after her.

"Yes," she answered.

"I need you to fill out this information sheet for our files.'

Sonya took the sheet and went to sit next to Carmen's desk.

"He's handsome, isn't he?" Carmen said, watching Sonya.

"Pardon me?" Sonya glanced over to Carmen.

"Mr. Hamilton. He's quite a catch, wouldn't you say?"

"I haven't noticed," Sonya answered.

Carmen sat down behind her desk. "Really?" she said,

sounding unconvinced. "Are you available yourself? I mean, I didn't see a ring or anything."

Sonya finished filling out the sheet and placed it on Carmen's desk. She knew what Carmen was trying to do. "That's not any of your business."

"I tend to make anything dealing with Dwayne my business."

Sonya wasn't sure if Carmen's eyes flared with anger. It was hard to tell through the secretary's green contact lenses.

"Does Dwayne know about your overprotectiveness?" Sonya used his first name to irritate Carmen. This time she was sure her eyes flared angrily.

Carmen stood so she could be at eye level with Sonya. "Enough with the games—he's mine. So back off!"

Sonya squared her shoulders and glared at the witless secretary. "I don't see any rings on your fingers, either. So that makes him fair game. Don't you think?"

"I'm warning you," Carmen hissed.

"Don't you ever threaten me. You don't have the slightest idea who you are dealing with."

The women exchanged venomous looks until they heard the door to Dwayne's office open. Sonya then witnessed a miraculous change in Carmen's attitude. "Thank you, Miss Walters. I'll make sure Mr. Hamilton receives this." Carmen held up the completed information sheet.

Unsmiling, Sonya turned and left Carmen's desk, storming past Dwayne.

"What has gotten into her?" Dwayne asked once Sonya was out of earshot.

"She's probably just stressed out," Carmen lied easily.

Dwayne turned to face his secretary. "Yeah, that's probably it. Did you make those phone calls?"

"I was about to get right on it."

Dwayne smiled and walked back into his office. It was well past six now. It was time to go home. He had promised Bridget that he would be home for dinner. He grabbed his briefcase and jacket and left.

He pulled into his driveway thirty minutes later. At least Bridget was home. Her blue Samurai Jeep was already parked in the driveway.

When he opened the door to the house, Buffy greeted him. "Hello, girl. How was your day?" he asked the black Lab.

The dog excitedly licked his face. "Good girl. Have you eaten yet—"

"Of course she's eaten," Bridget interrupted.

Dwayne looked up at his sixteen-year-old daughter with a crooked grin. His smile faded when he noticed what she was wearing. "Please say you didn't wear that to school."

Bridget looked down at her three-sizes-too-big jeans and midriff tank top. "What's wrong with what I have on?" she asked seriously.

Dwayne shook his head, not wanting to have this discussion tonight. He then noticed she had the cordless phone held under her ear. "Who are you on the phone with?"

"Shock G."

"Shock who?" he asked, walking past her and heading up the stairs.

"Shock G., my boyfriend."

Dwayne stopped in the middle of the staircase. "Boyfriend? What happened to—"

Bridget held up her finger, signaling for him to be quiet.

"Bridget, it's time for you to get off the phone. I have some important calls to make."

"Baby, I'm going to have to call you back. Yes. Okay. I love you, too. Bye."

Dwayne forgot what he was about to do and descended the stairs to follow Bridget into the kitchen.

" 'Baby? I love you?' What in the hell is going on?"

Bridget checked the food on the stove. "Oh, Daddy, calm down. Nothing's going on, we're just friends."

"A minute ago he was your boyfriend," he said, assessing his little girl's figure. He realized she wasn't a little girl anymore. She was five-foot-five and with curves he swore weren't there last year.

"Oh, Daddy, I just tell them that. I don't really mean it."

"Them?" Dwayne felt feverish. "Just how many are there?"

Bridget smiled at her father. "Just a couple."

"You're grounded."

Bridget's smile vanished. "Grounded? Why?"

"Because I said so," he thundered. "My daughter is not some nappy-headed boy's hangout!" Dwayne stormed out of the kitchen.

"But, Daddy," Bridget said, following behind him.

"Don't 'but Daddy' me, Bridget. I don't even know these boys: Ice Pick, K. Dog, Chili, and every once in a while you'll date someone with a normal name. Now this Shock G."

"You know George, Daddy. He lives down the street."

Dwayne's face registered shock. "Little George? The Whitfield's boy?"

Bridget crossed her arms and looked impatiently at her father. "Little George is eighteen."

"Eighteen? When did that happen?"

"You're overreacting, Daddy. Besides, I've already promised we would catch a movie tonight."

"I thought we were having dinner together tonight."

"We are"—Bridget shrugged her shoulders—"but afterward I have a date."

"No, it's a school night." Dwayne turned and headed up the stairs.

"Daddy, please."

"No. You have only a week until school is out for summer break," Dwayne said without looking back at her.

"Well, how long am I grounded?"

"Until your hormones calm down, or I'm in a nursing home. Whichever comes first," he shouted from the top of the stairs.

The phone rang. Dwayne knew Bridget would answer it. He started undressing and headed for the shower when Bridget knocked on the door. "I'm not dressed, Bridget. What do you need?"

"That was Aunt Sharon on the phone. She said she needs you down at the hospital."

Dwayne put on his robe and opened his door. "Why, what happened?" he asked frantically.

"She said some lady is being rushed to Northside Hospital."

Dwayne shifted his weight from one foot to another, irritated that Bridget couldn't take better messages. "What lady, Bridget? Did she say a name?"

Bridget squeezed her eyes tight, trying to remember what her aunt said.

"Oh, I remember. Some lady named Sonya."

Chapter Five

"I'm here to see Sonya Walters," Dwayne told the nurse at the hospital reception desk.

She smiled politely and roamed her finger down a clipboard. "She's in room 712."

"Thank you." Dwayne rushed in the nurse's pointed direction. The long, vacant hallway enunciated the sound of his shoes pounding against the linoleum floor. He arrived at Sonya's room and knocked. When he pushed the door open, he found Sonya lying against a stack of white pillows. But what disturbed him most was the instant frown that creased her face the moment their eyes met.

"How are you doing?" he asked, stepping into the room. Once inside, he saw Sharon sitting next to Sonya's bed.

"Oh, thank goodness you came." Sharon rushed from her chair to greet him.

Dwayne shared a quick hug, but his attention quickly focused back to Sonya.

Sharon continued to talk as Dwayne headed closer to the bed. "You won't believe what happened. Sonya walked in on a burglary."

Alarmed, Dwayne touched Sonya's shoulder. She pulled away, puzzling him more. "Are you all right?" He lifted his hand to the small patch against her head.

"I'm fine," she answered in a muffled whisper, then drew away from his touch.

Dwayne dropped his hand in frustration. "So what happened?"

Sonya closed her eyes before responding. "When I arrived home from our earlier appointment, I discovered the house door was open. I stopped briefly and tried to remember if I forgot to lock up the house before storming over to Laura's last night. I couldn't remember. Everything was one big blur. So I went inside. The house had been ransacked. Tables, chairs—you name it—had been overturned."

A knock sounded from the door. Everyone looked to see James Ellis walking in.

Sharon raced to greet her husband at the door.

"I came when I read your message on the refrigerator." He looked at Dwayne. "I didn't know you knew Sonya, Dwayne."

"Miss Walters's a client of mine," Dwayne answered absently, then turned his attention to Sonya.

Sharon walked back to the bed and touched Sonya's shoulder. "Finish telling Dwayne what happened."

"As I was saying—I found my house in shambles. So I immediately went to find a phone. Then I thought I heard something in the kitchen. I remained cautious, but before I knew it everything went black."

"You could have been killed," Sharon moaned, covering her mouth.

James nodded in agreement while Dwayne mulled her story over in his head. He pinched the tip of his chin and wondered if there was a connection to Curtis's murder and Sonya's burglary.

"What do you make of it?" Sharon asked him.

Dwayne turned toward the rest of the group and shook his head. "I don't know, but I can't chalk up the incident as coincidence."

She dropped her head back and closed her eyes again. "I don't see how they are related."

"Why not? You do realize, if your sister didn't kill her husband, someone else did?"

"Killed her husband?" James asked incredulously. "Curtis is dead?"

"I'll explain later, honey," Sharon said.

Sonya opened her eyes but said nothing.

"Sonya?" Sharon asked.

"I guess I hadn't thought about it that way."

Dwayne recognized the fear in her voice for what it was. "Don't get upset. We could very well be grasping at straws."

Sonya shook her head.

"Tina Hudson, Sonya's secretary," Sharon went on to tell Dwayne, "arrived to deliver some charts for Sonya to look over. She found Sonya unconscious on the kitchen floor."

"I see," Dwayne said thoughtfully. "Where is she now?"

"She went home. She had two kids to pick up from day care."

"I wonder what they were looking for," Dwayne wondered aloud.

"Have you seen her place?" James looked to Dwayne. "It's a fortress."

"You have to admit, your being broken into right after Curtis's murder is a bit suspicious," Sharon agreed.

"Well, I don't see a connection," Sonya admitted.

A light tap at the door caused everyone to turn around. Sonya moaned when a police officer walked through the door. "Sergeant Freeman."

"Hello, Miss Walters. Dr. Johnson said that you were up and about."

"I don't want to answer any of your questions," Sonya said too rudely and received open stares from everyone. "He's the same arresting officer on my sister's case," she offered as an explanation.

"Laura killed Curtis?" James asked, looking to his wife.

"Shh, honey. I'll explain later."

Dwayne walked over and shook Sergeant Freeman's hands. "Ah, Mr. Hamilton. What are you doing here?"

"I'm handling the Durden case."

"Oh, I see. Miss Walters went out and hired the best lawyer money could buy, eh? Well, it doesn't matter. There's very little to this case. Mrs. Durden already admitted to stabbing her husband. It's an open-and-shut case."

Dwayne's smile faded. "I doubt that Sergeant. I doubt that. Tell me, what brings you out here?"

"I need Miss Walters to answer a few questions. She seemed too busy in the past twenty-four hours to discuss her involvement with the case."

"Involvement?" Sonya sat upright to glare at the sergeant.

"I don't think this is a good time to talk about this. Perhaps after you obtain a subpoena?" Dwayne asked casually.

Sergeant Freeman smiled tightly. "I don't see why you would want to do things the hard way. I thought that Miss Walters was smart enough to come in voluntarily. I was mistaken."

Sonya struggled out of her bed. Sharon tried to pull her back, but Sonya wouldn't oblige. "I think it's time you left Sergeant," Sonya replied with a razor-sharp attitude. Freeman's eyes leveled with Sonya's. "I will get you in for questioning."

"Perhaps this isn't an open-and-shut case." Dwayne interjected.

Sergeant Freeman gave Dwayne an angry glance, then turned to leave the room. "We'll talk later, Miss Walters."

Sonya touched Dwayne's arm. "Not without my lawyer present."

Sergeant Freeman gave a slight nod and then disappeared out of the room.

"Well, can you believe that?" Sharon said from beside the bed.

"Actually I'm having a hard time believing any of this." James rubbed his head.

Sonya looked up and smiled at Dwayne. "Thanks."

"Ouch. I'm sure that hurt. Have you ever told anybody thanks in your life?" Dwayne teased.

Sonya smiled. "Once."

"Well, sister-girl, I think it's time we went home." Sharon pulled her husband along.

"But I thought we were—"

Sharon stomped on James's foot. "We have to get home. James hasn't even unpacked from his trip."

"What's the rush?" Sonya asked, looking at Sharon.

"Hospitals make me nervous," Sharon offered as an excuse. "Oh, before I go, you left this in the spare bedroom."

Sonya took the gold coin necklace and shook her head. "The clasp is loose on this thing. I have to get it fixed."

"Well, see you guys later."

Dwayne knew what his sister was thinking. Sharon, the hopeless romantic, was obviously trying to leave them alone. But before he could stop them from leaving, they were out the door.

"Umm, I wonder what got into her." Sonya settled back into the bed.

"You can never tell with Sharon. Can I get you anything?"

"No. The doctor wants to watch me for twenty-four hours. Are you still going to see my sister tomorrow morning?"

"First thing."

"That's good. I want you to call me after you do."

"Yes, sir."

Sonya looked annoyed. She looked down to study her hands. "Just see to my sister."

"You and your sister seem very close," Dwayne noted, looking down at her.

"Not as close as I would like us to be."

"Do you have any other family?"

"My mother. My father died years ago."

"Where is your mother?"

Sonya didn't answer.

Dwayne watched as tears gathered in her eyes.

"Mr. Hamilton . . ."

"Please, call me Dwayne."

Sonya smiled weakly at him. "Dwayne, I would like to be alone now, please."

Dwayne nodded in understanding. Walking to the door, he turned a final time to see her staring toward the window, deep in thought. His heart pounded against his chest. She was so beautiful with her hair hanging free in tiny ringlets. It affected him deeply to have witnessed the pain reflecting in her hazel eyes. He felt a strong need to protect her from the pain that was visible on her face.

He left the room quietly and walked out to his car, still in deep thought. The picture of her looking fragile remained with him as he drove home.

Later that night, he dreamed of her. Dreamed of holding her and protecting her. The next morning, he hardly remembered talking to Bridget through breakfast or even driving to work.

When Carmen entered his office with his requested information, he missed the sarcastic smile displayed across her lips.

"I have something that you're not going to believe," she cooed, sitting in the chair in front of his desk.

"Oh?" Dwayne leaned back into his chair.

"Yes. It seems that Miss Walters has a family secret."

Carmen had his full attention now. "What do you mean?"

"I received this fax from Mr. Hill down at the *Atlanta Journal*. The clipping is dated June 4, 1976."

"Well, what does it say? I have to go down to the jailhouse to meet Mrs. Durden." He began gathering things up from his desk.

"The clipping is about a housewife who stabbed her husband to death."

"So?"

"So the housewife's name is Dorothy L. Walters. Sonya and Laura's mother."

Chapter Six

"Let me see that!" Dwayne stormed.

A tight, smug expression possessed Carmen's lips as she handed him the article.

"I don't believe this!" He stared at the newspaper clipping.

"Believe it," Carmen chimed in.

Dwayne leaned against his desk and continued to read. "The article states that Mrs. Walters claimed she didn't remember the incident, then later changed her story admitting to the crime."

"Sound familiar?"

Anger replaced his frustrations. "Why in the hell didn't she tell me?" He flung the article onto his desk.

Carmen stood motionless with a satisfied look plastered into place.

"Carmen, see if Anthony is back, then have him get me as much information as he can concerning that case."

"I'm sure he's just returned from his vacation. He's not due in the office until tomorrow."

"Call him anyway. I need an extra person on this," Dwayne said, unconcerned.

"You're going to keep the case?" Carmen asked, shocked.

"That remains to be seen." Dwayne grabbed his briefcase and stormed out of the office, his anger evident in his powerful strides. He made it to the jailhouse in half the time. He was anxious to meet Sonya's sister.

Dwayne knew he should drop this case. He'd specifically told Sonya how much he hated surprises, and this definitely qualified as a surprise. Yet when Carmen asked if he were still handling the case, he was unable to follow his strict policy, and Sonya's solemn face still haunted him from yesterday.

After waiting for what seemed like eternity, Dwayne was ushered in to see his client.

The small sad face of the distraught woman glanced up to greet him. There was no display of any other emotion. She wasn't what he expected. He had envisioned a replica of Sonya: a fiery, hazel-eyed woman with a domineering aura. However, this woman was the opposite of that vision. She seemed too meek and fragile to be Sonya's sister. He searched her pained expression for similarities but found none. She looked to have weighed about one hundred pounds. Her complexion was a rich mocha with a kiss of cinnamon, except for the discolored bruises across her face. Her unbrushed hair hung long enough to lie comfortably on her shoulders. When he finally met her soft brown eyes, an instant brotherly protectiveness attacked his heart. He knew then that he was going to do all he could to help her.

"Hello, Mrs. Durden," he said, extending his hand. "My name is Dwayne Hamilton." Her soft chilled hands escalated his protectiveness. "Your sister has hired me to defend you."

Laura nodded in understanding.

Dwayne took his seat and prepared to take notes. Yet at his client's unnerving silence, he put down his pen. "Perhaps you should begin by telling me your version of what happened, Mrs. Durden."

"I killed my husband."

Dwayne flinched at the emotionless confession. When she didn't continue, Dwayne tried again.

"Did you tell anyone else this?"

"No," she whispered.

"Good, I suggest that you don't."

A lone tear streaked down her face.

"Your sister has, of course, given me a different scenario. May I ask which I am supposed to believe?"

Laura's bottom lip began to tremble as she attempted to dry her face. She didn't answer his question.

"Mrs. Durden, I can't help you if you don't help me. You refused to post bail. I doubt that your sister knows that. Do you mind telling me why?"

"Because I feel so guilty."

"You don't remember killing your husband, isn't that correct?"

Laura hesitated again, then slowly nodded her head.

"Then you have no reason to feel guilty," Dwayne reasoned, reaching out to take her hand.

Laura quickly pulled back. "I have every right to feel this way," she began. "I am guilty. I may or may not have physically killed him, but in my heart . . . I wanted to."

Dwayne leaned away from her and watched fresh tears roll down her face.

"I loved him. I always thought that I could make this marriage work. He made me feel as if everything that was wrong was my fault. I wanted him to love me."

Dwayne's jaw tightened as he listened to her confession. Her whole body shook as she wept. "I understand what you're going though, Laura. There is no way we can change what has happened. It's okay to feel this way—"

"No," she interrupted, shaking her head. "It's worse than that. I don't know when I stopped loving him and started hating him."

Dwayne shook his head, not believing her words. "Laura, this man hurt you. He took your love, your trust, and anything else you had to offer and just threw it away. I think you know exactly when you stopped loving him."

Laura closed her eyes and laughed softly to herself. "You sound like my sister."

"Your sister is right. You deserve better."

Laura fell silent again and nodded her head. A long pause hung in the air between them.

Dwayne again noticed the purple and blue bruises across her face and felt his own anger mount at the animal who could inflict such brutality on his own wife. "Mrs. Durden, should I come back?"

She shook her head.

"First, I'm going to arrange your bail," Dwayne said.

Laura looked neither happy nor disappointed at the news. She just sat there as if she was lost in a trance.

"Mrs. Durden?"

More tears rolled down her swollen cheeks. "I feel very confident about your innocence, and I know that your sister does, too.

"Yeah," Laura answered, dropping her head down to stare at her feet. "Good ole Sonya coming to the rescue."

Dwayne frowned at the sarcasm in her voice.

"I'm sorry," she said as if reading his mind. "It's just that I'm so scared."

Dwayne nodded his head in understanding. "I'll get you out of here. I'll talk to your sister about your bail."

Laura shook her head. "I don't want you going to my sister about my bail money. I have some money in the bank. I insist on using it."

"Do you know how much your bail will be?"

"I don't care. I'll use the house if I have to," Laura answered, looking up to stare at him.

Again Dwayne nodded. He didn't quite understand what was going on, but if this was what she wanted to do, then so be it.

A prison guard entered the room, and both Dwayne and Laura stood up. Dwayne remained watching Laura as she departed. He tried to absorb what had just happened. He sat down in his chair and let his mind drift to what he would've done had it been his sister behind these bars. Hell, if he even thought that James lifted a finger to his sister, it would've been him waiting to stand trial for murder. He reached for his pen as he wondered, what if it had been Bridget? His anger quickly returned as his pen snapped in half as he entertained such a thought. The ink oozing from his pen brought his attention back to reality. "Damn!" he cursed, jumping to his feet. He didn't expect to feel so emotional about this case. Another rule he was breaking. What was it about these sisters that kept him on the edge?

He left the small holding room to call his office.

"Hamilton, Locke, and Associates."

"Hello, Carmen. This is Dwayne. Did you get hold of Anthony for me?"

"Yes, and I was right. He wasn't too happy about cutting his trip short."

"Never mind that. Was he able to get any information?"

"He hasn't checked back in with me."

"Well, give me a call the minute he has something."

"Yes, sir."

"Okay, thanks."

"Oh, Dwayne?"

"Yes?"

"Miss Walters has called, looking for you."

"Did she call from the hospital?"

"No. She's at her office downtown. Would you like the number? She has already called here three times."

"No, just give me the address. I think I'd like to pay her a visit in person." Dwayne took down the information and hung up. *What in the hell was she doing at work?*

Sonya sat uninterested in the proceedings that surrounded her. She kept watching the clock on the wall. Why hadn't she heard anything by now? She had called Dwayne's office three times this morning, and still there was nothing.

The hospital had released her at nine o'clock this morning. She couldn't take staring at those dull white walls in the hospital. By ten o'clock, she was home and was bored. When she remembered that she had a financial status meeting scheduled for eleven-thirty, she rushed to the office.

She could tell by the many shocked faces at her office that they didn't expect her to be in today, especially Sharon. She'd walked into her office to find Sharon's legs kicked up on her desk and barking orders at her employees. Sonya laughed as Sharon nearly fell out of her chair, trying to get up. Now stuck in this meeting, she prayed that Dwayne would call her soon.

"Excuse me," she said, getting up from the table in the middle of one of her chief accountant's speeches. She slipped quietly out of the conference room and rushed down to her office. She ignored the large stacks of paper on her desk as she reached for the phone.

"Hamilton, Locke, and Associates," came the familiar chirp from Carmen.

"Yes, is Mr. Hamilton in yet?"

Carmen's voice lost its merry tune as she replied, "No, Miss Walters, he's not in. Would you like to leave yet another message?"

"Miss Walters?" Tina interrupted.

"Not now, Tina," Sonya scolded without turning to look at her secretary. "As for you, Miss Deaton, I think that I've had just about enough of your attitude today," Sonya continued into the phone. "You will either talk to me with the proper respect or—"

"Miss Walters, I'm afraid there is a Mr—"

"Not now, Tina!" Sonya screamed turning to face her secretary but was shocked to see Dwayne towering behind Tina's five-foot-two frame. Sonya instantly hung up the phone with an angry Carmen shouting on the other end.

"As I was saying, Miss Walters, there is a Dwayne Hamilton here to see you."

"I can see that, Tina. Thank you. You may leave now," Sonya said, going to sit in her chair. She knew her flushed cheeks gave away her embarrassment. "Won't you please have a seat?" she offered, gesturing to a chair in front of her desk.

Dwayne took a brief look around her spacious office, nodding his head. "Nice," he said casually as he took his seat.

"Thank you."

"I thought you were supposed to stay in the hospital for twenty-four hours?" he asked. His voice held concern.

Sonya glanced away from his probing eyes. "I was, but I was beginning to feel the walls closing in on me."

"I see," Dwayne answered, standing up to walk toward her.

Sonya's eyes widened in alarm as his hand reached up to feel her head. She started to pull away, but she felt the firm hold at the back of her neck.

"Be still. I just want to examine your bruise."

"Are you going to tell me that you're a doctor as well as a defense lawyer?"

Dwayne let out a deep chuckle. "Are you always so defensive when someone is trying to help you?"

Sonya flinched when his hand caressed her tender bruise. "Maybe you should have stayed a little longer at the hospital."

Sonya wanted to pull away again. Dwayne's nearness was playing havoc on her emotions. There was a wondrous fragrance that surrounded him that held her prisoner. "Have you gone to see my sister?" she managed to ask in a low voice, while focusing her eyes on a loose thread that hung from her fuchsia pantsuit.

Dwayne returned to his chair satisfied with his inspection. "I have, and I've gotten her bail arranged. She'll be released by three o'clock today—"

"Whatever it takes, I'll pay it," Sonya cut in.

"Your sister wants to post her own bail," Dwayne said matter-of-factly.

Sonya swirled her chair to face the long wall of open windows. She stared at the beautiful skyline of downtown Atlanta. She was hurt by her sister's decision. She only wanted to help, but once again Laura saw this as an opportunity to declare her independence.

How many times had Laura claimed that she didn't need or want any help from her? Laura always saw Sonya's concern as an act of interference. "Does she have enough money?" she finally asked in a low voice.

"She wants to put up her house."

Sonya squared her shoulders, gathered her courage, and stood up from her chair. "So are you here to also tell me that you're no longer working for me?" Sonya asked, her sarcasm sharp enough to cut through the thickest glass. She didn't want this man to see how much her sister's decision affected her.

"No, Miss Walters. I'm simply saying that Laura desires to pay her own bail."

"But not her own lawyer?"

Dwayne shrugged his shoulders.

"Okay, so she posted her own bail."

"I only came over because you wanted me to keep you informed," Dwayne answered.

Sonya walked from the window. "So what's next?"

"Next I begin working on your sister's defense. I'll compile the police reports and go over the crime scene. Which brings me to my next subject, which I hope you can help me with. Personally I prefer it if you keep a close eye on your sister. She has a very bad case of the guilts, and I want her heavily watched. Do you think that you could do that?"

Sonya crossed her arms. "Of course I can. She'll stay with me."

"It may not be as easy as that. There might be a slight chance that she doesn't want to stay with you."

"Are you telling me that my sister doesn't want to stay with me, either?" Sonya asked, this time unable to hide her hurt expression.

"I'm not saying that. I just got the impression that she may be a little resentful right now."

"Resentful? About what?"

"I don't know. I'm telling you what I picked up from her attitude."

"Now you listen here. My sister will want to stay with me. We've always been close and she . . . she would tell me if . . . if I've done anything to upset her. Now, in ten minutes, you've told me that she doesn't want me to pay her bail and that she may or may not want to stay with me!"

Dwayne let out an exasperated sigh. "I didn't mean to upset

you. What I need for you to remember is that your sister may not act like herself. She's going through a lot. What you think is helping her may not be.''

Sonya's shoulders slumped in defeat. She knew what Dwayne said made perfect sense. ''Okay, I'll back off.''

Dwayne flashed her a breathtaking smile, causing Sonya to shift her weight nervously on her heels.

''I must be going,'' he said, pulling his eyes away from hers.

Sonya watched as Dwayne began to say something else, then stopped. ''I'll talk to you later.'' He got up from the chair. Just as Dwayne reached for the door to leave her office, Sonya stopped him.

''You know, don't you?''

Dwayne turned back around to face her. ''Excuse me?''

''My mother. You know, don't you?''

Dwayne nodded his head. ''Why didn't you tell me?'' he asked, his eyes leveling with her own.

Sonya took a deep breath, then walked over to stand in front of him. ''Would you have taken the case if I had told you that mother was serving time for the exact crime my sister is charged with?''

Dwayne's expression told her the answer to that question. ''But you knew I would find out.''

''Maybe I was just trying to buy some time,'' she said, looking away from his intense stare.

''Time for what?'' Dwayne asked as she walked back to the window to look out at the tiny people below.

''I knew if you met my sister that you would know the kind of person she is, and that this is really two different cases.''

The room was silent. Sonya was too afraid to turn around. She didn't want this man to see her tears. She had already let him see her cry before, and she refused to let that happen again. Sonya inhaled his fragrance and knew that he was now standing behind her. Suddenly it became difficult to breathe and her stomach was doing those funny tricks again.

''You're right,'' she heard him say, his breath warm against her neck. ''I can't turn down this case now.'' Sonya's knees grew weaker by the seconds. Slowly she turned around to face him. He was standing closer than she thought. Their eyes held each other spellbound, and Sonya couldn't pull away if she had tried. She noticed how curly his lashes were. He was leaning closer, and Sonya's heart felt like it was about to explode in her chest. He was going to kiss her. Sonya knew it as she tilted her face upward in anticipation, her eyes closed.

"Miss Walters?" Tina said, bolting through the door.

Sonya jumped away from Dwayne and looked away toward her desk. She could feel her cheeks flame from embarrassment.

"I must be going," Dwayne said, his own voice cracking. "I'll talk with you later, Miss Walters."

Sonya nodded in response, refusing to look at him. When she heard the door close behind him, she released her breath that she had unconsciously held. She looked over at Tina, who was smiling from ear to ear. "This better be important."

Chapter Seven

One week later . . .

"Daddy, time to get up!" Bridget yelled.

Dwayne peered up at his clock which read five-thirty. *Does that girl ever sleep?* He couldn't fathom ever having so much energy. He heard Bridget's stereo blasting well past two o'clock this morning, and now she was waking him up. *Aging is such a cruel joke.*

Finally Dwayne mustered up the strength to throw one leg over the edge of the bed and then the other one. He appreciated the fresh aroma of coffee brewing downstairs. The girl did have her good qualities, he thought, smiling.

After his morning shower, he made it down the stairs dressed in his blue Father's Day robe. He poured his ritual cup of coffee and turned on the nine-inch TV that sat on the kitchen counter.

"Today in local news, Sergeant Freeman of the Atlanta Police Department announced the department's new plan of affirmative action to help prevent crime."

Dwayne sipped at his coffee as he watched the graying sergeant take the podium.

"Good morning, ladies and gentlemen. On behalf of the Atlanta Police Department, I'd like to address our current problem with the alarming number of homicide cases. In May, we had a record high of fifty-two cases. And already for the first week in June, we've had fifteen cases—"

"What's the department's plan, Sergeant?" a reporter butted in.

"To enforce tougher sentences on these horrendous crimes and put more officers on patrol," came his confident reply.

"Sergeant Freeman, Sergeant Freeman ... " the reporters chanted in unison.

Dwayne switched off the television. "Law and order at its best," he mumbled. Dwayne agreed that crime in Atlanta was at an all-time high, but Sergeant Freeman's suggestions wouldn't do much to stop it. It was just the department's way to let the public know that they were aware of the situation. Nothing else. Who was going to follow up to see if there were more men patrolling an area than there were last month? Nobody. Just a lot of talk and no action. "Hold it right there, young lady!" Dwayne bellowed, catching a glimpse of his daughter sneaking down the stairs. "Just where do you think you're off to dressed like that?"

"Like what?" Bridget asked, her innocent face carefully in place.

"That dress is too short and too tight, for starters. And you have on entirely too much makeup."

"Daddy, this is the style—get with it. Besides, it's the last day of school. All the girls are going to be dressed like this."

"You're not. Get upstairs and put on something decent!"

"But, Daddy—"

"Bridget Elizabeth Hamilton, you get upstairs this minute

and put on some clothes. Not something too tight or anything so loose it's hanging to your kneecaps. Do I make myself clear?''

Bridget sucked in her breath and nodded angrily at her father.

''And wash that junk off your face. No daughter of mine is running out of here looking like the red-light special on Hooker Avenue.''

Bridget flew up the stairs to her room, but not before Dwayne noticed the bright tears that glistened in the corner of her eyes.

''Damn!'' He realized he'd been too tough on her. At the sound of her stereo blaring, he knew she wouldn't open the door if he went to apologize. Teenagers, he thought. They should come with an instruction manual. He finished his coffee and went upstairs to get ready to attend Curtis Durden's funeral.

Sonya changed seven times before deciding on her black pantsuit. What did it matter anyway? She would probably be the only one there with a dry face. Who would notice? Laura had been crying since her release from jail. In the beginning, Sonya was sympathetic, but now she wished that her sister would start thinking about her pending case. Everything, it seemed, sent Laura in a crying frenzy. Last night, the cook made the mistake of making mashed potatoes and steak. It was the same dinner that Laura had prepared for her husband the night he was killed. The next thing Sonya knew, Laura was crying a river of tears. Now Richard Durden, Curtis's brother, had showed up at her doorstep, insisting that he overlook the plans for Curtis's funeral. Hell, she thought, I didn't even know the bum had a family, and frankly, Sonya hadn't started any proceedings to bury Curtis.

Laura went out her way to avoid Richard, saying that she couldn't bear looking into those familiar dark eyes. Sonya believed it was all in Laura's head, since she didn't see any similarity. However, that really didn't mean anything. People had for years told her that she and Laura looked nothing alike.

The fact of the matter was Sonya took after her father, and Laura was the exact replica of their mother.

Sonya always hated her looks. Even now, looking back at her reflection in the mirror, she hated the face that stared back at her. As much as she wanted to forget, she knew she would always remember . . .

"Shh, be quiet," a younger Sonya whispered to her six-year-old sister.

Laura nodded her head, yet Sonya saw fear reflected in her eyes there. Their parents had been fighting for more than an hour, and their mother's screams were growing louder by the second. There were a few times Sonya caught herself jumping at the sounds of broken glass being shattered against the walls downstairs.

Suddenly the room flooded with light. Sonya watched in horror as their mother stumbled toward them. Laura grabbed Sonya's arm so tightly, she could feel her tiny nails digging into her skin.

"Come on, babies," their mother gestured.

Neither girl moved. They were too scared to even breathe.

"Come on, babies. Please, come to Mama. We're leaving."

At the thought of being able to leave, Sonya inched her way toward her mother. She flinched slightly at the sight of her mother's bruised face.

Laura's grip wasn't easing up any, either, but she didn't want to pry her sister's fingers loose. It was important to keep Laura calm, she kept telling herself. She looked back at Laura and then to her mother, who was frantically waving for her daughters to hurry.

Once they were in arm's reach, she could feel Laura being snatched up by their mother, who also grabbed her hand to ensure that Sonya followed her.

They all raced down the stairs and headed toward the door. But before they could reach the knob, Sonya heard the familiar bellow from her father.

"Just where in the hell do you think you're going?"

Sonya knew they were in trouble. She could feel her mother's fingers tremble madly in her hand as Laura began to cry.

"Nowhere," she heard her mother lie. Laura was placed beside her once again as her mother took a protective stand in front of them. Yet, Sonya realized, there was no one there to protect her mother from her father.

"Dorothy, don't you lie to me, damn it! Where are you going?"

Sonya peeked around her mother's leg to look at her father's snarling face. He was going to hit her mother again, she could tell. She felt her mother's body vibrate with fear in front of her. Sonya quietly pulled her sister closer to her.

Before she knew what happened, her mother was being dragged off by her hair into the living room, kicking and screaming the entire way . . .

Sonya closed her eyes to the painful memory. Her entire body shook as she turned away from the mirror. Why couldn't she forget? she asked herself, but her troubled thoughts were interrupted by a soft knock at the door. "Who is it?"

"It's me. Laura."

"Come in." Sonya turned to face her sister. When she saw Laura still dressed in her house robe, Sonya became suspicious.

"I don't think I'm going," Laura said, looking down at her feet.

"What do you mean?" Sonya's voice rose an octave.

"I . . . I just don't think I'm up to it," came her excuse.

Sonya tried to calm down. She did, after all, expect this from Laura. "It's your husband's funeral," Sonya said reasonably.

"I know. I just don't think that I can go through with this."

"What will it look like if you don't attend the funeral? Have you thought about that?"

"I don't care what it looks like, Sonya. I said I'm not going!" Laura declared, then thrust her chin upward.

Sonya knew she couldn't make Laura attend the funeral. Yet

she wished that she could make Laura see that she was only hurting her case by not attending.

"Laura," Sonya began patiently, but she held her tongue the moment she noticed Laura's eyes take on a glossy sheen. She turned away and shook her head wearily. "I'll make your apologies at the funeral."

"Thank you."

Sonya heard the door close behind Laura, and she turned to stare at the door. "Great," she mumbled to herself. "Just great." She closed her eyes as she felt the beginnings of a major migraine.

"It was beautiful service," Sharon complimented, patting Sonya on the back.

"Don't thank me. Richard made all the arrangements." Sonya took a sip of her Coke.

"Who's Richard?" James handed his wife a glass of Coke for herself.

"Curtis's brother—"

"I didn't know that Curtis had a brother," Sharon interrupted.

"Join the family," Sonya answered.

"Are there any other members from Curtis's family here?" James asked, scanning the room.

"That I couldn't tell you. I don't know half the people here."

"Why didn't Laura attend?" Sharon inquired.

"Trust me. I tried to get her to attend, but she is still too distraught over this whole situation."

"They brought so much food," Sharon observed. "Good thing he was cremated. I don't think I would've been too comfortable staring in the face of that evil man," Sharon added.

Sonya looked around the room for the millionth time.

"Looking for someone?" Sharon asked, following Sonya's eyes.

"Yes . . . no. I was hoping to talk to Dwayne on how the case is going."

"Dwayne is it now?" Sharon arched a curious brow.

Sonya rolled her eyes heavenward.

"There you are," Dwayne said, walking up to the small group.

"Hello, brother dear." Sharon reached up to deliver a kiss to his right cheek. "We were just talking about you."

"Anything good?" he asked, looking directly at Sonya.

Sonya's stomach performed acrobatics.

"It was a good service," he commented.

"Curtis's brother, Richard, arranged the service," Sonya answered stiffly.

"Oh, I see." Dwayne nodded.

Sonya caught Sharon elbowing her husband.

"We must be going now," James cut in, finally catching on to his wife's meaning.

"Yes, James has a flight for New York to finish preparing for," Sharon added.

"And I also have to get back home," Dwayne excused himself.

"Is it my perfume?" Sonya joked.

"A woman with a sense of humor," Dwayne teased. "I like that."

Sonya's shoulders took their regular position as she started to return with a smart remark, but thought better of it. "Good day, Mr. Hamilton," she finally said with a forced smile and turned away from the group.

"Fascinating," Dwayne mumbled.

"So you do like her?" Sharon asked with a hopeful gleam in her eyes.

"What's not to like?" he asked halfway to himself.

"Good. I think she likes you, too," Sharon said, continuing to play Cupid.

Dwayne turned and looked skeptically at his sister. "How can you tell that? By the fireballs she launches with her eyes

or the heavy sarcasm she tosses my way whenever she sees
me?''

"Don't pay any of that any attention. I think she's warming
up to you."

Dwayne rolled his eyes at his sister, then he walked away.

"I do, I really do," Sharon called after him.

"Come on, sweetheart." James said, taking her by the arm.
"I think it's time we left."

Dwayne arrived home early. He was hoping to get some
work done. He could take only so much sitting in his office.
Seeing Bridget's Jeep parked in the garage instantly flared his
curiosity. *I thought she was going over to Sylvia's house.*

Entering through the kitchen, his body froze at hearing the
familiar laughter of his daughter mingled with a heavy baritone.
Finally he pushed open the kitchen door which led to the living
room. His eyes widened with alarm at seeing his daughter half
dressed and in the arms of a strange boy. Her giggling instantly
ceased as father and daughter's eyes clashed together.

"Daddy!"

Chapter Eight

Dwayne sat on the edge of his bed and stared at his shaking hands. He could still feel Shock G.'s neck between his fingers. He couldn't remember the last time he'd been so angry. When he saw George's arms laced possessively around his baby, he wanted to tear the boy from limb to limb. Even now, he wondered if he should have let the boy go. He could tell George was relieved, by the way he stumbled over the furniture on the way out of the house.

Dwayne ordered Bridget to her room with the promise that he would deal with her later. Right now, it was in her best interest to let him calm down. *Where did I go wrong? Am I doing such a bad job of raising her?*

He reflected on his discipline tactics in the past years, and felt he had been both fair and lenient. He couldn't remember whether he gave his parents as much grief when he was a teenager. If so, he wished he could apologize.

They weren't able to see their granddaughter, but he knew that they would be proud of her. His parents had both passed away by the time he entered his first year of college. He wished he could seek some parental advice from his mother on how to handle Bridget.

Dwayne glanced at Theresa's picture that sat on his nightstand. He missed her. He missed her warm laughter and kind heart. He picked up the small silver frame and traced his finger along the sharp edges. *How would she handle this situation?*

Dwayne studied her light brown eyes and gentle smile and felt a dull ache in his chest. Lying back on his bed, still holding the frame, he remembered the day his dreams came to a crashing halt . . .

"Theresa, are you all right?" Dwayne demanded, while he banged on the bathroom door. She had been in there for thirty minutes, and he could hear her soft sobs through the door. "Theresa, sweetheart, please let me in," he pleaded. There was a long silence before he heard the lock turn.

When he saw the redness of her eyes and nose, he instantly drew her to him. He held her for a long time, as her tears drenched his shirt.

Theresa drew herself away from her husband and forced a smile for his benefit as she wiped her tears with the back of her hand.

Dwayne gently reached up and began stroking her long hair. "Are you okay?" he asked, looking into her eyes.

She avoided his eyes and nodded.

"Come here," he instructed her. He took her by the hand and pulled her into their bedroom. She sat down on the bed, while Dwayne kneeled down in front of her and took her delicate hands into his own.

"Theresa, please tell me what happened at the doctor's office today."

Again there was an unnerving silence that hung in the air between them. When she at last was ready to speak, she lifted her chin and held Dwayne's gaze. "I've been diagnosed with breast cancer."

Dwayne felt the force of her words and exactly what they meant. He wanted desperately for her to take them back, to say that it wasn't true. *Cancer? She couldn't have cancer. She's too young. She was only twenty-two. They had their whole life ahead of them.* "We'll get a second opinion," Dwayne stammered.

"That was the third doctor I've seen. I couldn't tell you until I was sure."

"How far along?"

"It's serious, Dwayne. I found out too late."

Dwayne thought of their two-year-old daughter that lay sleeping in her bed. He thought about how Theresa had sacrificed her medical studies to send him through law school. He was a second-year student. When he was able, he'd planned to send her back to med school. He thought of their plans together and felt them all slipping away. "We'll get through this," he said as tears gathered in his eyes.

"Of course we will," she said, hugging him close to her. It was her turn to comfort him.

Dwayne wanted desperately for there to be a mistake. His tears shook his entire body as he held on to his wife.

Theresa fought for as long as she could, but the disease proved to be too much for her. She died a year later.

Dwayne knocked lightly on Bridget's door. "Bridget, let me in."

"Go away!" she screamed.

Dwayne took a deep breath and tried again. "Bridget, please open up." After a brief moment, Bridget unlocked the door.

"Are you going to start yelling again?" she asked.

Dwayne noticed her red eyes. "No," he answered gently.

She allowed him entrance. Dwayne avoided stepping on the large piles of clothes spread throughout her floor. Posters of her favorite rap artists hung from every wall, as well as famous basketball stars.

Dwayne took a seat on the edge of her bed and hoped that he

hadn't crushed anything valuable. "Have a seat," he directed, patting the spot next to him.

Bridget plopped next to her father and avoided making eye contact. Dwayne leaned over and took her chin between his fingers, forcing her to look at him.

"My beautiful little girl." He brushed a lock of curls from her face. "Why do you want to grow up so fast?"

She pulled her chin away and looked down at her braided fingers.

"Bridget, I want to understand what's wrong. Maybe you can help me. All I know is, in the past year, you've got it in your head that you're going to do what you want to do, when you want to do it. I can't have that. There's only room for one adult in this house—and that's me. Some of the things you pull, you know better. The rules of this house haven't changed. I expect your homework and chores done without me having to follow up behind you. Lately all you think about are boys, boys, boys—"

"Daddy, you don't understand," Bridget interrupted.

"I do understand. I was a boy once, you know. I'm here to tell you—those boys want one thing and one thing only."

"Nothing happened, Daddy," Bridget said matter-of-factly.

Dwayne's shoulders slumped in relief. "What would have happened if I didn't come home?"

"Nothing. Don't you trust me?" Bridget frowned.

"Of course I trust you. It's those street thugs I don't trust."

Bridget rolled her eyes at her father and looked as if she was bored by his logic.

Dwayne counted to ten before he spoke again. Bridget was normally a sweet girl, but since she turned sixteen, she acted as if she knew everything. "Bridget, you're a pretty girl. You remind me so much of your mother. I'm trying to raise you to have more pride in yourself. I know you're young, but you're not that young. You're a lady, and you should demand respect for who you are."

Dwayne took another moment before he spoke again. "Don't let anyone dictate to you that you deserve nothing less than the best. You're too smart for that. I want my daughter to have the best of everything. I made that promise to your mother a long time ago, and it's a promise I intend to keep.''

By the way Bridget began to hold herself upright, Dwayne knew his words were getting through. He placed a kiss on his daughter's forehead, then stood up from the bed. ''Please feel like you can come to me or Aunt Sharon when something is troubling you.''

Bridget gave him a brief smile, then he turned to leave the room. ''Oh, about this afternoon. You know you're grounded, right?''

Bridget's smile faded. ''Of course.''

Chapter Nine

Laura stepped from her bath water wrapped in a fluffy, pink towel. She felt better today yet she wasn't sure about facing the world so soon. However, she was grateful how Sonya's estate separated her from the real world, even if it was for only a little while. Laura walked into the accompanying bedroom as she dried herself.

There were so many things she wanted to get accomplished today. First, she wanted to contact Mr. Hamilton. She hadn't been very cooperative since this whole ordeal began, but today she wanted to start helping with her own defense. She wasn't looking forward to returning to jail. Laura hated having to lean on her sister for help. In her heart, she truly loved Sonya and knew, for the most part, she was only trying to help. Yet sometimes she didn't want Sonya to interfere so much. However, she did realize—had she listened to Sonya—she wouldn't be in this predicament.

Laura reflected on the many arguments between she and Sonya over the past years. She hated to admit it, but Sonya had been right most of the time. Sonya'd warned her about dropping out of college to marry Curtis. Laura's eyes swept

Adrianne Byrd

across the beautiful decorated room and felt a sense of pride for her sister. Laura often wondered what she could have achieved had she stayed in school.

Throughout her academic career, she had also made good grades, but she lacked the determination to succeed that drove Sonya. Her sister had desperately wanted to make it out of Techwood, a housing project in downtown Atlanta. If she could just do it all again, there would be so many things that she would change. If she only knew then what she knew now. But hindsight is always twenty-twenty, she thought. Right now she wanted to concentrate on her future.

Laura slipped into a pair of white shorts and matching T-shirt. When she turned around to leave, she released a startled gasp at seeing a large man dominating the doorway. "Richard, what are you doing here?"

An excited Anthony Payne burst through Dwayne's office door, waving a small sheaf of papers in front of him. "I think I got something," he boasted confidently as he dropped the loose papers on Dwayne's desk.

"What is it?" Dwayne leaned back in his chair.

"Richard Durden."

"What about him?" Dwayne asked, watching the younger man take a seat.

"He doesn't exist," Anthony said, also leaning back in his chair, momentarily frightened of tipping over.

Dwayne shook his head at his overzealous assistant, who unfortunately was touched with a bit of clumsiness. "What do you mean, he doesn't exist? I met the man at his brother's funeral."

"Then you met an impostor."

"So are you going to tell me what you mean, or are we going to play twenty questions?" Dwayne asked, a little irritated.

"Well, according to this background check, Curtis was born to one Patricia and Jeremy Durden. His mother gave birth when she was just fifteen years old. His father was a young gang member who didn't live to see his twenties."

"And?" Dwayne rolled his hand, wanting him to speed up the story.

"And," Anthony continued, "due to a series of complications in her pregnancy, Patricia was unable to have any more children."

Dwayne leaned forward with that information. "What are you saying?"

"I'm saying according to my research, Curtis was an only child." Anthony leaned back farther in his chair. This time he did capsize, sending his tall body across the emerald carpet.

Dwayne shook his head at his assistant, who immediately sprang from the floor as if he intended to fall on his face on purpose. "Are you all right?" Dwayne asked in mock concern.

"Of course, sir," he answered, clearing his throat. He never once showed his embarrassment.

Dwayne shuffled through the papers sprawled across his desk until he found what he was looking for. "According to this, it was Richard Durden who identified Curtis's body."

Anthony shrugged his shoulders. "You're positive Miss Walters said Richard was Curtis's brother? Perhaps he was a cousin or something."

"No, she definitely said brother. This report also lists him as a brother." Dwayne picked up his phone to call Sonya, but before he could dial, Anthony's hand stopped him. "There's more."

Tina buzzed in over the small intercom. "Miss Walters, there's a Mr. Hamilton here to see you."

"Show him in." Sonya quickly refreshed her lipstick and checked her hair to make sure the pins still held it in a perfect French roll. By the time Dwayne entered the room, Sonya had picked up her pen and pretended to be engrossed with her work.

"Miss Walters?" Tina interrupted.

Sonya glanced up and placed her pen down on the desk.

"Mr. Hamilton, won't you have a seat?" She gestured to one of the vacant chairs in front of her desk.

Tina smiled seductively at Dwayne and left the room, unaware of Sonya's intense gaze on her retreating figure.

Dwayne took a seat and cleared his throat. "Miss Walters, I apologize for showing up on such short notice, but we've just discovered some disturbing news."

Sonya took a deep breath. "Is it about Curtis?"

Dwayne nodded. "I found out through my assistant, Anthony, your sister's husband had an interesting occupation. He was, as we say, a representative for a pharmaceutical company?"

Sonya knew what she was about to say would start an argument, so she braced herself. "I know Curtis was a drug dealer," she said softly.

Dwayne's jaw clamped shut. Sonya could see the tiny muscles along his jawline twitch in obvious frustration. He silently unbuttoned his gray jacket and loosened his tie. "Do you want to tell me how something like that just slipped your mind?"

He had every right to be angry, Sonya told herself. "I didn't think it was important at the time."

"How could you have possibly thought that? That bit of information opens up a new avenue of suspects," he reasoned.

Sonya nodded in agreement.

"You have nothing else to say?" Dwayne asked, staring at her.

"I was wrong not to have mentioned it," Sonya admitted.

Dwayne took a deep breath and glanced up at the ceiling as if he were looking for help from a higher power. "Is there something else you're hiding from me? Anything else you don't consider important?"

Sonya shifted in her chair. "No," she answered with a great deal of patience.

"Good. But I warn you, if I find any more surprises, I'm dropping this case. Understand?" Dwayne informed as he held Sonya's gaze.

Sonya nodded, hating his parental tone.

"Anthony has also brought another disturbing matter to my attention. I had a background check done on Curtis. I've discovered that Curtis Durden's parents are both dead—"

"I knew that," Sonya cut in.

"Let me finish," Dwayne instructed her patiently. "As a child, Curtis bounced back and forth through our wonderful judicial system. He went from one foster home to another."

"Explains a lot," Sonya commented.

Dwayne nodded. "At fifteen he had his first brush with the police. He was charged with burglary."

Sonya absently twirled the gold coin around her neck while deep in thought. "So you're telling me it wasn't Curtis's fault he was a jerk."

"No. But maybe he got caught up in the system," Dwayne reasoned.

Sonya rolled her eyes at his explanation.

"But that's not all. We were unable to come up with any record of a Richard Durden."

Sonya stopped twirling her necklace. "No record?"

Dwayne stood up from his chair and began to pace across the floor. "So you're as shocked as I am?"

Sonya's mind raced a mile a minute. "Then who is the man that's been living under my roof for the past week?"

"I haven't the slightest idea. Not only that, this Richard identified Curtis's body, according to the police reports."

Sonya placed her fingers to her temples. What Dwayne was saying wasn't making any sense.

"Is this man still at your home?" Dwayne asked, straightening his jacket.

Sonya came out of her chair. "Laura!"

Sonya snatched up the phone to dial home. If this man wasn't who he said he was, then she wanted Laura away from him. The phone continued to ring. Sonya gave Dwayne a worried glance. *Why isn't she answering the phone?* The answering machine picked up on the fifth ring, and Sonya slammed down the phone. *Something's wrong.* "I have to get over there." Sonya grabbed her purse.

"Maybe she's at a friend's house," Dwayne reasoned.

Sonya paused at the door. "Laura hasn't left the house since she was released from jail," she answered.

"Then I'll come with you." Dwayne followed her out of her office door. Racing down the small aisle of cubicles, Sonya saw the curious stares from her employees as she passed by. They reached the elevator bay and waited impatiently for one to arrive. Sonya tried to convince herself Laura wasn't in any danger, but she failed miserably.

When the elevator arrived, both Dwayne and Sonya rushed in. She glanced at Dwayne once and noticed the genuine concern. They reached the lobby and flew across the hard marbled floor. Outside, Dwayne grabbed her hand. "We'll take my car."

Sonya looked quizzically at him.

"You're not exactly a safe driver under stressful conditions," he explained.

Sonya gave no argument as she ran along with him, giving no thought to her three-inch pumps as she kept up with Dwayne's pace.

Dwayne pulled out his keys and pushed the small button to disengage the alarm system. He jumped into a black Porsche, leaned over, and unlocked the passenger's side.

In the next moment, Sonya searched desperately for her seat belt. Dwayne sped around corners and changed lanes like a madman. A few times, Sonya cringed when he came entirely too close to another vehicle. *He thought I was a reckless driver?* She was relieved when they reached the highway. There weren't too many cars for her to worry about.

They arrived at Sonya's house in record time. Sonya bolted for the door, and Sonya quickly turned off the alarm. Dwayne entered right behind her. "Laura!" they both screamed in unison. No answer.

"I'll check upstairs," Sonya said, racing up the long spiral staircase.

Sonya darted in and out of the six bedrooms, frantically

searching for Laura. Each room was empty. Dwayne's thundering voice caused her to rush back to the staircase.

"I found a note," he said, waving a thin piece of paper.

Sonya flew downstairs. Fear gripped her heart as Dwayne handed her the letter.

Dear Sonya,
Stepped out for a moment with Richard. Will return soon.
                                                    Laura

Chapter Ten

The moon hung high while filtered rays pierced through the Palladian windows, serving as the only light in Sonya's living room.

"She should have been home by now," Sonya fretted. She paced across the polished marble for the millionth time.

"Are you sure you called all her friends?" Dwayne asked without looking up. He held his head between his hands and stared down at the floor.

"Everyone that I know of. Laura doesn't have many friends."

Dwayne searched for words that would soothe her but could think of none.

"What can the police do?" Sonya asked.

"We've already gone over this. The police will think she skipped bail."

"But she *wouldn't* skip bail. She wouldn't do anything that stupid."

"Please sit down, Sonya. You're making me a nervous wreck."

Sonya looked as if she wanted to argue, but sat in the cream-colored love seat on the opposite side of him. She crossed her long, slender legs, and Dwayne caught his breath at the sight of the moonlight caressing their shapely form. His eyes slowly traveled to her form-fitting dress that glowed in the luminous light. When he looked up to meet her worried expression, he felt a tight knot form in the pit of his stomach. She looked beautiful with the radiant moonlight dancing along each curl of her hair.

Dwayne's eyes traveled to her flawless shaped lips. He could feel himself being drawn to them. When he looked back into her eyes, he noticed they seemed to glow with passion.

Suddenly she stood up, never taking her eyes from his. She reached behind her dress and pulled the zipper in the back. Mesmerized, he watched the dress slide to the floor. Shimmering lights kissed the various parts of her glorious body that stood before him. His breathing became shallow as he looked upon his Venus. Her firm legs led him to a flat, tight stomach that promised him a world of wonder and discovery. His eyes traveled to her ample breasts that demanded attention. Dwayne felt his passion rising.

"Dwayne, do you hear me? Dwayne!" Sonya's voice boomed, shattering his romantic vision.

Dwayne looked guiltily at Sonya, who sat fully clothed in the love seat opposite him.

"Hello, is anyone home?" Sonya said, waving her hand in front of his face.

"I . . . Uh. Yes, I'm sorry," Dwayne sputtered, jumping to his feet.

"Where are you going?" Sonya asked, her eyes widening in alarm.

"I . . . I need to use the phone," he said, wanting to leave the room.

"Well, there's one beside you." Sonya pointed to a gold phone sitting on the glass table beside the sofa.

"It's a personal call," he offered as an explanation.

"Oh," Sonya said, standing. "Follow me, there's one in the kitchen."

Crossing the spacious living room, Dwayne searched for something, anything, to say. "When did you redecorate?"

"I reordered my furniture the same day I was released from the hospital." They entered the kitchen. "There's the phone." Sonya pointed.

She left him alone in the kitchen to make his call.

What is wrong with me? He waited a few minutes to gain his composure before he dialed home.

"Hamilton residence," Bridget answered pertly.

"Hello, honey, it's me."

"Oh, hello, sweetheart," Bridget answered too seductively.

"Sweetheart?"

"I'm joking, Dad."

Dwayne shook his head against the phone. "I'm calling to let you know that I'm coming home late tonight, so don't wait up."

"Ah, sugar-daddy got a date," Bridget teased.

"On the contrary. I'm waiting for a client."

Sonya returned to the kitchen and headed to the refrigerator. "I'll see you when I get home," Dwayne said, watching Sonya from the corner of his eye. "All right, I love you, too. Bye."

Sonya placed the bottled water back in the refrigerator. She stiffened at hearing Dwayne's words.

"Mind if I get something to drink myself? I'm dying of thirst," he asked from behind. His rich voice sent chills down her spine.

"Of course," she said, refusing to look back at him. "What would you like? I have Coke, Sprite, and just about any kind of fruit juice you like."

"Do you have anything stronger?" He peered over her shoulder to look for himself.

Dwayne's nearness caused a deep blush to stain her cheeks. "I . . . ah think I have some Merlot. I really don't keep anything stronger than wine."

"Then Merlot it is. We need something to soothe our nerves."

Sonya turned to retrieve glasses from the cupboard. Moments later, they sat in the living room, sipping on the rich taste of Sonya's favorite red wine.

"Tell me a little about yourself," Dwayne asked, staring directly into Sonya's eyes.

Sonya didn't know whether it was the wine or his intense gaze that caused her to feel warm. "There's nothing to tell." She rolled her finger around the glass rim.

"Oh, I doubt that."

Sonya smiled awkwardly. "I'm sure you've already ran a background check on me, so you already know everything."

Dwayne returned her smile. "I know the basics. You've accomplished a lot to get where you are and in such a short time. President of your own advertising company. That's very impressive."

"A great deal of it came from being in the right place at the right time."

"You graduated cum laude from Harvard. I think you're being too modest. Surely there's more?"

"No, that's about it."

"And your sister?" he asked, changing the subject.

"What about her?"

"You both are so . . . different."

"On the surface maybe, but in here"—Sonya pointed to her heart—"we are very much the same."

"Why haven't you ever married?" Dwayne asked after a long pause.

Sonya chose her words carefully before speaking again. "I'm not so sure if I believe in marriage." She didn't try to hide the pain covering her face. "Would you like some more wine?" Sonya offered, as she got up and headed toward the kitchen without waiting for an answer. Once in the kitchen, she wiped her forehead with the back of her hand. What was it about this man that caused her to react this way? She had never discussed such a personal question before, not even with Laura.

Only fools believed in marriage, she thought. Men looked at the institution as if it meant ownership. It was no more than a license for them to treat their wives like a piece of meat. She remembered the times she had to cover her ears from hearing the beatings her father rained nightly on her mother. She remembered, vividly, the black eyes and broken noses as if it was yesterday.

Once Laura made the comment that their parents' situation was their mother's fault, but Laura was too young to know any better. It was probably how she adopted the notion that when Curtis abused her, it was somehow her fault.

Sonya decided in her heart, a long time ago, that she would never marry. She fought to get out of the projects and make something of herself. Now she had accomplished everything she had dreamed of, and she did it without the help of a man.

"Sonya, are you all right in there?" Dwayne called.

"Yes. I'll be right there," she answered. She wiped a lone tear from her eye and returned to the living room with a new bottle of wine.

When she entered the room, Dwayne had taken off his jacket and tie and was now busy loosening his collar. When their eyes locked again, Sonya fought a powerful urge to go to him. It was a feeling that confused her.

Dwayne pulled his eyes away first. "If I didn't know better, Miss Walters, I would think you were trying to get me drunk."

Sonya smiled and sat the new bottle of Merlot between them. "I thought about what you said," Dwayne spoke seriously again. "I have to disagree with you. I believe marriage to be a beautiful institution. Men and women were ultimately put on this earth to coexist together."

"Then why aren't you married, Mr. Hamilton?" Sonya asked with a sarcastic smile.

"I was married once," Dwayne said, looking down at his glass. "My wife passed away almost thirteen years ago."

Sonya felt his pain instantly. "I'm sorry," she whispered, leaning forward to take his hand. The unexpected electrical current from his touch caused her to release it.

Silent moments passed between them before Dwayne spoke again. This time there was a small tremor to his voice. "Why don't you believe in marriage?" he asked softly.

Sonya closed her eyes. She didn't want to answer nor did she want to open herself up to this man. "It's just my silly opinion." She tried laughing off his question, but the serious look on Dwayne's face told her that he didn't accept her explanation.

"Sonya, not every man is like Curtis." This time he leaned in to take her hand. There was a softness in his eyes that made her want to trust him. She wondered what it would be like to trust a man with all her doubts and uncertainties. A warning bell rang loud in her head. Sonya pulled her hand from his touch and faked her self-confidence. "I'm sure you feel that you're the spokesman for your gender, Mr. Hamilton, but the truth is, I've never met a man worthy of my love."

Dwayne's eyes didn't lose their softness. "Maybe one day you will, Miss Walters."

Again Sonya felt uncomfortable with their conversation. "It's getting late." She stood and walked away from him. She paused beside one of the windows and gazed out. Her instincts told her that Dwayne was standing behind her.

"What are you afraid of, Sonya? Love? Companionship? I assure you, these things are nothing to fear."

Sonya attempted to laugh at his observation but failed. Her voice cracked, and she knew then she was caught. She turned around to face him, knowing he could see the tears gathering in her eyes. "It's been my experience, Mr. Hamilton, that a woman's love is something very fragile. Unfortunately it's also something too many women give away carelessly. I don't plan to make that same mistake. I fought for too long to prove that I define my happiness. I don't need or want to depend on anyone else to give me what I am capable of doing myself."

Dwayne's face softened under the tranquil glow cascading through the window. "I know you've been hurt, Sonya." He reached up and gently began to caress her cheek. "Don't let the ignorance of a couple of men rule your heart against the rest of us.''

''Are you considering yourself in a different class than Curtis, Mr. Hamilton?'' Sonya wanted to pull away but couldn't.

Dwayne smiled. ''I think you already know the answer to that question.''

This time Sonya did pull away. ''I think it's time you left, Mr. Hamilton.''

''Are you going to be all right tonight? Maybe I should take one of the extra bedrooms upstairs. I don't like the thought of you being left alone,'' Dwayne said with concern in his voice.

Sonya's stomach tightened at the thought of them sleeping under the same roof. She was still too confused about the strong emotions exploding within her just from looking at him. Yet what could she say? She definitely had enough room, and she would be lying if she said that today's events didn't leave her shaken up a bit. She was grateful he'd stayed this long, but she didn't want him to continue with his interrogation.

''Sonya?''

Acknowledging she didn't feel safe alone, she looked back into his probing eyes. ''I would like it very much if . . . you would stay the night, Mr. Hamilton.''

Dwayne glanced at the clock beside his bed. Three fifteen, five minutes since the last time he'd checked. The guest room Sonya gave him was directly across from her room, a thought he was unable to forget. He wondered if he should call Sharon again to check on Bridget.

He had called Bridget after deciding to stay the night with Sonya. He didn't want to leave his daughter home, so he instructed her to spend the night at her aunt's house. He had also called three times after she arrived safely at Sharon's to check up on her. He knew Bridget could be a handful and was probably trying to see how much she could pull over her aunt's eyes. Looking at the clock again, he decided against it. Sharon was no pushover—surely she had things under control.

Dwayne pulled himself into a sitting position, realizing he wasn't about to get to sleep anytime soon. He let the moonlight serve as his light as he stood up from the bed. The unpleasant feeling of cold marbled floors sent shivers to his spine as pulled on his pants and headed toward the door. He successfully made it out of his room without making a sound, then headed toward the staircase.

As he descended, he admired Sonya's palatial house. The elaborate style was indeed impressive, yet he felt the grand home didn't quite fit the woman he saw in Sonya. There was no doubt in his mind that she was a strong, intelligent, and classy woman, but he had the distinct impression this house represented a wall, perhaps a fortress, she built around herself. The house was beautiful, but it lacked the warmth and laughter it needed to turn it into a home.

Dwayne remembered the pain reflected in Sonya's eyes earlier that evening, and suddenly the answer became crystal clear to him. She was afraid. Of what, he didn't know and found himself wishing that he did. The protectiveness he felt for her grew with each passing day.

Dwayne shook the thoughts forming in his mind. He should be thinking of other matters, such as his missing client.

The sight of flickering lights caught Dwayne's attention. He headed toward the living room to find out its source. Stepping into the spacious room, he didn't expect the lovely vision of Sonya dressed in a blue lace nightgown. She sat prettily on the couch with the added light from the candles illuminated around her. He couldn't figure out why she had at least a dozen or more candles lit in the living room as she seemed engrossed in something she was holding.

Dwayne didn't want to disturb her, so he started to head back to his room. If it wasn't for the sniffling he heard, he would have carried out his plans.

"Sonya?" he asked, stepping back into the room. If she heard him, she didn't show it. She continued studying something in her lap. "Sonya, are you all right?"

This time Sonya did look up, her eyes puffy and red. It was

obvious to him that she'd been crying. "You're wrong. All men are alike." Her words slurred together as her lips trembled.

"You're drunk," Dwayne said, coming toward her. He noticed another empty bottle of Merlot in front of her.

"I'm not drunk." Sonya tossed what looked to be a small picture frame to the opposite end of the couch. Dwayne's curiosity caused him to look toward the frame.

"I think I need to get you to bed," he said, picking her up. She didn't seem to realize that Dwayne was carrying her up the stairs as she continued to pout. "I'm not sleepy," she recited.

Dwayne smiled down at her, enjoying the feel of her in his arms. She rested her head against his shoulders and sighed. Dwayne worried that she would hear the hard pounding of his heart. He kicked her bedroom door open and headed to the king-sized canopy bed that sat like a golden throne in the middle of the room.

He tucked her in, and despite her protests, she closed her eyes the moment her head hit the pillow. Dwayne could do no more than gaze at her. She was more beautiful in her sleep than at any other time he'd studied her.

Slowly he turned from the room and succeeded in not disturbing her. He went back down the stairs to the living room and blew out a few of the candles before his curiosity returned to the discarded picture frame. Dwayne picked up the small frame and viewed the four people in the photograph. It wasn't a happy picture. No one in the picture was smiling. The dark, heavyset man in the photo had his arm draped possessively around a slender woman who looked repulsed by his touch. The young girls standing in front of the unhappy couple resembled their parents but not each other.

He recognized Sonya instantly. Her hair was parted in the middle and pulled into two tight ponytails. She resembled a sad angel dressed in a dingy white dress. Sonya's hands held those of the smaller sister standing beside her. Laura wore the same dress, however, in a smaller size. She was the only one not looking in the direction of the camera. She stood staring toward her older sister. Her face held such adoration for Sonya. It was obvious to Dwayne that Sonya has always been Laura's protector.

Dwayne thought of what Sonya had said earlier. "You're wrong. All men are alike." He also remembered the rest of the article Carmen had given him. Dorothy Walters was a battered housewife. For the first time, he understood what Sonya meant and what she must have gone through as a child. No wonder she felt all men were the same. She had seen nothing but violence in men.

Dwayne studied Sonya again, and this time he let his finger trail around the frame of her face. She looked so sad. Slowly he placed the picture back on the sofa and blew out the rest of the candles.

Walking back up the stairs, his thoughts wandered back to the picture. He was beginning to understand Sonya's determination to prove to herself that she could handle everything on her own. The house was a fortress she had built to protect what she held so dear: her heart.

Sleep wouldn't come as the clock now read four forty-five. There was a sudden thrashing sound coming from outside his room. Dwayne left to investigate. The sound was coming from Sonya's room. He gently pushed open her door.

There, in her silken sheet haven, Sonya thrashed about. *She's having a bad dream.* Instantly Dwayne was there, gathering her into his arms. "Shh, I'm here," he whispered. Her thrashing ceased almost immediately. Her body molded itself against his chest in total relaxation.

Dwayne rocked Sonya until he felt his own sleepiness. Gently, he laid her back in the bed. A small whimper escaped Sonya's lips as she unconsciously clung to him. Without hesitation, he slid into bed beside her. Within minutes, he was asleep. Soon the first rays of dawn trickled through the windows to kiss the couple's faces as they lay sleeping peacefully.

Chapter Eleven

Bridget sat next to her aunt and uncle, bored with their conversation. They talked about different computer programs and diagnostics tests her uncle James had handled in the past week. She couldn't understand how Aunt Sharon sat there, nodding her head, as if she were truly interested in this stuff.

Neither of them noticed that she was bored out of her mind. She dipped her spoon in and out of her soggy cereal, praying that her father would call or show up to save her at any moment. She looked down disgustedly at the knee-length, pastel dress her aunt Sharon made her wear today. If anyone she knew saw her dressed like this, she would die of humiliation.

"Bridget, don't play with your food," Sharon instructed with a smile. "And sit up straight. Young ladies don't slouch like that."

Bridget refrained from rolling her eyes as she straightened herself in the chair. Uncle James ended his story with a boring computer joke someone told at work. Aunt Sharon laughed heartily while Bridget tried to figure out the punch line.

James turned his attention to her. "So, Bridget, you have

only one year left of high school. Any thoughts about what your plans are after college?''

After college? That's at least five years away. How would I know? "I'm not quite sure what I want to do yet," she said simply.

"It's never too soon to start planning, and trust me, computers are the future," James said. He nodded his head toward her as if he were trying to get her to agree with him.

"Well, do you have any hobbies or interests you'd like to pursue?" Sharon jumped in.

Bridget let out a small sigh. This was going to be a long and painful conversation, she just knew it. *Hurry up and call, Daddy.* "I like music and I thought about, maybe, modeling." That was the wrong answer, judging by the looks that passed between them. *Maybe I should've said I was thinking about becoming a doctor or lawyer.*

"Is there anything else you enjoy doing? Perhaps you have a favorite subject in school?" Sharon asked with hope laced in her voice.

"No, not really. I don't think school really agrees with me," she answered honestly.

"How about another hobby?" James asked a little too eager.

"I like collecting coins. I have over two thousand that I've collected over the years. It's really neat. Maybe you would like to see them?" She looked from her uncle to her aunt who gave her odd looks.

"Does your father know about you not preparing for your future?" Sharon asked, not bothering to hide her displeasure.

Bridget slumped her shoulders but quickly corrected herself at Sharon's disapproving look. "Dad says that I should take my time deciding what I want to do, and that no matter what I choose, he would stand behind me." That wasn't completely true. What he had said was for her to start getting serious about life and get her head out of the clouds. But she wasn't about to tell them that.

The breakfast table grew quiet as everyone finished their meal. Bridget didn't see what the big deal was. Everyone acted as if she were supposed to already have her whole life planned. *I'm sixteen. What's the rush?*

"Are you all packed?" James asked Sharon when she stood to clear the dishes.

"Yes. Our reservations are confirmed. We leave tomorrow at eleven."

Bridget helped clear the table. As her aunt and uncle talked about attending some banquet in James's honor in California, Bridget blocked out the rest of their conversation. She thought about her future. She liked the idea of pursuing a career involving precious coins. The subject fascinated her.

After the dishes were all cleared away, Bridget returned to the guest room to give Sharon and James their privacy. Once she was alone in her room, she let her shoulders slump to their regular position. She felt hurt by her aunt and uncle's lack of support. *Whose life is it, anyway?*

She waited patiently for her father to call. Being on restriction was a drag. She couldn't believe he told her aunt that she was not to leave the house until he had personally called for her to do so.

Another hour passed, and Bridget grew restless. Aunt Sharon knocked on the door and peeked in. "What are you doing?" she asked, smiling.

"Thinking," Bridget answered.

"About what?" she asked, walking into the room.

Bridget shook her head. "I don't think you want to hear about it."

Sharon lifted a questioning brow. "Of course I would. Why would you think that?"

"I don't think anyone cares about what I really want to do. Just what they think I should do."

Sharon sat beside Bridget with a hurtful expression. "That's not true, Bridget. I'm always here when you want to talk."

Bridget took a deep breath, then began talking carefully. "I'm hurt by how you and Uncle James made me feel at breakfast. I'm not some silly teenager. I mean, you made me feel like my suggestions for a career were stupid or something."

"Honey, we didn't mean to offend you. It's just that we want the best for you. That includes the best schools and the best career."

"I know, but maybe I should have a say on what I think is best for me. Every time I come over here, I get hit with questions on my career choices or advice on how to catch a husband once I'm in college. I might not want to get married. Maybe I don't want to go to college."

"Not go to college?"

Bridget dropped her head. *Here we go again.* Adults didn't mind her expressing her opinion as long as it didn't differ from theirs. "That's an option. College isn't for everyone, you know."

Sharon smiled tightly. "Maybe we should discuss this with your father."

Bridget threw her hand up. "Why? It's not my father's decision. It's mine. I kinda like the idea of dealing with coins. Perhaps I could be some kind of dealer or something."

"Without a college education?" Sharon asked skeptically.

"College doesn't guarantee you a job, Aunt Sharon," Bridget said, placing her hands on her hips.

Sharon continued to shake her head. "Your father isn't going to like this."

Bridget gave up. Aunt Sharon hadn't heard a word she'd said. She put her face in the palm of her hand and chose to ignore the rest of her aunt's words. If Aunt Sharon wanted to tell her father, she would just have to prepare herself to go through this speech when she got home. Again she wished that he would hurry up and call.

Sonya rolled over and bumped her head against something hard. Slowly she opened her eyes to see a broad chest lying beside her. Her heart skipped a beat as she allowed her eyes to travel upward. Her entire body quivered in shock at discovering Dwayne sleeping beside her.

Desperately she searched her memory for an explanation.

She remembered not being able to sleep, then going downstairs to have another glass of wine. Bits and pieces of her drinking more than just one glass of Merlot flooded her mind. A remorseful moan sounded deep within herself. *What have I done?*

Dwayne's arms tightened around her waist as he snuggled closer. Her eyes widened in alarm as her voice failed her. She was speechless. She allowed herself a moment to think before she decided to ease away from him. It was easier said than done. His arms were too heavy for her to lift. They seemed to weigh a ton.

Sonya gave up after the fifth try. She needed a better plan, but she couldn't think of another way of escaping his embrace. Surely she didn't let her first time result from a drunken stupor. She found comfort in the fact that she was still dressed in her nightgown. *That could only mean nothing happened. Right? Why can't I remember?* Sonya felt her anger rise. *How dare he take advantage of me when I obviously couldn't defend myself. What kind of man was he?*

Sonya allowed her fury to build while she imagined wild scenarios that led them to being in bed together. She never once believed she played a guilty role, resulting in them lying in bed together. She blamed Dwayne for taking advantage of the situation.

Her anger gave her strength to start pounding on Dwayne's chest, waking him instantly.

"What the hell?" Dwayne demanded, warding off one of her punches.

Sonya's fury was at full swing as she continued to land punches at different parts of his body. "You bastard!"

In one quick motion, Dwayne stood and dragged her out of bed. "What is your problem?" he commanded, glaring at her.

"How dare you take advantage of me!" Sonya hissed back at him.

"Take advantage?" Dwayne gave her a disgusted scowl. He saw her wince in pain from his tight grip, so he dropped his hands and proceeded to shout at her, "Is that what you honestly think I did? Do you believe that I would even consider doing such a thing?''

Sonya's face registered disbelief. *Did he plan to deny the obvious?* ''Apparently you get your kicks by seducing women when they are defenseless.''

''You mean drunk, don't you?'' Dwayne sneered.

Sonya clenched her hands into tight fists. ''I don't care what I was, it still gave you no right to seduce me!''

Dwayne found her reaction comical. ''Seduce? Have you lost your mind?'' He gave a lustful smile. ''After the way you entwined your body all over me last night?''

Sonya's face turned deep red. ''That's a lie,'' she accused, refusing to believe him.

''Trust me, if anyone seduced anyone, it was you seducing me. I couldn't pry your body off me if I wanted to,'' Dwayne continued, smiling down at her.

''Liar!'' she said, backing away.

Dwayne tensed at her viciousness. ''How would you know? You were too drunk to remember. And I'll tell you one thing: you're quite the tigress when you're drunk. When you're sober, you won't ever have to worry about a man wanting to touch you. You are the most dispassionate, uptight woman I've ever known!''

Sonya put all her strength into the powerful slap that stung her hand. She watched the dark imprint from her hand surface against his smooth skin. She closed her eyes, sure that he would no doubt retaliate.

Dwayne turned and left the room without saying another word to her. When the door closed behind him, Sonya opened her eyes, puzzled. She continued to stand in the middle of her room long after she heard him walk out of the guest room and out of the house. The sound of his car's engine revving caused her to go to the window. She watched regretfully as he sped down the driveway.

She wiped away the tears trickling down her face. *Damn him!* She looked away from the window as a sense of loneliness engulfed her. A voice deep within her screamed that she had made a mistake.

Standing in the shower, Sonya cursed herself for the zillionth time. She was convinced she had overreacted. There had to be a reasonable explanation for what happened, she just wished she knew what it was.

By the time she had dressed and called the police to report Laura missing, Sonya was riddled with guilt. The front doorbell rang, and Sonya went downstairs to answer it.

"Good morning, Miss Walters," Sergeant Freeman greeted.

Sonya shook her head, not believing her luck. "Are you the only police officer that works in Atlanta?"

"It would seem so. May I come in?"

Sonya stepped aside to allow the sergeant to enter. She started to close the door behind him when another officer appeared.

"Miss Walters, this is Sergeant Anderson with the Roswell Police Department. I took the liberty of having his precinct inform me when anything dealing with you or your sister came up."

"How kind of you," she answered.

"Good morning, Miss Walters," Sergeant Anderson greeted finally. Sonya nodded in acknowledgment.

"You called to report Laura missing?" Freeman asked.

Sonya hated Freeman's tone and cringed from the mere thought of having to tell this man her sister was missing. She knew what this report would do to Laura's bond.

"Miss Walters?" Freeman broke into her private thoughts.

"Yes. My sister is missing."

"Missing, or has she skipped town?"

Sonya bit her lip to prevent herself from saying what she really wanted. Freeman was riding her nerves. Every time she turned around, it seemed, he was looking over her shoulders.

"Miss Walters, you do realize there is a possibility that Laura left on her own?" Freeman added.

"I doubt that," Sonya answered, walking away from the

door to stand directly in front of Sergeant Freeman. "I believe my sister was taken against her will."

Freeman erupted in laughter. Evidently he didn't believe her. Sonya moved away from him to stand in front of Sergeant Anderson.

"You look like a man who takes his job seriously." She gave Freeman a disgusted look. "Are you going to do your job and take my statement or not?"

Sergeant Anderson looked from her to Freeman. "May I ask why you believe your sister was physically taken?" he asked, pulling out a pen and a small notepad to take down her response.

"My sister's disappearance occurred the same day we discovered her husband's brother to be an imposter."

"We?" Anderson asked, looking up.

"Yes. My sister's lawyer, Dwayne Hamilton, discovered this yesterday."

"Maybe your sister and this man are in collaboration with each other," Freeman suggested.

Sonya glared at Freeman, causing him to become serious. "As I was saying, Dwayne's, I mean Mr. Hamilton's, office did a background check on Curtis's family and discovered that Curtis was an only child. If Sergeant Freeman's department had done their homework, they would also know this."

"What does that have to with your sister murdering her husband? Why would we care if you were housing a stranger?"

"Because according to your own paperwork, you have Richard Durden listed as identifying Curtis's body. Surely that sounds like a crime worth investigating."

Freeman's jaw twitched. "Perhaps Richard Durden is Curtis's stepbrother. Did you ever think of that? Perhaps they shared the same father and not the same mother."

Sonya reflected on his words for a moment, then shook her head. "No. That wouldn't work, either. This man said he was Curtis's younger brother."

"So?" Freeman asked impatiently.

"So he claimed he was five years younger. Dwayne said Curtis's father died when Curtis was two years old."

This succeeded in getting Sergeant Anderson to take her claims seriously. For the next hour, she went over everything she knew. Most of it was from what Dwayne told her last night. Freeman's scowl remained on his face the whole time. When Sergeant Anderson announced that this indeed sounded like a kidnapping case, Sergeant Freeman began muttering to himself. Neither Sonya nor Sergeant Anderson paid him any attention.

Sonya watched the police cars drive down the driveway. She'd hoped that filing that report would at least make her feel as though she was doing something to help her sister; it didn't. The problem was, she didn't understand the whole situation. Why would this man want to cause Laura harm? What was the connection between Richard Durden—whoever he was—and her sister?

The phone rang, startling Sonya out of her deep thoughts. She reached for the phone, praying it was good news. "Hello?"

"Hello, Sonya? This is Tina." Sonya's hopes crashed.

"Good morning, Tina."

"Good morning. I called because I was checking to see if you forgot your one o'clock appointment with Mr. Packard?"

Sonya moaned into the phone. She did forget. "Cancel it. I'm dealing with a family emergency." Sonya didn't want to go into any details. She made a point to keep her professional and personal life separate. Sharon had been the only exception to the rule.

"Actually, Miss Walters, I had a hard enough time trying to get you in for this appointment. It may be months before Mr. Packard agrees to another one."

Sonya cursed at her luck. She reluctantly informed Tina she would be there in time for her appointment. She entertained the thought of passing up the Packard Steel line but thought better of it. She had worked too hard to let this pass up. *I will just go in for a few hours. If everything goes as planned, I will be home by five.*

She ran upstairs to get dressed. She selected a peach-colored dress with matching pumps. When she finished, she looked herself over in the mirror. She succeeded in presenting herself as a self-confident businesswoman, everything she wasn't feeling. *Come on girl, it's just for a few hours.*

Sonya's meeting with Mr. Packard went well. She won the Packard Steel account and soon found herself working later than she intended.

When she looked up at her clock, it read eight-thirty. She decided to stay another hour to clear some more paperwork that was stacking high on her desk. It was late, and everyone had gone home for the evening. It was the best time to get it done.

Sonya buried herself in her work, and before she knew it, it was eleven thirty. Had it not been for her stomach growling like a fierce lion, she would have worked through the night. She leaned back into her chair and closed her eyes. *I have to get something to eat.*

She thought about calling Dwayne, but she was sure he would have contacted her if there were any new developments in Laura's case. She stared at the phone, wanting to call him anyway. She shook her head at her foolishness, then decided to go home.

Sonya stood up from her chair and began gathering her things. She was disappointed that the police department hadn't tried to contact her. She desperately wanted to believe that no news was good news.

She closed her office door and headed toward the elevators. Something fell. *What was that?* She held her breath and waited to see if she would hear it again. Nothing. *I must be hearing things.* She shook her head and continued toward the elevator. *There it is again.* Sonya's heart pounded loudly in her ears. The roots of her hair stood at attention.

Slowly she glanced around the large office. "Who's there?" she called out. No answer. Sonya expelled the breath she unconsciously held. She continued to creep toward the elevator bay, which seemed miles away. This time she heard something fall, and she took off running. She dropped a trail of paper as she raced through the large office.

Footsteps! She heard someone following her. Yet her fear refused to let her turn around. She reached the elevators and frantically started pushing buttons. A bell sounded as an elevator door began to open.

Running for the opening door, Sonya took a quick glance behind her. She let out a horrified scream as she bumped solidly into a figure stepping from the elevator.

Chapter Twelve

Dwayne sat next to his brother-in-law at Fat Tuesdays, James's favorite bar at Underground Atlanta. James ordered another drink from the passing waitress. The music was loud, and the smoke stung Dwayne's eyes but this had always been his and James's favorite hang out.

"I'm glad you were able to make it," James shouted over the music.

Dwayne smiled and ordered another Coke. He didn't want to touch anything alcoholic, knowing he had to drive home. However, after what he went through this morning with Sonya, a drink was what he sorely needed. "Bridget gave me the message to meet you here. What on earth happened between her and Sharon last night?"

"More like this morning. Sharon told me they had discussed Bridget attending college. I don't think that your daughter is too keen on the idea."

"Oh," Dwayne said, with some thought. He'd attempted the same subject with Bridget and knew he had handled the situation wrong. He'd succeeded only in getting his daughter upset, leaving him frustrated. "What brought up the topic?"

"Who remembers? I just know that after Sharon talked to Bridget, she was snapping at me."

"That explains why you're here." Dwayne smiled.

"I don't see anything funny about this. We are supposed to leave for the banquet tomorrow. This is the last thing I need right now."

Dwayne nodded. "Congratulations. Sharon told me about the banquet in your honor."

James held Dwayne's friendly gaze. "Thank you."

Dwayne looked around, soaking up the atmosphere. He recognized a few faces from his firm and nodded in acknowledgment.

"How is Laura Durden's case going?" James yelled over the music.

Dwayne rolled his eyes and shook his head. "I have a missing client."

"What? She jumped bail?" James asked incredulous. "I bet Sonya is livid. For a woman who's supposed to be so cold, she has a temper so hot she could start a fire with her eyes."

Dwayne shrugged his shoulders. "Tell me about it. I got burned by one of those flames this morning."

James curiosity perked up. "This morning?"

Dwayne closed his eyes while pinching the bridge of his nose. "I wish I could just figure her out. Or figure out a way to tear down that invincible wall she's got up."

James leaned onto one elbow then placed his chin within the palm of his hand and just listened.

"I mean, I know where she's coming from. I can only imagine the hurt she has gone through being from an abusive home. I know she fought like hell to get out of the Projects. And on top of that I feel a deep sense of responsibility for her sister's mistakes. But . . ." Dwayne fell silent. "I guess after putting it all like that, I can understand perfectly why she shuts men out."

James gave a sly grin then shifted his weight to lean closer to Dwayne then jab him playfully in his side. "I can't believe it. You like the Ice Queen."

Dwayne chuckled. "The Ice Queen?"

"Yeah, Sharon told me that the men in their office had labeled her that. I have to admit, whenever I talk with her, she holds a cold disposition."

Dwayne continued smiling. "At least I know it's not me."

Sharon screamed as she and Sonya fell to the floor. Sonya jumped away, momentarily unable to recognize her. "My God, Sharon, you scared the hell out of me!" Sonya held a hand over her pounding heart.

"It's good to see you, too."

"Are you all right?" Sonya asked, standing up.

"I think I broke my butt bone. Why on earth are you running through here screaming like a madwoman?"

"I thought I heard someone in the office." Sonya's face grew serious as she remembered the footsteps.

Sharon was finally able to stand up but not without rubbing her butt to emphasize the pain she was experiencing. "I see," Sharon said, unconvinced. "I don't see anybody. I think you need to start giving up such long hours."

Sonya ignored her criticism. "Someone *was* behind me."

"Look at this," Sharon said, bending to pick up sheets of paper. "You have paper everywhere."

Sonya began picking up the loose paper, but she kept her eyes toward the office. She knew she didn't imagine the whole thing.

"Sonya, do you hear me?" Sharon tapped her shoulder.

"Yes," she lied. "Come on, let's hurry and get out of here." Sonya followed the paper trail leading back to her office. The whole time, she kept looking over her shoulder.

After they finished, Sonya wanted to leave.

"Wait up, Sonya. I came to get a file off my desk." Sharon walked toward her own office. "I figured that I might as well get some work done on the flight to California tomorrow."

When Sonya didn't respond, Sharon hurried past her. "Come on, girl. You're starting to spook me." Just as she was able to get the words out, the entire office went black. "What the hell?" Sharon said, edging closer to Sonya.

Sonya drew in a sharp breath. "Let's go." Slowly they moved in the direction of the elevator bay. Sonya's ears strained to listen.

"Maybe it's just a power outage," Sharon whispered.

Sonya shook her head. "I don't think so. The backup generator would have kicked in—besides, look over there."

Sharon's eyes swept around the room, not knowing what Sonya wanted her to see, but she was able to make out the building across the way. The lights were on. "I don't like this," she finally said.

Sonya's thoughts exactly. It seemed like eternity before they reached the elevator bay. The elevators were dead also. "My God, the generator to the elevators is shut off, too."

"The staircase is over here." Sharon took Sonya's hand and led her farther down the hall. A loud thundering noise rang out behind Sonya as she felt something whiz by her ear. *Someone is shooting!*

The women screamed as they ran into the dark stairwell. They took off down the stairs. Sonya kicked off her shoes to maintain the same urgent pace with Sharon. When the stairwell's door crashed open above them, Sharon and Sonya picked up speed. Neither of them looked behind them as they took two or three steps at a time.

What floor were they on now? Sonya wondered. Nine? Eight? Sharon stumbled but lost no time getting back to her feet. Sonya glanced to make sure she was all right but couldn't stop to make sure.

Sonya saw a door on the next level of stairs and grabbed Sharon's hand and pulled her through it. She wasn't confident they would beat their attacker down the stairwell. The door led them to another office. Which one she didn't know or care. "This way!" she hissed. They needed to find a hiding place.

The stairwell door smashed open, and Sonya suppressed a scream. "Get down!" she commanded, dropping to the floor.

"Over here!" Sharon whispered, crawling under a desk. Sonya squeezed in and held her breath.

Dwayne felt his pager vibrate against his leg. He glanced at the number displayed on the tiny screen. "Excuse me, I have to make a phone call," he told James and left to use the phone at the bar.

"Hello, Bridget. What's up?"

"I was wondering if it was okay if I go over to Sylvia's house. I'm bored," she pouted.

"You're supposed to be bored, remember? You're grounded."

"Please, Daddy? I've done all my chores today and everything. Please?"

Dwayne wanted to give in to his daughter, but he knew he had to hold his ground. Besides, Bridget probably had no intention of going to Sylvia's house. "No, Bridget."

She let out an exaggerated sigh. "Well, how long am I on restriction?" she asked, her annoyance evident in her voice.

"Until I say you're off," Dwayne answered sternly.

"Then can I have company come over?"

"Bridget, you know the rules. No company. I'm on my way home. Maybe I can keep you company," he teased.

"I can hardly wait," she groaned.

Dwayne laughed. "Bye, Bridget. I'll see you in a little while." He hung up the phone, still smiling.

"Important call?" James asked when he returned to the table.

"No, it was just Bridget wanting to go over to a friend's house."

James shook his head. "You have your hands full with that one."

"Yes, but she's well worth it. I think I'd better cut the evening short and get back home. For all I know, there could be a party going on at the house."

James laughed. "I see a lot of you in her. You know you weren't always on the right side of the law."

Dwayne's eyes twinkled. "I know. That's why I'm going home, to make sure she doesn't follow in my footsteps." James roared with laughter as he watched Dwayne's departing figure.

An overly made-up woman threw her hands around Dwayne's neck and smiled seductively at him. "Want to dance, stranger?"

Dwayne shook his head politely. "I was just leaving."

"Ooh, that sounds like a great idea. Mind if I tag along?"

Dwayne lifted an amused brow. "Thanks, but I'll have to take a rain check."

She shrugged her shoulders as if it made no difference to her. "Maybe next time, sexy."

Dwayne smiled and gently pushed past her and through the growing crowd. The party scene was no longer his thing. It faded out of his mind when he met his wife. She had waitressed at a local club that he and James hung out in college. He made it to his car in the parking deck, relieved to be heading home.

Sonya heard the light footsteps stop in front of the desk. She felt Sharon's hand tremble in hers, yet neither made a sound. She wished that she could at least see who their attacker was but didn't risk it. Moments later, the footsteps walked in the opposite direction. Sonya relaxed against the desk. "Who is that?" Sharon whispered.

Sonya placed her hand over Sharon's mouth. She didn't want to get too comfortable until they could get out of the building. She crawled from under the desk and tried to look around. Sharon crawled out beside her. "Is he gone?"

"Shh." Sonya reached for the phone on the desk. It was dead. "Damn!" she whispered.

"What's wrong?" Sharon inquired, looking over her shoulder.

"It's dead—come on," Sonya instructed, crawling farther down the aisles. Each phone she checked gave her the same results. "We are going to have to get back to the stairwell— we have no other choice." She made out Sharon's figure in the darkness and saw that she nodded her head in agreement. "Are you ready?" Sharon nodded again. "Let's go!"

The women headed back toward the stairwell. Sonya cautioned Sharon to be as quiet as possible. They were still unsure exactly where their predator was. They made it without an incident. Sharon lost a shoe as she struggled to keep up with Sonya.

Silently the women headed down the stairs. This time, they stopped every once in a while whenever they thought they heard something or someone following them. Sonya didn't realize how loud breathing was until now. She heard everything, it seemed, intensified a thousand times. She was able to make out the number three imprinted on the next stair level. *Only a couple more to go.*

A door crashed open above them, and the women quickly picked up speed. "Go, go, go!" Sonya hissed behind Sharon. The run was awkward for Sharon, who ran with only one shoe on. Level two, then one quickly came into view. The women stormed out of the stairwell and down the lobby. Sonya's bare feet made no sound as she dashed across the hard marble floor, while Sharon's one sneaker made a clapping sound as she followed.

Sonya passed the security desk and noticed the officer slumped over his chair. Sharon let out a startled scream when she noticed the body. Sonya looked sharply at her. Sharon gave an apologetic expression as she realized what she'd done. The stairwell's door burst open, and the women continued running toward the front door.

A brief sense of freedom engulfed Sonya as they made it to one of the glass doors. Sharon screamed just as she was able to make it through the door behind Sonya. At that exact moment, the glass door beside her shattered into a million pieces. Their stalker was shooting again.

Sharon's car was parked in front but had four flat tires.

"Damn!" This meant they would have to go to the fifth-level parking deck to make it to her car. Sonya ignored the small pebbles and sharp objects that continued to poke at her toes through her thin nylon stockings.

There was no one at the security booth at the parking deck, and Sonya's fear escalated. "We're going to have to find a place we can use a phone. Come on," Sonya said, heading toward the street.

"I thought we were going to your car?" Sharon complained, following Sonya.

"There was no security guard. I have a feeling my car probably has four slashed tires, too," she reasoned, jogging down the dark street. Sharon clutched her side as she struggled to catch up with Sonya.

It wasn't long before a car screeched behind them, flaring its bright headlights, chasing the women down the darkened street.

Sonya ran harder. *Dear God, save us.*

Chapter Thirteen

What started as drizzle soon became a downpour. Dwayne turned on his windshield wipers and squinted at the road. He switched on the defroster and waited for the fog to clear. The car phone rang, and Dwayne picked it up.

"Hello?"

"Dwayne?" came a shaky voice.

"Sharon? Sharon, is that you?" Dwayne asked with instant concern.

"Dwayne, we need you to come and pick us up," she said, sounding out of breath.

"Where are you?"

"I don't know. Sonya, where are we?" Sharon asked.

Dwayne's heart picked up its pace.

"Dwayne?" Sonya's voice came on the line.

"Yes. What's going on? Where are you?"

"We're at a place called Ray's Barbecue. It's on the corner of Hope Street, downtown. Do you know where that is?"

Dwayne exited off I-285 to turn around. "Yes, I know where it is. What are you doing there? What's going on?"

"We'll tell you when you get here. Please, hurry. We need you." The line went dead.

Dwayne floored the accelerator. In record time, he was back downtown. *Why on earth were they in that section of town?* Ray's Barbecue had been closed for years. He turned down Hope Street and searched for the two women.

When he pulled up to the old, deserted building, he was even more puzzled. He turned off the engine and stepped out of the car. His clothes molded against him as the rain descended heavily. "Sharon? Sonya? Are you in there?"

He walked up to the door and tried to enter. It was locked. He went to the window and peered through the boarded frame. *This doesn't make any sense.* He walked to the back of the building to see if he could see anything. He called their names again.

"Dwayne?" Sharon asked, looking around the corner of the building.

"Sharon!"

Sharon ran to him with outstretched arms. She allowed him to crush her body to his. She trembled violently as Dwayne hugged her in a protective embrace.

"Are you all right?"

Sharon nodded as her tears mingled with the rain. Dwayne sighed in relief. He looked around, half-expecting Sonya to appear. After a moment, he eased Sharon from his arms to stare down at her. "Where's Sonya?"

"I forgot. She's around here. Help me. She's hurt."

"Hurt?" Dwayne said, following close behind her.

There, behind a thick bush, Sonya sat clutching her ankle. "I thought you forgot all about me," she said, looking at Sharon.

"Let me help you to the car," Dwayne offered, bending to pick her up.

Sonya waved off his hands as she attempted to stand on her bad ankle. "I can walk on my own." She winced in pain.

So she was still playing the tough role. "You couldn't last night," he retaliated low enough for only her to hear.

"Come on, I'd like to get to my husband tonight," Sharon said, looking around the area.

Dwayne watched Sonya limp to the car. She looked like a drowned rat. Her torn peach colored dress left little to the imagination. Yet in her ragged state, she still walked with her head held high and her shoulders thrust back. He knew she wasn't going to ask for help. *Stubborn woman.*

The threesome squeezed into the two-seater Porsche with Sharon crammed in the middle. Dwayne started up the car. He cursed at the fierce rain that attacked his windshield. "Will someone please tell me what is going on?" Dwayne said after neither woman spoke.

"I'm still not sure what happened," Sharon answered. "It seemed like it was all part of some terrible dream."

"A nightmare," Sonya said softly.

"What happened?" Dwayne asked, anxious to get a satisfying answer.

Sonya took a deep breath and told Dwayne everything that took placed at her office. Sharon cut in every once in a while to correct whenever she felt Sonya wasn't adding enough suspense.

Dwayne's eyes grew wide in horror. When they finished, it was a moment before Dwayne spoke.

"Are you both all right?"

Both women nodded.

"We're going to the police," he decided.

The police station felt crowded to Sonya as she sat in a tiny chair outside Sergeant Freeman's office. Their statements had been taken hours ago, and now they waited for Freeman and his men to return from the crime scene. Dwayne stayed with the women after they both threatened his very life if he left them alone.

James sat holding Sharon as she still trembled from the night's events. A few times the women gave each other encouraging smiles.

Dwayne returned from using the phone. He called home a lot, Sonya observed. Probably to check on his girlfriend, she thought. She was jealous. It was a feeling that disturbed her, no matter how hard she tried to deny it.

"Are you all right?" Dwayne asked, coming to sit beside her.

Sonya didn't trust herself to speak, so she nodded her head. It wasn't the truth. She felt cold and frightened. Someone tried to kill her tonight. How could she possibly be all right?

"Here, put this on," Dwayne said, taking off his jacket.

As much as Sonya didn't want to accept his help, she took the jacket. There was no reason for her to freeze to death. "Thank you," she managed to whisper.

Dwayne's eyes softened. "You're welcome."

Was it his voice that caused her to shiver, or was she still cold? Their last conversation came to mind and Sonya felt herself wanting to apologize. Dwayne had shown her nothing but kindness and she . . . well, she had been unfair to him since the beginning. She opened her mouth to say something when Freeman came storming down the hallway.

"Mrs. Ellis and Miss Walters, will you please come into my office? You're welcome to come, Mr. Hamilton."

"I'm coming too," James said, walking beside his wife. Everyone found a seat in the tiny office. James and Sharon sat together, Sonya and Dwayne sat side by side. When Dwayne reached out to take her hand, Sonya smiled. She needed his comfort now.

"It's been a long day, Miss Walters—forgive my bruskness. My men and I've gone over the crime scene and we are going to treat this case with as much discretion as possible. It seems that I owe you an apology, Miss Walters. There were two unconcious people found at the scene."

"Two?" Sonya and Sharon asked in unison.

"We found the security guard in the lobby, just like you said. There was also a guard in the parking deck."

Sonya remembered her decision not to go to her car and breathed a sigh of relief.

"I can offer you police protection, if you'd like."

Sonya looked at Dwayne.

"How much protection and for how long?" Dwayne asked the sergeant.

"I can put one officer with her. I can't spare more than that."

Dwayne shook his head. "Only one man? Her sister is missing, and now someone is trying to kill her. It could be the same people that got to Curtis."

Freeman held up his hand. "I understand where you're coming from, Mr. Hamilton, but I don't do magic tricks. I can't get you something I don't have. And as far as this being related to Mr. Durden's case, I'm not ready to draw those same conclusions."

Sonya shook her head disbelievingly at the sergeant. "And why not? Can't you see that there's more here than meets the eye?"

"And what is that, Miss Walters? I don't see the connection at all. Your sister kills her husband in a domestic violence case, then she skips town: case closed. As far as someone trying to kill you, maybe it's from something you did. Lord knows, you don't exactly rain sunshine on anyone."

"Sergeant Freeman, I suggest you stick to the facts and keep your personal opinion to yourself," Dwayne said, coming to her defense.

"I don't want to fight about this. I'm just trying to say that this doesn't prove there is a connection. Now do you want police protection or not?"

"No, thanks. From what I've seen, I can't tell the police from the criminals," Sonya answered.

"Suit yourself. I do, however, suggest that you keep a low profile."

Sonya stood. "Can we leave now?"

Freeman tilted his head toward the door, and everyone filed out of the office.

"What a jerk!" Sharon hissed once they were back in the hallway.

"You're being too nice," Sonya said, coming up beside her.

"Are you ready to go home?" James asked Sharon.

Sharon nodded her head, then turned to Dwayne and Sonya. "I'll talk to you when I get back. Dwayne, you look after her. If she won't accept police protection, then you watch out for her."

Dwayne winked at Sharon, then leaned in to place a kiss on her forehead. "I'll call you when I get home."

James took his wife's arm and led her out of the police station.

"Are you ready?" Dwayne said, looking at Sonya.

Another cold shiver raced down Sonya's spine as she nodded. The sooner she could get out of this place, the better, she thought.

Sonya stepped outside with Dwayne close behind her. The rain had stopped, but the air felt cool. She continued to limp as her ankle still pained her.

"Do you want to go to the hospital and have a doctor take a look at your ankle?"

"No. Right now I would kill for a warm bath and a soft bed. I can see a doctor tomorrow."

Dwayne opened the car door for her. She got in and waited for him.

When Dwayne took his seat, he didn't start the car. "I don't think it's a good idea that you go home tonight. I don't think you'll be safe."

Sonya was relieved and afraid when he mentioned this. "I could stay at a hotel tonight. I'd be safe there."

"I think you would be safer at my place."

Sonya digested his statement. Stay with him and his girl-friend? She didn't like that idea, but she couldn't think of a better one. She really didn't know how safe she would be in a hotel, either.

"Look, Sonya, I have to tell you. Nothing happened between us last night. You were having a bad dream, and I just came in to comfort you. I mean, I just calmed you down."

"I know nothing happened," Sonya answered.

"I just want you to trust me. You'll be safe at my place."

Sonya was unable to suppress a smile. "Okay, I'll stay at your place tonight."

Dwayne smiled and started the engine. He tuned the radio to a soothing jazz station, and Sonya let herself relax. Every bone in her body ached as she tried to massage her neck muscles.

"You're sure you don't want to go to the hospital?" Dwayne asked again.

"Yeah, I'm just tired, that's all." Sonya leaned her head back and stared at the ceiling of the car and tried to rest. She touched her neck and realized that it was bare. Just then a car behind them banged into Dwayne's back bumper. Dwayne switched lanes but not without the car behind him following.

"What the hell?" Dwayne cursed.

"I don't believe this!" Sonya cried, locking her seat belt into place.

Dwayne turned onto Highway 316, trying to outrun a Calloway Corvette from behind them. But the car was just as fast. Suddenly the car appeared beside them and tried to sideswipe him.

"Dwayne!" Sonya screamed.

The mysterious car smashed into the driver's side, pushing Dwayne into the opposite lane. Sonya held on to the dashboard as she heard Dwayne curse violently. A loud bang rang out, and Sonya watched Dwayne's window shatter into a shower of broken glass.

"Get down!" Dwayne commanded.

Sonya unbuckled her seat belt and squeezed herself down on the floor. Another shot rang out, and more glass covered the passenger seat.

Dwayne was having trouble with the gears. Sonya's heart pounded wildly against her chest. She heard another curse from Dwayne as the car was forced off the road. Pain spread throughout her body as she felt something crush her.

The black Porsche crashed into the trees off the side of Highway 316. The horn blared into the night air as Dwayne's heavy body slumped against the steering wheel.

Chapter Fourteen

Sonya heard footsteps approaching outside the car. The mere thought of moving caused pain to shoot across her body. Both doors of the car flew open, and Sonya felt rough hands search her body.

"I don't see it," a man whispered above her.

"Keep looking. It has to be around here somewhere."

Dwayne's moan caused the men to hesitate. Sonya kept her eyes closed and prayed Dwayne wouldn't say anything else. She feared what these men would do to them. When Dwayne quieted down, the men continued their search.

"Hurry. We've got to get out of here!"

It seemed like hours before Sonya finally heard them give up. A car's engine started in the distance before Sonya opened her eyes. Except for every bone in her body crying out in agony, and a thunderous migraine, she felt okay. Somewhere deep within herself, she found the strength to pull out from the floorboard. She saw numerous cuts and bruises over her arm as she made it out of the pile of glass that covered her.

Her eyes quickly focused on Dwayne's body slumped over the steering wheel. Tears stung her eyes as she struggled to get to him. She ignored the pain throbbing in her hands as she pulled his body off the car horn.

Blood oozed from a deep cut above his right eye, Sonya panicked. "Dwayne, Dwayne," she called out, firmly shaking him. She continued rocking him until she heard him moan. Relief swept through her body, when his eyes fluttered open to look at her. She felt a river of tears flow down her bruised face. She buried her head against his chest, overwhelmed by emotion.

Dwayne lifted his right hand and gently stroked her loose hair. She sobbed against his chest. "I didn't know what to think. I thought you were—"

"Shh, don't say it," Dwayne comforted, but Sonya heard the pain laced in his voice.

Sonya allowed him to caress her hair while she sought comfort from his body. When her tears subsided, she pulled away embarrassed. "I'm sorry."

"Don't be," he answered, flinching.

"You're hurt." She shifted her weight from him. Dwayne just smiled, then closed his eyes. "Dwayne?"

"I'm all right. I just need to rest a bit."

Sonya looked around after remembering the car phone. It was on the mat between Dwayne's legs. "I'll call for help." She scrambled to reach the phone. She plugged the cord into the cigarette lighter and tried to call 911. It took several tries before she could get the call through.

"Nine-one-one."

"I need help. I've been in a car crash off, I believe, Highway 316," Sonya informed the operator while talking a mile a minute.

"Okay, calm down. You're crashed off Highway 316?"

"Yes." She nodded her head as she responded. Dwayne still hadn't moved again.

"Okay, ma'am. I need to know where off 316 are you located."

Sonya looked around the car to see if she could see a landmark or something that would give her an idea of her location. But she couldn't see much through the mass of trees surrounding them.

"I'm not sure. I can't see anything," she said frantically.

"I need you to remain calm, ma'am. Which direction on Highway 316 were you traveling on?"

"I think north. Yes, north . . . Hello?" The line was dead.

"Damn!" She tried to call again, but each time the call was dumped.

Dwayne moaned, and Sonya scurried back to his side. "Dwayne?"

"My head," he mumbled, lifting his hand to touch the cut above his eye.

Sonya leaned over him, examining the wound. "We're going to have to get you to the hospital," she observed. Their eyes met in a fervent gaze. Sonya felt his eyes gently caressing her face as she was unable to pull away. She smiled sweetly, wanting to offer some kind of encouragement.

Dwayne gave a small chuckle. "You mean I had to have a near-death experience to get you to smile at me?"

Sonya returned the laugh. "I deserved that."

Dwayne tried to lift his head but quickly laid it back down again. "I think I like this position better."

"I called for help, but I was cut off. The calls keep getting dumped."

"The wonderful world of technology," Dwayne joked.

Sonya wondered how he could play at a time like this. "Can you move?"

"Not without experiencing an extreme amount of pain."

"Maybe I should go for help," Sonya suggested, looking out the window but was unable to see anything other than trees.

"I don't know if that's a safe idea," he said, closing his eyes again.

"I don't think just sitting here is going to help our situation any. I have to at least try to find help."

"Some protector. I was supposed to look after you." The sincerity in his voice touched her.

"It's not your fault," she consoled, taking his hand into

hers. She was aware of the warmth spreading through her hand that held his.

"What happened?"

"I'm not sure, but we're going to be all right. They'll send someone to search even with the call getting dumped, so help is on the way."

"You're good at taking care of people," Dwayne complimented. "Your sister is very lucky to have someone like you looking after her."

Sonya forced herself to keep smiling, although she was afraid for her sister. Where was she? Was she safe?

Dwayne squeezed her hand as if he could read her mind. "We're going to find her."

"I hope so."

Dwayne closed his eyes, leaving Sonya to stare at his stilled form. The blood oozing down his face unsettled her. She reached down and struggled to tear a strip from her dress. When she successfully tore a long strip, she tenderly cleaned his wound. She also took this time to study his strong features. His skin felt warm but was soft against her hand. His eyelashes curled neatly against his face, making him appear younger.

She didn't know what to do. She didn't know how long she should wait for help to come. It could be minutes or it could be hours—there was no way for her to know. Yet staring into his peaceful face, she couldn't bring herself to leave him. She tried the phone again but without success. She could only pray that someone would find them.

"Ma'am, are you hurt?" a voice broke through her dream.

Sonya flinched from the bright light the voice's owner was flashing directly into her face. She shook her head as the man moved the flashlight from her face. Blue and orange lights swarmed around the car. We're being rescued, she thought happily. But when she looked in the driver's seat, Dwayne was gone.

"He's in the ambulance, ma'am," the voice said to her frantic look.

"Is he all right?" she said, trying to get out of the car.

"Yes, ma'am," he answered, helping her from the car. "Donny, we need someone to look this lady over," he called out.

Sonya pushed past the paramedics and ignored him as he called for her to wait for someone to examine her. She watched the men busily attend to Dwayne, who lay on a stretcher. The ambulance started its engine and Sonya quickly stopped one of the paramedics from closing the back door.

"I want to ride with him."

"Are you a family member?" he asked.

Sonya nodded to the man, and he helped her into the ambulance. She found a small spot and sat next to Dwayne. When he opened his eyes, she summoned a smile.

"I need you to call Bridget," he whispered.

"What?" she asked, not able to hear his request.

"Call my house and tell Bridget to come to the hospital."

Sonya blinked as she realized what he was saying. He was asking her to call his girlfriend. Somehow she found the courage to nod her head at his request. Sonya felt her heart numbing at the intense pain she felt through the rest of the ride to the hospital.

Of course he would ask for his girlfriend. Who was she to him?

Gwinnett Hospital came into view, and Sonya gave Dwayne an encouraging smile. In a flash, the men moved urgently to get Dwayne through the emergency room. She followed as if in a daze. She was instructed to wait in the emergency room while doctors and nurses swarmed around Dwayne.

An hour later, someone finally saw to her small bruises and twisted ankle. Yet at every moment, her thoughts were consumed by visions of Dwayne's condition. It was only after she told one of the nurses that she was Mrs. Hamilton did anyone inform her of Dwayne's condition. He had slipped into a coma.

Sonya dreaded the phone call she had to make. She called Sharon's house and informed her of what happened.

James took the phone from a near hysterical Sharon and informed Sonya they would be there as soon as possible. Sonya relayed the message to have someone call Bridget. James promised that he would. After hanging up, Sonya felt first helpless, then guilty. She sat in the waiting room with her face cupped in her hands as depression crept into her heart.

Another hour passed before Sonya caught a glimpse of a doctor she had seen hovering over Dwayne. She rushed from her chair and approached the doctor.

"Do you know anything about my husband? Do you know whether or not he's okay?"

"I'm sorry. Dr. Hillion is examining your husband. I'll let the doctor know you're waiting to hear about his condition."

Sonya blinked at the small lie she had to tell the staff in order to keep informed on Dwayne's prognosis.

"There you are!"

Sonya looked up to see Sharon and James running toward her. "You made it," Sonya said, relieved to see a familiar face.

"Of course we made it. How are you doing?" Sharon asked, concerned.

"I've definitely seen better days."

James stepped beside Sonya and his wife. "I think you should have accepted Sergeant Freeman's police protection."

Sharon nodded her head in agreement. "Sonya, this is serious. Someone wants to hurt you."

"Well, I think that they succeeded in that."

"Do you have any idea who it could be?" Sharon probed.

"None. Perhaps it's the same man that's holding Laura," Sonya suggested.

"I'll tell you later." Sharon took Sonya's hand.

"Mrs. Hamilton?" a dark-skinned doctor asked, peering around the door.

"Yes," Sonya answered, then blushed at the startled expressions on both James and Sharon's faces.

"I wanted to inform you of your husband's condition."

"Please come in, Dr. Hillion."

"Yes. Well, your husband has a concussion and is being monitored. We don't know how long he will remain unconscious. It could be hours, days, or weeks."

"Or years," a voice full of pain echoed through the room.

The small group turned to see a young woman entering the waiting room.

"Bridget," Sharon said, opening her arms for the smaller woman to embrace her.

Sonya found herself curiously studying the girl that clung to Sharon. She was young, too young. James pulled the doctor aside and continued talking to him while Sharon talked to the young girl in soft, loving tones. Suddenly Sonya felt like an outsider. This was Dwayne's family, and she didn't belong here.

Sonya turned and walked toward a vending machine pretending to be interested in buying something while the family talked. She returned much later and sat in an empty chair. Her guilt escalated as she continued to blame herself for the incident. She leaned her head back against the wall. Soon her exhaustion ravaged her weary body, and within minutes, she was asleep.

Sonya opened her eyes to a throbbing headache pounding against her temples. *Is it morning?* If it was, she didn't feel like she had slept long at all. She looked around the emergency room, taking a moment to remember what happened. A vision of Dwayne lying in the ambulance flashed through her mind.

Sonya stood up from the uncomfortable chair, feeling sore and stiff. She walked past Sharon and James, who had also fallen asleep in the waiting room chairs. Steadily she looked through each room, trying to locate Dwayne. When she found his room, she was unprepared to see the younger woman, Bridget, draped across his body. She was crying. Sonya watched the girl's body shake from her deep sobs.

Sonya looked toward the ceiling, praying for strength. She

didn't understand the urge to comfort this woman. When she stepped farther into the room, the younger girl looked up at her with red-stained eyes. She was shocked by her familiar gray eyes. She has his eyes, she thought, confused.

Bridget wiped her eyes with the back of her hand and tried to stop sniffling. "I'm scared," she whispered. "I can't lose my father, too."

Sonya's heart broke as she opened her arms. Bridget raced to embrace her in a powerful hug. "He's going to be all right," Sonya said, stroking her hair.

"How do you know?" Bridget pulled away to look into Sonya's eyes.

There was so much trust and hope in the young girl's eyes when she held Sonya's gaze. "I just know," she whispered.

Bridget embraced Sonya again and cried. Moments later, Sonya gave in and cried, too.

Chapter Fifteen

Dwayne felt as if a freight train had run over him. His temples throbbed, his face ached, and his tongue felt like dried leather. When he strained to open his eyes, it caused his head to pound. He attempted to ask for water, but no words would come, just a deep burning sensation that scorched his throat. *Someone's crying.* He tried again to open his eyes, this time succeeding. He saw a blurred vision of two women crying at the foot of his bed. *Why are they crying?* He tried to open his mouth to say something, but pain throbbed in his jaw.

"Look!" one of the ladies cried before she ran over to take his hand.

He recognized the woman who gazed lovingly at him. "Theresa," he whispered.

"No, Daddy. It's me, Bridget." She leaned in and kissed his forehead.

Dwayne's eyes closed. Theresa was gone. When he heard the other woman step behind Bridget, he slowly opened his eyes. A beautiful mixed shade of green and brown stared down at him through eyes brimmed with tears. He gave a lazy smile. He wanted to comfort the beautiful woman. It wasn't until she reached for his hand did he realize her grief was for him. He looked over at Bridget to see love shining in her face. When he looked back at the other woman, there was a similar look in her expression.

"Water," he managed to say, but the effort sent him into a coughing frenzy.

Bridget ran to the bathroom and returned with a small Dixie cup filled with water.

"It's good to have you back," the woman—who he swore was an angel—said.

Bridget helped him tilt his head to drink the water. It felt wonderful as it slid down his parched throat. Images of two cars racing down a lone highway filled his head. Then a horrible vision of a car crash brought his memory back to the present.

"Sonya?" he asked, testing his memory.

"Yes, I'm here." She smiled.

The door to his room opened, and a doctor strolled in. The doctor looked at him, at first startled, then with a proud grin that covered his entire face. "Welcome back, Mr. Hamilton."

Bridget and Sonya stepped back and allowed the doctor to examine him. Satisfied with the results, he turned to Sonya and Bridget.

"Mrs. Hamilton, if you and your daughter would step into the waiting room, I'll call you when it's okay to visit."

Mrs. Hamilton? Maybe he didn't remember everything.

Sonya and Bridget walked into the waiting room where Sharon and James were just waking up. Bridget ran to the comfort of her aunt's arms.

"How is he?" Sharon asked, smoothing the child's hair.

"He's awake," Bridget answered, still shaken.

When Dr. Hillion walked into the waiting room, he was bombarded with questions. He held up his hand to quiet them. "He's fine. He's resting."

Relief swept through Sonya's body. She was visibly shaken. What if it had been fatal? It would have been her fault. She was the one that had put everyone's life in jeopardy. She listened intently as the doctor continued to talk with the family.

"Mr. Hamilton will probably be able to leave Friday. That will give us enough time to monitor him. It appears he's suffering from a severe concussion. We'll keep him for observation."

Sharon hugged James as tears glistened her eyes. Bridget did the same. Sonya needed comforting, too, but didn't want to intrude on the family. She stood there not knowing whether she should cry from relief or guilt. Instead she returned to Dwayne's room.

He was resting again, so Sonya pulled a chair closer to his bed and sat beside him. She wasn't sure how long she just stared at his stilted figure. All she could do was think of what to do next. Should she keep a low profile? Where should she go? She didn't know who she was hiding from. She also thought about her sister. Was there a chance that she was still alive? Was she in any danger? Sonya allowed her tears to flow because she had no answers.

Everything was out of control. She no longer knew what to do or how to do it. Dwayne had offered to protect her but look what happened. She was on her own now. Laura was her responsibility, not Dwayne's. Tomorrow she would think of something, she promised, before drifting to sleep.

"You finally decided to wake up?" Sharon teased.

"Where am I?" Sonya asked, sitting up.

"Gwinnett Hospital," Sharon said, squeezing her hand.

"I feel awful," Sonya commented, rubbing her head.

"You should, girl. You had quite a night."

Sonya glanced to the empty bed beside her. "Where's Dwayne?"

"They moved him into another room a moment ago," Sharon said.

"How is he?"

"Better. He can probably leave tomorrow. You need to wake up. Bridget and I are going to treat you to lunch."

"Is that a safe idea?"

"Maybe we should sneak you into the back of McDonald's," Sharon joked.

"I'm serious, Sharon. Maybe I should go to Sergeant Freeman. Someone means business."

"What do you want to do?" Sharon asked seriously.

"I don't know, but I can't put anyone else's life in danger. First, it was you, and now your brother."

"So you're going to hide until when?"

Sonya shook her head. "I don't know, Sharon. I don't have any answers."

"Aunt Sharon?" Bridget peeked around the door.

"Come in, Bridget." Sharon motioned for her to enter.

Bridget entered the room, wearing a blue and pink pastel dress. She'd brushed her hair into a tight ponytail at the nape of her neck. She's pretty, Sonya thought.

"How are you feeling?" Bridget asked politely.

"I feel better now that I've had some sleep. How are you doing?"

Bridget took a deep breath and nodded. "I went home to take a bath and tried to relax. I think it helped."

"A bath. Now that sounds wonderful," Sonya commented.

Bridget held out a Macy's bag and handed it to Sonya. "Aunt Sharon asked me to pick you up something on my way back to the hospital. A size six, right?"

Sonya looked over to Sharon.

"I figured you needed some clean clothes. I wasn't about to go to your house. Who knows what I would have found there?" Sharon said, shrugging her shoulders.

Sonya agreed with Sharon. She couldn't go home, and the police weren't exactly helpful. Sonya hoped the nurses wouldn't find her sneaking a shower as she stood and walked to the bathroom. When she stepped out, wearing a pair of button-fly jeans and white T-shirt, she felt better.

"I don't think I've ever seen you in jeans before," Sharon said.

"It's been years," Sonya agreed. She brushed her hair back into a tight ponytail.

"I'm sorry. I didn't know what you would like. I figured I couldn't go wrong with jeans and a T-shirt," Bridget explained.

"You did fine. Besides, if I have to do any more running, I'm dressed appropriately," Sonya said, stepping into a pair of Reeboks.

"Do they fit?" Sharon asked. "I had to guess your size."

"Perfect."

"Are we going to see Daddy before we leave?" Bridget asked, looking at her aunt.

"You go on ahead. We'll be right behind you."

Bridget left, and Sharon turned to Sonya. "Dwayne wants us to take you to his house. We've talked this morning."

Sonya shook her head. "I don't think that's a good idea. Look what happened when he tried to protect me last time."

"Do you have a better idea?"

Sonya started to argue further, but she realized she didn't have a better plan. The only thing she knew was, she was frightened. "No."

"Then let Dwayne help."

"All right." She held up her hands in mock surrender.

"Come on, let's go see Dwayne." Sharon looped her arm around Sonya's shoulders.

"Did you cancel your flight?" Sonya asked as they walked toward Dwayne's room.

"James went alone. I couldn't leave with Dwayne like this. But I'm joining him tomorrow after Dwayne's discharge from the hospital."

As they entered Dwayne's room, Bridget's soft laughter greeted them. Dwayne was smiling at his daughter, but his smile grew wider at the sight of Sonya.

"If I didn't know better, Mr. Hamilton, I would think that you're faking all of this just to get attention," Sonya teased.

Dwayne held his hand over his heart. "Oh, you wound me to the quick, Mrs. Hamilton."

Sonya blushed while everyone in the room started laughing.

"They wouldn't let me ride here with you. I had to be a family member," she offered as an explanation.

Carmen and Anthony knocked, then entered the room.

"I see you're recovering just fine." Anthony laughed. "You're surrounded by beautiful women."

Dwayne smiled. "It's heaven, Anthony."

Sonya saw Carmen's bloodshot eyes. Had she been crying? "Oh, Dwayne, when I heard the news I was devastated." She headed toward him.

Bridget stepped between Carmen and her father.

"I'm sorry to have worried you both," Dwayne answered, giving Bridget a bewildered look.

Everyone exchanged pleasantries, but the room soon grew uncomfortably silent. Sonya didn't miss any of Carmen's evil glares.

"Maybe we should be leaving," Sharon said, after no one spoke.

"Yeah, me, too," Anthony agreed. He looked at his watch but accidentally knocked the flowers from Carmen's hands. "Excuse me." He bent to pick up the flowers the same time as Carmen, which caused their heads to bump.

"Anthony!" she hissed.

"Sorry."

Dwayne hid a smile and winked at Sonya.

Sonya felt flirtatious and winked back. Sharon leaned down and kissed Dwayne's forehead. "We'll be back later."

Bridget hesitated, then followed behind her aunt. "Check you later, sugar-daddy."

Dwayne watched his family leave the room and sighed. At least by tomorrow, he would be back home. After everything that happened, he was concerned about his family's safety.

"I think you need to drop this case," Carmen complained. "I mean, look at you. You're a lawyer, not some superhero."

Anthony stood behind Carmen and shook his head. Dwayne couldn't fault Carmen. She was just concerned for his welfare. He blocked out the rest of Carmen's ranting and concentrated

on what happened last night. One thing he was sure of—he
wasn't going to get any answers sitting in this hospital bed.

"Carmen, could you leave me and Anthony alone for a
minute? I want to talk to him in private."

Carmen looked insulted that he had cut her off in the middle
of a sentence.

"Please?" he added.

Picking up the purse she had lain on the bed, she left the
room without another word. Dwayne and Anthony shook their
heads.

"She's quite a woman," Anthony commented, grinning.

Dwayne found Anthony's infatuation with Carmen humorous. "If you say so." Dwayne continued to shake his head.
"Look, I need you to do me a favor. Can you do some investigating for me? You think you can handle that?"

"Sure thing, boss."

Sonya, Bridget, and Sharon arrived at the Hamilton residence
later that evening. Sonya admired the beautiful two-story home
as she entered. Just moments after opening the front door, an
excited black Lab jumped onto Bridget's legs.

"Hey, Buffy!" Bridget smiled, happily petting the dog. "Did
you miss me, girl?" Bridget continued to coo.

Buffy wasted no time jumping from Bridget to Sonya. Sonya
laughed at the dog's eagerness.

"I think she likes you," Bridget observed.

"I believe I like her, too."

"Did you put some food down for her?" Sharon asked,
going into the kitchen.

Bridget twisted her face into an amused frown. "I forgot.
Come on, Buffy," Bridget called, patting her leg for the dog
to follow her.

Sonya trailed behind everyone into the kitchen. She found
the western-style kitchen a cute decorative idea. Bridget followed her gaze. "Do you like it?"

"Yes, it's different."

"Dad let me decorate it. I also did the bathrooms, his study, and of course, my room."

"So you like decorating?" Sonya asked.

Sharon lifted a curious brow.

"I never thought about it really. I had a good time decorating the rooms, so yeah, I guess I do." Bridget pulled out a large bag of dog food and poured some into Buffy's bowl. Buffy immediately buried her face in the bowl.

"It's a wonder why that dog never turns on you. She hardly ever eats," Sharon commented, shaking her head.

Bridget shrugged her shoulders as if she wanted to avoid the subject.

"Where should I put my things?" Sonya said, regarding the bags of clothes they had just bought at Bridget's favorite department store.

"I'll show you." Bridget sprang up from the floor and led Sonya up the stairs to the guest room.

The room was small but charming, with its pastel floral designs. "You're right across the hall from my bedroom." Bridget smiled. "We'll share the bathroom. It's the room at the end of the hallway." Bridget continued showing her the upstairs. "And that's Daddy's bedroom."

Sonya stared at the closed door that was at the opposite end of the hallway. She wondered what Dwayne's room looked like—but of course she wouldn't dare satisfy her curiosity, not in front of Bridget anyway.

Sharon called them from downstairs, and Bridget motioned for her to follow.

"I'm going to run and pick us up some movies and popcorn. Maybe we can have an old-fashioned slumber party tonight. Hopefully that will relieve some tension around here," Sharon said, picking up her purse.

"Great!" Bridget agreed.

Sonya relaxed. They were doing their best to make her feel at home, and she knew it. "Is there anything I can do?" she offered.

"No, I think I have everything under control. I'll be back

in about an hour. I also have to pick up my bags and bring them over, so I'll be ready to leave tomorrow after Dwayne comes home. Sonya, you get some more rest." Sharon turned to Bridget. "How are you doing?"

"Better, now that I know he'll be home tomorrow."

Sharon kissed her niece's forehead. "I'll be back in an hour." She waved to Sonya and slipped out the door.

Bridget turned to Sonya. "Are you tired?"

"No." She eyed her cautiously.

"Good, let's go try on the outfits we bought!"

Sonya laughed as she allowed the young girl to lead her back up the stairs.

Sonya, Bridget, and Sharon reached for the last Kleenex simultaneously. They were near the end of the four-hour epic, *Gone with the Wind*.

"This is so sad," Bridget whispered, capturing the last tissue.

"This is my all-time favorite movie," Sharon sniffled.

"Mine, too," Sonya agreed.

"Where is he going?" Bridget asked as Rhett Butler headed for the door.

"She realized what she had too late," Sharon whispered.

The three women held their breaths as they waited for Rhett Butler to deliver his signature line.

"He's going to leave her like that?" Bridget asked, shocked.

"Shh," both Sharon and Sonya instructed Bridget.

Not another word was uttered as Scarlet looked into the camera and envisioned what tomorrow would bring. The credits were rolling when Sharon stood and turned on the lights in the living room.

"That was a great movie." Bridget blew her nose. "I thought it was going to be a lame movie, but it turned out to be awesome."

"Sonya, I didn't think you liked romance movies," Sharon commented.

"I just know the difference between reality and fantasy. I'll take Hollywood's fantasy over reality anytime."

"Well, I think I'm going to go to bed. I'll take Dwayne's room," Sharon said, yawning.

"Oh, no, you don't. Both of you are helping me clean up this mess. Daddy comes home tomorrow, and I won't have him think I've neglected my chores."

Sharon gave Sonya an amused look. "Okay, we'll help."

Sharon stood and took the two bowls of half-eaten popcorn into the kitchen.

Sonya picked up the pillows from the floor and went to rewind the videotape in the VCR. When she selected the appropriate button, she noticed a picture of a beautiful woman smiling in a wooden-framed picture.

She had a friendly smile, Sonya observed, picking up the frame. She didn't know that Bridget stood behind her until she spoke.

"That's my mother," she boasted proudly.

"She's beautiful," Sonya commented, swallowing a lump in her throat.

"Daddy says that I take after her, but I think I look like him," Bridget said, continuing to look at the picture behind Sonya.

"I definitely see a strong resemblance between you and your mother, but you have your father's eyes." Sonya placed the frame back.

Both women studied the angelic image in the picture frame.

"I wish I could remember her," Bridget finally said.

Sonya turned curious eyes toward Bridget. Bridget gave her a half smile. "She died when I was a baby."

"I'm sorry," Sonya said, reaching to push a loose curl from Bridget's face.

"It's okay. It was a long time ago."

"What are you ladies in here chatting about?" Sharon asked, entering the room.

"Nothing," both Sonya and Bridget answered in unison. They looked at each other and gave friendly smiles.

"Let's finish getting this mess cleaned up," Sonya said, turning her attention back to the living room.

The next evening, Dwayne entered the house, happy to be home.

"Daddy!" Bridget yelled from the top of the stairs and flew into her father's arms, nearly knocking him over. Dwayne held his daughter tightly. Buffy was next to greet him at the door.

"Hello, girl," Dwayne knelt down to pet the dog.

Dwayne felt the room charge with energy the moment Sonya walked into the room. "Hello," he greeted, unaware of his voice deepening.

"Welcome home."

Dwayne felt his heart pound wildly at the sight of her dressed in a short white sundress. Her hair hung in loose curls past her shoulders. He saw where she tried to hide a bruise on her left cheek with makeup, but there was still a purple shadow.

"Are you going to stand in this hallway all day, or are you going in?" Sharon scolded, pushing Dwayne farther into the house.

Dwayne felt the pain in his leg vanish somewhat. He knew by the silence that the women were holding their breath as he walked to a nearby chair. When he sat, everyone beamed with pride.

"We've fixed you a welcome-home dinner," Bridget said.

"We?"

"Sonya and I. You're going to love it!"

Dwayne smiled. For the first time, he noticed Bridget wore the exact outfit Sonya wore. Apparently they were becoming fast friends. He was also relieved that there hadn't been any further incidents. Sonya was safe here, and even more shocking, she hadn't put up much of a fuss about it.

"Do you need any help in the kitchen?" Sharon asked, walking behind the two women.

When the doorbell rang, Dwayne stopped Sharon from answering it. "I'll get it. You go help in the kitchen. I'm hungry enough to eat a horse.'' Sharon laughed as she went into the kitchen.

Dwayne made it to the door, ignoring the pain shooting up his leg. "Ah, Anthony. Come in."

"I think I have something," Anthony said angrily.

"What did you get?" Dwayne asked, stepping aside to allow him entrance.

"I sneaked into Walters Intercorp to do some investigating of my own. I looked to see if I could find something that perhaps the police had missed."

Anthony had Dwayne's full attention. "And what did you find?"

Anthony took a deep breath and pulled out a small plastic bag. "I discovered it in the stairwell."

Dwayne took the plastic bag and unwrapped it. What he saw made him catch his breath. "I don't believe it."

Chapter Sixteen

"I believe this belongs to you."

"Oh, Sharon, you found it!" Sonya said, taking the gold chain from her.

"Tina found it on the accounting floor."

Sonya nodded at the memory of them hiding under a desk. "Tell them I'm grateful."

Bridget gathered plates from the cabinet while rapping along to her favorite rap song. Sonya smiled at her teenage antics. She found Bridget to be a treasure. In the past two days together, she was beginning to think that Bridget's carefree ways were rubbing off on her.

"I swear that child is going to go deaf listening to that CD player blaring in her ears. Bridget!"

" 'What's up, what's up, what's up with the Bankhead bounce, shortie!' " Bridget sang at the top of her lungs.

"Bridget!" Sharon continued to shout. Sonya tried not to laugh.

Bridget snatched off the headset. "Did you say something, Aunt Sharon?"

"How on earth can you listen to that music so loud?"

Bridget frowned. "This is the jam, Auntie."

Sharon shook her head. "I don't know what you kids are listening to today with that rap stuff. Now back in my day, we had music."

Sonya nodded, agreeing with her. "Groups like Earth, Wind and Fire, The Commodores, Michael Jackson."

"I listen to Michael," Bridget defended.

"Yeah, but not with songs like 'Off the Wall' or 'I Wanna Rock With You.' " Sharon and Sonya jumped up as if on cue and began singing their rendition of Michael's classic.

"Oh, I know," Sonya interrupted with an idea of her own. " 'She's a bad Mamma Jamma—' " Sharon joined in, singing at the top of her lungs.

Dwayne entered the kitchen, holding his ears. "What are you women doing in here?"

"Aunt Sharon and Sonya are trying to convince me that the music they grew up listening to is supposedly better than today's music."

"I thought you were strangling a cat in here," Dwayne joked. Bridget laughed. "But of course the best music was in the midseventies, something your aunt knows little about. Songs like 'For the Love of Money'." Dwayne began to sing.

Sonya was surprised by Dwayne's voice. *He has a wonderful singing voice.*

"And the love ballad are still classics," Dwayne added. "Songs like 'Killing Me Softly.' "

Sonya quickly joined in singing with Dwayne. Startled looks passed between Sharon and Bridget. Sonya turned toward Dwayne while singing her part. His laughing eyes gave her the courage to sway to the tune playing in her head. She was having fun.

Dwayne took his turn, leaning gently into her. He had no idea that his seductive voice was causing goose bumps to spread across Sonya's body. They finished the song with their bodies only inches apart. Sonya felt the throbbing energy pulse from him.

Sharon and Bridget clapped loudly. Bridget put her fingers in her mouth and whistled.

"You have quite a voice, Sonya," he complimented.

"Thank you. May I pay you the same compliment?"

"Well, I was impressed," Sharon teased.

"Is that yours?" Bridget asked, pointing to Sonya's gold coin around her neck.

"Yes, it is. My sister gave it to me on my last birthday. Do you want to see it?"

Bridget nodded and walked closer to get a better view. "It's gorgeous. Where did she get it?"

"She didn't tell me. She knows that I love coins, so she got this for me."

"You do? I love collecting!" Bridget said, clutching her arm. Sonya laughed at her excitement. "Do you want to see it?"

"I'd love to—"

"After dinner," Sharon interrupted. Bridget frowned but proceeded to finish setting the table.

Sonya helped but kept noticing the worried look on Dwayne's face. A couple of times, it seemed as though he wanted to say something but decided against it.

After dinner, Sharon called a taxi to go to the airport. She had turned down Dwayne's offer to drive, claiming she wanted him to rest. When Bridget offered to drive, she claimed that her heart couldn't endure her driving.

For the next hour, Sonya enjoyed looking through Bridget's vast coin collection. "I can't believe you actually love coin collecting," she said, handing Sonya another Aztec coin.

"I don't collect them. I just find them intriguing. This one's pretty," Sonya said, picking up one of her coins.

"Oh, my boyfriend got me that one."

"Boyfriend?" Sonya asked teasingly.

"Well, he's kinda my boyfriend, but don't tell Daddy."

"Your father doesn't approve of him?"

Bridget leaned back on her bed. "My father believes I'm too young to have a boyfriend."

"And what do you think?"

Bridget shrugged her shoulders. "All my friends date."

Sonya shook her head. "That's not what I asked you. What do you think about having a boyfriend at your age? Don't think about what your friends are doing. They're probably going along with the crowd, too."

"I don't think that I'm too young. Women in earlier times were getting married at thirteen."

"Ah, you like history."

Bridget nodded her head as if she hadn't realized she enjoyed the subject.

"But that still doesn't answer the question. Women in those times didn't have a choice. You do."

Bridget looked at Sonya strangely. "I like boys."

"More than yourself?"

"I don't understand."

"Tell me—what do you want out of life?"

Bridget sighed. "I don't think I'm up for another 'What do you want to be' speech."

"Do you want to talk about it after you're grown and wondering where you went wrong?" Sonya covered Bridget's hand with hers. "Just remember, when you fail to plan, you plan to fail."

Bridget was silent for moment. "I want to do something dealing with coins."

"Have you gone to the library to see what career options there are in that field?" When Bridget shook her head, Sonya said, "Then I suggest we do that first thing Monday."

Bridget smiled. "You don't think that it's a stupid career choice?"

"It doesn't matter what I think. You have to find gratification within yourself. Worry about men and marriage later—I'm sure it will come in time."

Dwayne smiled beside his daughter's closed door. He was grateful Sonya could do what he couldn't. He had tried to explain self-love to Bridget. Maybe what Bridget needed was another woman to talk to. He also saw a change in Sonya. She seemed more relaxed around Bridget.

He recalled her singing along with him in the kitchen and laughed quietly to himself. There was a playful side to her. That was the side he wished to see more of. He left the women alone and went back downstairs. Sonya and Bridget returned and washed the dishes together. That was an amazing feat. Bridget didn't like doing chores, but around Sonya, he noticed, she didn't seem to mind.

Dwayne turned down the lights and played his favorite jazz station. He wanted to relax, and jazz had a way of doing that for him. He pulled the small plastic bag from his pocket and stared at it. What was he going to do now?

"Daddy?" Bridget appeared from around the corner.

"Oh, come on in, Bridget."

Bridget walked in slowly. "I want to ask a favor."

"I can tell. What can I do for my favorite daughter?"

"I'm your only daughter," Bridget said simply.

"So you are. What can I do for you?"

"I know that this is your homecoming, and that I'm on restriction, but I was hoping that I could go over to Sylvia's house. She leaves tomorrow to go her grandparents house in Tennessee for the summer."

Dwayne smiled. "Okay, I'll let you go this time."

Bridget threw her arms around her father and gave him a quick peck on the cheek. "Thank you, Daddy."

Dwayne shook his head as he watched his daughter race out of the living room. Within minutes, she had a small bag packed.

"I'll be back first thing in the morning. Sylvia's flight is at eight o'clock."

Dwayne nodded his head and waved to his daughter. He felt good for giving in to her this time.

"Dwayne?" Sonya asked, peering around the corner. "There you are. Mind if I join you?"

Dwayne grinned. "Of course I don't mind. Please have a

seat.'' He watched her move slowly to the recliner chair across from him.

"I wanted to thank you."

"For what?"

"For everything. I can't begin to tell you how guilty I feel about everything that I've put you through. I mean, putting your sister in danger, and then your car accident. And still you invite me into your house. You have a beautiful home and a wonderful daughter."

"Thank you. She seems to like you."

"I like her."

"You mustn't feel guilty for anything. It's not your fault that any of this happened. You're as much a victim as the rest of us."

Sonya wiped away a stray tear. "I can't stay here forever, Dwayne. Eventually I'll have to come out of hiding and get on with my life."

Dwayne squeezed the plastic bag tighter. *Should I tell her who may be responsible for this?* "Will you give me the chance to find out who's doing all of this?"

She shook her head. "You're a lawyer, not a superhero, remember?"

"So you heard that, did you?"

"Who didn't? You could hear her halfway down the hallway." Sonya's face grew serious. "Are you involved with Carmen?"

Dwayne lifted a startled brow. "Do I dare hope there's jealousy in your voice?" Sonya squared her shoulders, and Dwayne held up his hands in surrender. "No"

"Oh," was her soft response.

"You sound disappointed."

"Does she know that?"

"Know what?" he looked at her confused.

"Nothing. I don't know why I brought it up." She stood to leave, but Dwayne stood also.

"Don't leave," his voice pleaded.

Sonya felt her legs tremble beneath her. She didn't know

why she cared whether or not this man slept with his secretary. When she turned back to him, she felt a deep, longing stir within her. He had a way of looking at her that made her feel as if she were the most beautiful woman in the world. She couldn't turn away now if she wanted to.

She watched, hypnotized, as Dwayne walked closer to her. He closed the distance between them. ''I'm glad you brought it up.'' His hand reached out to stroke her cheek tenderly.

His touch was doing wondrous things to her body as she moved closer. His breath caressed her face. Her head felt dizzy as he leaned closer. His hands laced through her loose curls as he cradled her head closer. His lips touched hers softly at first, in a tantalizing butterfly kiss. If there was a token of resistance, it faded beneath his gentle persuasion. She felt herself losing all sense of reality, yet her senses seemed infinitely sharper. Sparks ignited within her causing her to return the kiss with as much fever and passion as he gave.

''I waited so long for this,'' Dwayne whispered against her ear. A wave of pleasure rippled across her skin. She wanted to get closer. She tugged at the tiny buttons of his shirt but sent most of them sprawling across the floor.

His lips brushed across her earlobe, turning her passion into an inferno. Her hands glided across the hard contours of his chest, enjoying the feel of his firm muscles. When her hand paused above his heart, she felt it beating as fast as her own.

Sonya's breath locked in her throat as his mouth skimmed hot and open along her neck. She tilted her head higher, allowing him to rain kisses across her throat. She trembled and moaned in irrepressible hunger. She couldn't think and wasn't sure that she wanted to. She didn't want to stop the blissful rapture that threatened to leave her paralyzed.

The sensual assault of his lips made her feel wanton, made her skin tingle with the hot flush of desire. She closed her eyes helplessly, her body trembling. Dwayne's fiery lips caused her to whisper his name repeatedly until his mouth silenced her words.

She had discovered the taste of heaven. The devastating

effect of his embrace was like nothing she had ever experienced. Her entire body tingled with anticipation, her skin sizzled from his touch. His fragrance wrapped itself around her senses, and she lost herself to the feel and taste of him. She laced her slender arms around his neck and brought his head even closer.

Dwayne slid both straps of her dress down her shoulders, then bent lower to trail kisses along her shoulder, setting fires that nearly consumed her.

Dwayne's hands glided up the middle of her back, pressing her even tighter against the hard, muscled length of him. Her skin felt like satin between his fingers. Her lips tasted like fine wine, and he was drunk from its potency. Her lips teased his earlobe, and a rush of warmth raged within him. Her hand roamed down his back and proceeded to travel even lower. This time it was he that moaned in undeniable pleasure. His shirt slid soundlessly to the floor. Unable to bear this sweet torture, he swept her light form into his arms and proceeded to carry her up the stairs.

Chapter Seventeen

Dwayne laid Sonya against the firm mattress. He pulled his lips away to gaze into her passion-filled eyes. "You're so beautiful," he whispered. When his lips returned, he heard a weak moan tumble from Sonya's lips. With skillful hands, he peeled Sonya's dress from her body.

Sonya's hands fumbled with Dwayne's pants.

"Here, let me," he offered. In a flash, he stripped from the rest of his clothes. "Your turn," he said seductively.

Sonya reached behind her and unfastened her bra. Dwayne drew in an audible gasp as he stared at her beautiful breasts. Sonya slid off the rest of her clothes and gazed at him.

Passion ate at Dwayne's soul when his eyes traced the curves of satin flesh that reminded him of a forbidden goddess. His hands moved to inspect what his gaze so hungrily devoured. The exquisite feel of her chipped at his sanity, making him want her more.

Sonya felt branded by a fire that burned from within. Another path of fire scalded her flesh as his caress roamed over her abdomen and descended lower. She felt dizzy from the sensations that pulsated through her as he aroused each sensitive point on her body. It seemed he had more than two hands as his fingertips kneaded her breast and strayed to her hips. She pressed closer to meet his ardent caresses. The sensations were indescribable as an ache of desire caused her to whimper.

Sonya gently twisted away, yearning to touch him as familiarly as he touched her. She wanted to satisfy her own curiosity of her Adonis. She combed her hands through the short crop of his hair, then brushed over the broad expanse of his chest to feel the beat of his heart beneath her palms.

Her eyes followed her curious touch, memorizing every inch of his sleek, muscular body, claiming it as her own. Dwayne sucked in his breath at the wondrous feelings he was experiencing. When their lips touched, Sonya felt certain she had surrendered her soul as she melted against him.

Dwayne heard the echo of his own sigh as she whispered his name against his ear. He moved above her, his body trembling with a fierce passion. He wanted to devour her and appease the tormenting craving her touch had stirred.

Sonya curled her arms over his shoulders and, unashamed, peered into his smoldering gray eyes. She saw a reflection of her own chaotic emotions.

''Sonya . . .'' Her name tumbled from his lips as he pressed boldly against her. His mouth moved on hers in a silent request to lose herself to him. His arms tightened around her.

Sonya drifted along clouds of ecstasy as she surrendered to the feelings he stirred within her. It took her a moment to realize that they were not perched on lofty clouds, but were swaying to the rhythm of their own heartbeats.

His hand captured a firm breast, then his lips abandoned hers to circle the tanned peak. A quiet moan tumbled free as a blistering heat wave swept across her flesh. Her own caresses grew bold as she lowered her hand below his abdomen.

Dwayne gasped. ''God, woman, you are driving me mad,'' he whispered.

Sonya discovered every inch of his body, teasing and taunting him until he groaned in torment. Her lips flicked his hard nipple and then descended across his belly. Her inquiring hands fanned across his chest and then followed in the wake of her kisses until she had touched and tasted all of him.

Dwayne's heart thundered furiously, and his lungs seemed inoperable. He couldn't breathe, he couldn't think, he could only respond to the rapturous hunger spurting through his body.

Rapture that defied reason gripped him as she continued to explore the sensitive points of his body. He shuddered and felt ready to explode if he couldn't bury himself in her soon. He was oblivious to everything but the maddening urge to end this wild torture by plunging into the blaze.

Sonya cried out as he lunged into her. Pain ripped through her, and she gasped for breath. She had forgotten there would be pain.

"Oh God!" Dwayne pulled away.

Sonya's eyes glazed with unshed tears as she gently pulled his head back to meet her hungry kiss. She wanted, needed, for him to continue. "Please," she whispered, urging him on.

This time, he entered slowly. Her arms slid around his back as she dug her fingernails into his skin. He thrust toward her and then withdrew, letting her adjust to the experience of accepting a man. It was with deliberate effort that Dwayne kept from ravishing her. He would not hurt her, he told himself repeatedly. But soon he found himself driving toward her, clutching her closer as a wild, budding pleasure gripped him.

She drew him to her as her nails dug deeper into the taut muscles of his back. And then she was soaring, reveling in the rapturous feeling that took her higher and higher. They were one, body and soul.

Forgetting his vow to be gentle, his muscles flexed as he raised her from the bed to meet his hard, driving thrusts. He was blind with passion and trembling with desire.

Sonya felt her soul draining from her body as he moved within her, claiming her as more than just his possession. She was shaky, breathless, seeking some distant, compulsive sensation that waited just beyond her grasp. She strained against him to appease this unfamiliar craving that left her trembling.

A strange, satisfying wave seemed to blossom somewhere

in the dark depths of her soul, vibrating through her entire body
until she was consumed by its magical, splendorous pleasure.
Ecstasy ran through her veins, leaving her oblivious to all
except this overwhelming sense of fulfillment.

Tears of pleasure rolled down her cheeks as he buried his
head against her shoulder. He groaned as his passion spilled
into her, leaving him drained of strength. His soul had abandoned him, leaving nothing more than an empty shell that was
devoid of all emotion. Just as he thought this wondrous world
had ended, she placed a tender kiss on his forehead, restoring
much of his strength.

Dwayne propped his forearms on either side of her and held
her head in his hands, keeping her face tilted toward him.
"Mine," he whispered, capturing her lips. Sonya snuggled
against him and felt his claim to be true. She had no memory
of what followed next as sleep quickly descended upon her.

Sonya woke to the rich smell of coffee brewing from downstairs. She stretched lazily against Dwayne while smiling her
contentment. "Morning, sleepyhead," Dwayne's seductive
voice greeted her.

She turned over to face him and smiled. "Good morning."

"Now that's how a woman is supposed to greet a man in
the morning, not with flying fists," Dwayne teased.

Sonya laughed. "Okay, I deserved that."

"You deserved a lot more than that." Dwayne bent his head
and kissed her passionately. When he pulled away, he saw her
eyes sparkled with mischief.

"Now that's how a man is supposed to greet a woman in
the morning, not with useless talk."

Dwayne laughed and hugged her closer to him. "Maybe
we should join Bridget downstairs. I smell her famous coffee
brewing. She must have made it home already."

Sonya pulled away from his embrace. "Do you think she
knows?"

"Not much gets past Bridget, I'm sorry to say. I have to

figure out the best way to handle this sticky situation,'' Dwayne reflected, shaking his head. ''After that recent talk we had, I feel like a hypocrite. Are you uncomfortable with this?''

Sonya's smile didn't quite reach her eyes. Things were happening too fast. She went from not wanting to depend on any man to wanting to please this man. Is this how most women felt? Is this where many women went wrong?

''Don't do this, Sonya,'' Dwayne warned, interrupting her thoughts.

''Don't do what?'' She pretended innocence.

''Don't put up that wall. I feel you doing it.''

''I don't know how I feel about anything anymore. Almost overnight my world has changed. I don't know how I feel about Bridget knowing about us. I don't even know how I feel about it. It's all so new to me.''

Dwayne kissed her tenderly. ''It's new to me, too. I haven't felt so strongly about another woman since my first wife. In truth, I don't know how I feel about Bridget knowing, either. I don't know how she will react. But I'm not going to hide my feelings for you.''

''What *are* your feelings?''

''I feel a sense of protectiveness toward you. I want nothing and no one to hurt you. I feel you light up a room whenever you walk into it. And I feel alive whenever you smile.''

Sonya blushed at his kind words, but he said nothing of love. Love? Is that what she truly wanted? For so long, she believed that it was the one thing she could live without.

She studied his strong features and wondered if that was what she felt for him. She certainly felt everything he'd just described. She loved the way he seemed to dominate a room whenever he entered. She loved the way he looked at her as if she were the most beautiful woman in the world. But did she love him?

She thought of her father and how much her mother had claimed to love him. She thought of Laura's marriage. How many times had Laura confessed that she loved Curtis?

When Sonya tensed in his embrace, he gently cupped her

chin forcing her to look at him. "Sonya, I'm not like your father. I would never hurt you." He brought his hands down and cupped her firm breast.

Sonya moaned despite herself. She wanted to believe him, but she couldn't. She tried to pull away from his touch. She couldn't think with him touching her like that.

Dwayne smiled warmly at her, but his expression quickly turned serious. "I can't believe that you . . . that you were . . ."

"A virgin?"

Dwayne nodded. "I mean I'm . . . I was . . ."

"Surprised?"

Dwayne nodded again. "Why did you wait?"

Sonya looked away. "I don't know why I waited so long. I guess I wanted something different. I wanted something special." Their eyes made contact. "And then came you."

Dwayne's lips covered hers in a spellbinding kiss. Sonya's arms instantly embraced him.

A soft knock sounded at the door. Sonya pushed Dwayne away and scrambled to cover herself.

"Just a minute," Dwayne called.

Sonya's eyes were wide as she looked up to him.

"She's not going to bite," he whispered.

Sonya remained still when he motioned for her stay in bed. The pain in his leg had returned briefly as he limped to retrieve his robe. He gave her an encouraging smile, then went to answer the door. He blocked the frame so Bridget would not see past him.

"Good morning, Daddy." She smiled.

"Good morning, Bridget."

Bridget jokingly tried to look around him. "I made breakfast this morning for you and Sonya."

"Thank you. That was very thoughtful of you. We'll be down in a minute."

Bridget giggled, then winked at her father as she turned to go back downstairs. He shook his head, then closed the door.

Sonya sat on the edge of the bed, shaking her head. "I'll

say that she didn't sound too disappointed to discover I'm in here.''

"No, I think that she was rather happy with the idea.''

Sonya smiled. "You seem rather pleased yourself.''

"Guilty,'' he said, coming toward the bed. In one quick motion, he swooped her up into his arms.

"Where are you taking me?''

"To the bathroom. I bet you never had a shower with a man before,'' he said, winking.

Bridget placed a jug of orange juice on the table just as a squeal descended from upstairs. She smiled inwardly. *It's about time he found someone.* Hopefully Sonya was just what he needed. He needed someone to take his mind from work. That was all he seemed to do: work and come home.

There were plenty of times, Bridget felt, that maybe it was somehow her fault. That she was responsible for him not enjoying life. Another squeal from upstairs caused her to giggle. She liked Sonya. And more importantly, she didn't treat her as if she were some mindless teenager. Yes, she thought, Sonya was just what her father needed.

Perhaps Ms. Deaton would stop calling so much. Carmen would call four or five times a night, wanting to talk to her father. And it was hardly ever business related.

The phone rang. "Hamilton residence.''

"Hello, Bridget.''

"Oh, hi, Aunt Sharon.''

"Good morning. I was calling to let you know that I made it in safely. Is everything okay?''

Bridget's smile widened. "Everything is wonderful.''

"Oh? So are you going to keep me in suspense?''

"I think you are going to have to wait and see for yourself.''

"That good, huh?''

"Better.'' Bridget giggled.

"Okay. Well, is your father in?''

Another squeal filled the house. "He's a little busy right now."

"Oh? How about Sonya, is she in?"

"I think she's a little busy, too." Bridget held the phone away from her ear as Sharon screamed excitedly in the phone.

"Bridget, tell me everything!"

Bridget heard her father's bedroom door open, then close. "I can't, Aunt Sharon. Call me back later." Bridget reached to hang up the phone. She heard Sharon calling for her as she placed the phone on the receiver.

Dwayne entered the kitchen dressed only in a pair of black, short pants. He immediately noticed the extravagant breakfast Bridget had prepared. There were plates of pancakes, sausages, bacon, and eggs. She had even cut up fresh fruit and placed it on the table.

"Are you expecting an army?"

"No, I was just in a cooking mood. I hope you like it."

"It smells delicious."

"Thank you." Both fell silent. Bridget bit her lip while plastering on a look of amusement.

Dwayne crossed his arms, then searched for the right words. "Bridget, I think we need to talk."

She nodded. "Okay."

Dwayne sat at the table, and Bridget pulled her chair beside him. When she took her seat, Dwayne reached for her hand. *Here goes.* "I want to talk to you about a very delicate matter."

Again Bridget nodded, her amused expression still in place.

"I want to talk to you about what happened last night."

"Mm-hmm," Bridget urged.

"It wasn't something planned." Dwayne couldn't think of where to go from there.

"I understand, Daddy. I'm cool with it."

Dwayne frowned. He wasn't handling this well. "You don't want to talk about this?"

"Daddy, I know what goes on between men and women. I'm not naive, you know." Bridget stood and walked to the cabinets.

Bridget's words shocked Dwayne. "What?"

Bridget jumped, causing a plate to slide out of her hand and crash loudly onto the floor.

"Just what do you mean by that?"

Bridget stepped back. "I just meant, I know about the birds and the bees."

"How do *you* know about the bird and the bees?"

Bridget dropped her shoulders and looked shocked by his question. "You can't be serious."

"Answer my question."

Bridget placed her hand on her hip. "They teach sex education in school."

Dwayne's face dropped. "Since when?"

"Come on, Daddy. What did you expect? Besides we have cable."

Suddenly Dwayne didn't want to pursue this conversation. He shook his head, not believing what he was hearing. For some reason, he believed that she would be naive about the subject until he was ready to approach the subject. Maybe he was naive.

"Is Sonya going to come down for breakfast?" Bridget asked, trying to change the subject. She reached for the broom and began sweeping up the broken glass.

"We'll finish this discussion when I'm able to get my hands on some heart medication." Dwayne left the kitchen. By the time he reached his bedroom, he had made a mental note to attend more PTA meetings.

"How did it go?" Sonya stood up from the bed. She had already dressed and returned quietly to his room. She wore a pair of baggy jeans and a midriff T-shirt. It was clear to him that Bridget had picked out most of her clothes.

"She handled it well."

"Tell me the truth, Dwayne. She was angry, wasn't she? She resents me. Oh, God, what a mess." She slumped onto the bed.

Dwayne sat beside her. "No. Believe me, she had no problems about this situation. In fact, she seems . . . content with it. She's waiting for us to join her for breakfast.'' He hugged her when he noticed her worried expression. "Trust me. She's fine with the idea.''

Sonya nodded as she pulled out of his arms. She hugged herself as she stood up from the bed. "Let's give it a try,'' she said bravely.

They left the bedroom and descended the stairs hand-in-hand. The doorbell rang, and Bridget raced from the kitchen to answer it. She stopped when she saw her father and Sonya on the staircase.

Relief swept through Sonya as Bridget gave her a heart-warming smile. Sonya returned the favor as the doorbell rang again.

"I'll get it,'' Bridget said.

Dwayne leaned in and gave Sonya a kiss on her cheek. Bridget opened the door just as Sonya returned his kiss, then she felt Dwayne's body stiffen. She pulled away from him and looked curiously at his expression. At that moment, a familiar syrupy voice echoed up the stairs.

"Good morning, Bridget. May I speak with your . . .''

Sonya turned her head, shocked to see Carmen at the door.

Chapter Eighteen

Carmen stood in the doorway dressed in an emerald, skin-tight, rayon dress that left little to the imagination. Sonya's eyes followed Carmen's long legs which trailed to a pair of matching pumps.

Carmen looked from Dwayne to Sonya. "I don't believe this," she announced, dropping her hands to cradle her hips. "Are we now sleeping with our clients? I didn't realize that business was so bad."

Before Sonya could respond, Dwayne released her hand and raced down the stairs. He took Carmen by the elbow and dragged her into his office.

Dwayne swirled Carmen around and glared at her. "That's enough, Carmen. What the hell do you want?"

"I'm sorry, did I interrupt something?" Carmen sneered.

"No. I just think we need to speak in private, Miss Greene."

"What happened, Dwayne? Or is this additional services provided by our firm?"

Dwayne's jaw clenched in outrage. "You're out of line."

Carmen's beautiful face turned sinister. "She can't have you."

Dwayne grabbed Carmen's forearm. He loosened his grip when a flash of pain crossed her features. "I think it's time you left. I don't know what has gotten into you."

Carmen stopped and gazed softly into his eyes. "You don't know, do you? You honestly don't know how I feel?"

Dwayne furious gazed turned into a questioning one.

Carmen shook her head and chuckled to herself. "You can't be that blind."

Dropping her shoulders, she looked defeated. She turned away from him.

Dwayne witnessed the tears glistening in her eyes and had the disturbing feeling of guilt attack his conscious. "Carmen," he called to her then walked over to stand in front of her. The misery etched in her features, tugged at his heart. He reached out to caress her cheek tenderly. "I'm sorry. I swear, I didn't know."

Sonya pushed open the door and stepped inside Dwayne's office. She stopped when she saw Dwayne caressing Carmen. A smothering heat of betrayal rose within her to melt her heart. She crucified herself for believing that Dwayne was different. Just as quietly, she turned and slipped out of the room.

Carmen attempted to wipe away her tears. "I must look like a fool to you." She smiled weakly at him.

Dwayne shook his head. "Not at all."

"Well, I feel like one." She managed to compose herself. "I came over to tell you that my contact at the police department informed me that they discovered two sets of bullets at Walters Intercorp."

Dwayne shook his head in confusion. "Two?"

Carmen nodded then crossed her arms. "I think we may be over our heads in this."

Dwayne thought heavily on their new discovery. "Whatever is going on, we can't just walk away."

"We? Or you?" Carmen asked then shook her head. "I'm sorry."

Dwayne looked into her eyes. "I mean me. I can't walk away."

Carmen smiled sadly. "Then maybe you should consider police protection."

Dwayne laughed. "That's not an option."

"I'm worried about you, Dwayne. This is too dangerous and you're not a . . ."

"A superhero?"

They both laughed.

Carmen became serious. "I must be going. Anthony went to see Malik for you. The sooner we find Laura the better."

"We?"

Carmen walked to the door then turned around to face him. "Of course. We are a team."

Dwayne walked her to the door and thanked her for the information.

"Just promise me one thing," Carmen said.

"What's that?"

"That you will take care of yourself."

Dwayne smiled broadly. "I promise."

Carmen walked out of the house and Dwayne headed to the kitchen to join Bridget and Sonya. But when he entered the kitchen, Bridget sat alone at the table.

"Where's Sonya?"

"She left ten minutes ago," she replied quietly.

"Damn!"

Anthony sat in Malik Moyers's office, tapping his pen against a small notepad. A single cigar that burned wastefully in an ashtray caused a thick cloud of smoke to fill the room.

Anthony looked around, noticing the furniture must have been purchased from garage sales. He never understood why Malik chose to keep his office this way. He was no cheap detective. But Malik would only say that he'd never forget his roots. Anthony could understand that, but the man still had a rotary telephone.

Malik sat opposite Anthony and was dressed head to toe in black leather, regardless of the ninety-degree weather outside.

Get **4 FREE** Arabesque Contemporary Romances Delivered to Your Doorstep and Join the Only New Book Club That Delivers These Bestselling African American Romances Directly to You Each Month!

No Obligation!

WE INVITE YOU TO JOIN THE ONLY BOOK CLUB THAT DELIVERS HEARTFELT ROMANCE FEATURING AFRICAN AMERICAN HEROES AND HEROINES IN STORIES THAT ARE RICH IN PASSION AND CULTURAL SPICE...

And Your First 4 Books Are FREE!

Arabesque is the newest contemporary romance line offered by Pinnacle Books. Arabesque has been so successful that our readers have asked us about direct home delivery. We responded to your requests. You can start receiving four bestselling Arabesque novels a month delivered right to your door. Subscribe now and you'll get:

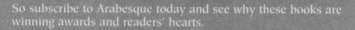

- ✦ 4 FREE Arabesque romances as our introductory gift—a value of almost $20! (pay only $1 to help cover postage & handling)
- ✦ 4 BRAND-NEW Arabesque romances delivered to your doorstep each month thereafter (usually arriving before they're available in bookstores!)
- ✦ 20% off each title—a savings of almost $4.00 each month
- ✦ FREE home delivery
- ✦ A FREE monthly newsletter, *Zebra/Pinnacle Romance News* that features author profiles, book previews and more
- ✦ No risks or obligations...in other words, you can cancel whenever you wish with no questions asked

So subscribe to Arabesque today and see why these books are winning awards and readers' hearts.

After you've enjoyed our FREE gift of 4 Arabesques, you'll begin to receive monthly shipments of the newest Arabesque titles. Each shipment will be yours to examine for 10 days. If you decide to keep the books, you'll pay the preferred subscriber's price of just $4.00 per title. That's $16 for all 4 books with FREE home delivery! And if you want us to stop sending books, just say the word...it's that simple.

See why reviewers are raving about ARABESQUE and order your FREE books today!

WE HAVE 4 FREE BOOKS FOR YOU!

ARABESQUE

(If the certificate is missing below, write to:
Zebra Home Subscription Service, Inc.,
120 Brighton Road, P.O. Box 5214, Clifton, New Jersey 07015-5214)

FREE BOOK CERTIFICATE

Yes! Please send me 4 *Arabesque* Contemporary Romances without cost or obligation, billing me just $1 to help cover postage and handling. I understand that each month, I will be able to preview 4 brand-new *Arabesque* Contemporary Romances FREE for 10 days. Then, if I decide to keep them, I will pay the money-saving preferred subscriber's price of just $16.00 for all 4...that's a savings of almost $4 off the publisher's price with no additional charge for shipping and handling. I may return any shipment within 10 days and owe nothing, and I may cancel this subscription at any time. My 4 FREE books will be mine to keep in any case.

Name _____

Address _____ Apt. _____

City _____ State _____ Zip _____

Telephone ( ) _____

Signature _____ AR1197
(If under 18, parent or guardian must sign.)

Terms and prices subject to change. Orders subject to acceptance by Zebra Home Subscription Service, Inc. .
Zebra Home Subscription Service, Inc. reserves the right to reject or cancel any subscription.

Leather had always been Malik's trademark. Rumors had it that Malik was kin to Iron Mike Tyson. Both resembled pit bulls, and both were known for their fighting ability. No one crossed Malik or at least no one lived to tell the tale. Muscles bulged throughout every inch of his body.

Malik was Atlanta's best detective, according to Dwayne. Anthony now shared that same opinion. The detective grew up on Atlanta's toughest streets and was well connected. Whenever Dwayne found himself in a jam, he would always call Malik for help. There wasn't anything that Malik couldn't find. Or anyone.

"So Dwayne needs another favor?" Malik laughed.

Anthony smiled. "Yes, and this time he wants you to report all information to me."

Malik leaned back in the wooden chair. "Ah, must be a woman he's looking for then." Both men enjoyed the joke before the detective said, "Is this the file?"

"Yes." Anthony turned serious and watched Malik open the small folder. "Her name is Laura Durden. Age, twenty-six. Height, five foot six." Anthony stopped when Malik peered at him over the folder. "Is something wrong?" he asked innocently.

"Despite popular opinion, I can read."

"Sorry."

"She's up on murder charges?" Malik read from the folder.

"I'm afraid so."

"So there may also be a bounty hunter on her trail?"

"It's possible."

"Sounds like an interesting case. Does she have any family she can run to? Any out-of-town friends?"

Anthony crossed his legs, resting his left ankle on his right knee. "According to my report, the only one she has is her sister, Sonya Walters. Her mother has been incarcerated for over fifteen years."

"Sonya Walters?" Malik looked up from the folder.

"Do you know her?"

Malik nodded with a crooked grin. "I know her."

Anthony's curiosity led him to probe further. "How do *you* know Miss Walters?"

"She wasn't always eating caviar. We go way back."

"Techwood," Anthony concluded. "You grew up with her in Techwood."

"Yeah. So this is Laura Walters? She has definitely grown up," he commented, taking the small photograph from the folder.

"If you think she's something, wait until you see Sonya," Anthony said, nodding his head in approval.

"Well, Sonya was always a looker. She was a little uptight, but she had all the brothers after her."

"Do you think you'll have any trouble finding Mrs. Durden?"

Malik laid the picture back in the folder. "If she's in Atlanta, I'll find her."

"Well, you're the man," Anthony said, standing up from his chair.

"As long as you stiff-shirts recognize," Malik laughed, then reached to hand Anthony a cigar.

"No, thanks. I'm trying to cut back," Anthony bluffed.

"Come on, man. Just try it."

Anthony knew it was an insult if he declined the cigar. "Thanks." Much to his horror, Malik pulled out a lighter. "I think I better save it for later."

Malik slowly shook his head as he flicked on the lighter. Anthony bit off the end of the cigar, something he saw Malik do, and accepted the flame offered to him.

Anthony inhaled and immediately felt sick while Malik commented on how green he looked. He coughed so hard and so long, he just knew he was going to lose a lung.

Malik roared with laughter while Anthony fought for oxygen. "I'll make a man out of you yet."

Tears stung Anthony's eyes as he struggled to breathe again. Maybe I shouldn't have inhaled, he thought bitterly. After he felt better, he handed the cigar back to Malik, vowing he'd never touch another one for the rest of his life.

* * *

"We've looked everywhere. We can't find it." Samuel shifted his weight from one foot to the other. His expression was apologetic. The dark scar that covered half his face help made him legendary on the streets but it was his loyalty to C.J. that made him deadly.

"If you don't have it, then you obviously haven't looked everywhere," his boss retorted.

Samuel retreated backward but stopped short when he bumped into a solid figure. He had forgotten about the two guards by the door.

C.J. stood from his chair as anger flashed in his midnight eyes. "We're running out of time," his voice thundered. He hovered above Samuel by a full foot, but it was his power that intimidated everyone.

Samuel watched the .45 lying inches away from his employer's hand. Sweat rolled down his forehead. His lips trembled as he tried to swallow the large lump in the middle of his throat.

"If you could just give us forty-eight hours, I know we can get your merchandise. Forty-eight hours, that's all I ask." Samuel's eyes widened when C.J. picked up the gun.

"You will come through for me this time." The statement was a command, not a question.

Samuel knew his life was at stake. "Yes, sir. We won't let you down this time."

Samuel watched C.J.'s towering frame return to his chair. The gun remained in his hand. Fear slithered down Samuel's spine when their eyes met.

"No, I don't think you'll disappoint me, Samuel. You got your forty-eight hours. I want you to keep Benjamin posted on your progress."

"Of course, sir."

C.J. fanned him away, and a pair of rough hands seized him by the collar. The guards lifted him in the air and tossed him from the private office.

Samuel crashed hard against the cement. The office door

slammed behind him. Pain ripped through his body as he pushed himself off the cement and looked back at the closed door. *Forty-eight hours.* The number loomed over his head. He had to work fast. He walked down Henderson Avenue, constantly glancing over his shoulder to ensure he wasn't followed.

He made it to the blue Nissan, parked two blocks up, confident he was alone.

"What happened?" Odell asked.

Samuel looked at his brother and shook his head. "It ain't good. Let's get out of here."

"What did he say?"

"We have forty-eight hours to get our hands on that merchandise. So far, I don't think he suspects we're also working for Frank. If he ever does, we're dead."

Odell started the car. They arrived in Kennesaw nearly an hour later. Both men were engrossed in their thoughts.

Odell turned off the headlights and pulled into the driveway leading to a small shack surrounded by large, looming trees. The men got out of the car and walked to the small house.

Samuel opened the door, then stepped inside. Odell followed but kept looking behind.

Once inside, the men walked along the creaking floor-boards toward the back of the house. Samuel placed his ear against the door before peeking inside. There, still tied to the small wooden chair, sat Laura Durden.

Chapter Nineteen

Dwayne returned home, slamming his car door. *Where could she be?* He had turned Atlanta upside down, searching for Sonya. She'd been gone now for over twenty-four hours. She hadn't returned home, and Walters Intercorp was still shut down due to the police investigation. *Didn't she realize her life was in danger?*

Yesterday's scene played over in his mind. *I shouldn't have left her alone to draw her own conclusion. Why didn't I tell her everything last night?*

Dwayne leaned against the gold Lincoln Town Car, deep in thought. *She had to be somewhere, but where?* Tomorrow, Walters Intercorp's employees would return to work. Would she risk going there? At this point, he didn't know what Sonya would do.

Silence greeted Dwayne when he entered the house. Bridget was probably still upset with him. She hadn't said much about what happened, but her heated looks said enough. When the phone rang, Dwayne raced to answer it by the second ring.

"Hello?"

"Dwayne, I finally caught you."

"Hi, Sharon," he answered with disappointment.

"Well, I'm happy to hear from you, too."

"I'm sorry. Things are a little crazy right now."

"Did something else happen?"

"Let's see if I can sum this up." Dwayne thought for a moment. He didn't really want to tell Sharon all that went on between him and Sonya. After all, they were good friends.

"I'm waiting," Sharon persisted.

"It's a long story. Maybe I'll tell you when you get home."

"Is everything all right? Where's Sonya?"

She would ask that. "She's not here right now."

"What do you mean, she's not there? I thought that you were supposed to watch her?"

Dwayne became defensive. "I'm not her mother, Sharon. I can't" Dwayne got an idea—"I have to go, Sharon. I'll talk to you later. Bye." He ignored his sister's protests on the other end and hung up the phone. Within minutes, he was out the door. He knew where Sonya was.

Sonya pulled the Atlanta Braves baseball cap lower and pushed up her dark sunglasses. She observed the different people on the Marta bus, unsure if her disguise was convincing. She glanced at her attire again: a pair of oversized, faded blue jeans hung low enough to show her men's boxer shorts—it was something she had seen Bridget do. The midriff tank top displayed her flat stomach—it seemed to be the style with the other young girls on the bus.

A young boy winked at her. He had to be at least seventeen, she thought. *Do I look that young in this getup?* The boy stood, then strolled to the empty seat beside her. "What's up, shortie?"

Shortie? Sonya ignored him. Maybe he would get the hint and go away. He didn't.

"What's your name?" he asked in a fake baritone.

Sonya scooted farther away from him. She heard his disgust as he stood up from the chair mumbling, "Damn trick, thinks she's all that."

Sonya's eyes widened at his audacity. Maybe she went too far in her disguise. She fingered her big loop earrings. *How do these girls wear this stuff?* Habitually Sonya's hands went to her now short haircut. She remembered the shock of the hairdresser when she asked for her to cut it all off. Afterward, when she saw the long ringlets of hair sprawled across the floor, she felt her identity had been stripped from her.

She wondered what Dwayne would think of her new haircut. Did he like her long hair? Sonya cursed herself for even thinking about him.

She stared out the window and studied the trees as the bus passed by them. It had been ages since she rode Marta. It was once her only form of transportation. As a young girl, her parents could never afford a car, but she remembered her mother always promising to buy one. Sonya smiled at that thought. Her mother was always planning to do so many things.

Sonya recognized her stop and gathered her things. She waited along with the other passengers for a connecting bus. Bus number 124 pulled up, and Sonya got on. This time, she sat closer to the bus driver. She didn't like being in the back where most of the younger kids hung out. She noticed more approving stares from the younger boys on the bus.

Ten minutes later, the bus pulled up to her stop, and she got off. She stood in front of the big building, trying to gather her courage. She remembered the last time she was here. It was a hard time for her, and she didn't doubt that today would be any different.

Finally she took a deep breath and walked into the building. She stood at the reception desk for nearly fifteen minutes before the officer pulled herself from the phone.

"May I help you?" she asked politely.

Sonya smiled. "Yes, I would like to see my mother, Dorothy Walters."

Bridget propped open another book, fascinated by what she had discovered in the library. Why hadn't she come here before?

She had no idea there was so much information on coins. She flipped through the books, unaware that she had been in the library going on five hours.

She took notes on the different museums she wanted to visit. She had also listed all the different coin dealers in Atlanta. The excitement she felt was contagious as she looked up at Shock G.

"Hey, Bridge, check this out. Did you know that the coin your dad gave you last Christmas is listed in here?"

Bridget shook her head. "Let me see that."

Shock G. handed her the book while he grinned confidently at her.

"It's worth twelve hundred dollars," she said, shocked.

"We're rich."

Bridget frowned at him. "Rich? Not hardly." She continued to browse through his book. "This is interesting. Maybe I should check this one out. Perhaps we can see if I have one that would really make us rich."

Shock G. agreed. "We could be living large, Bridge. We could get married, buy us our own crib. That way we don't have to listen to your father."

Bridget laughed, but she remembered her conversation with Sonya. "Maybe we're too young to get married."

Shock G. looked at her as if she were an alien. "What? Are you going to start perpetrating 'cuz you might be rich?"

"No, George, I just think we're too young to get married," she said, shrugging her shoulders.

"Too young? Girl, you buggin'. I thought you wanted to get married."

Bridget looked around to see if anyone was listening to their conversation. "George—"

"And what's with this George? You know I go by Shock G."

Bridget took a deep breath and tried again. "Shock G., I just want to wait until after I go to college and start my own coin shop before I think about marriage."

"College? Since when did you want to go to college?"

Bridget leaned back in her chair and stared at him. Did she love George? He was fun, and it upset her father to think that she was with him, but the conversation with Sonya had her thinking. Wouldn't it be great to have a career of her own, to have her own sense of independence?

"George—I mean, Shock G.—don't you want to make something of yourself? What can we do with a basic education? Nothing. Things are changing all the time, and knowledge is our only defense."

George's mouth fell open. "Girl, who on earth have you been talking to?"

Bridget smiled. "Just a friend of my father's."

"A friend, huh? And what qualifies this friend as a keynote speaker? I mean that's all adults talk about. College. You don't need no fancy degree to get a good job. Look at my uncle Tyrone. He has his own business. He serves the best barbecue in Atlanta."

Bridget shook her head, not believing his logic and not believing she once listened. "Geor . . . Shock G., I don't want to serve barbecue for the rest of my life."

George pushed his chair away from the table. "Not serve barbecue? Girl, we'll be rolling in the dough when Uncle Tyrone leaves me the business. He's already said that I can start working for him next week. I figure I'll start now and learn the basics, you know, learn the ropes. In a few years, he'll want to retire and we can take over the business."

Bridget tossed her hands up. "It's getting late. We can talk about this later. I'm going to check out this book and go home. I'm supposed to be on restriction." She gave him a quick peck on the cheek and smiled. "Come on. We don't have to make any definite plans today."

That seemed to cheer him up as he got up to follow her to the checkout counter.

Laura greedily accepted the spoon of mashed potatoes from the man named Odell. He kept her tied to the chair as he fed her. She tried to keep her pride intact, but it was hard not to beg for mercy from this man.

The way his eyes swept over her figure, she didn't know whether or not he would act on what was obvious in his eyes. *He won't take liberties if his partner, Samuel, is around.*

Laura wanted to ask Odell questions. How long were they going to keep her? Would she ever leave this place alive?

She looked wearily at Odell. How could she have ever believed that he was Curtis's brother?

Laura finished the rest of the potatoes and waited for him to leave. But he didn't move. He lifted his dirty hand and caressed the left side of her face. She wished she could wash his touch from her skin. She grew nervous as his eyes studied her lips.

Odell's head lowered, and Laura twisted her face away from him. It didn't matter—he just began kissing her cheek. Laura cringed at the feel of his wet lips plastered to the side of her face. His fingers quickly grabbed her chin and pulled her face back to him.

Laura felt her lunch threaten to return when his lips finally made contact with hers. She refused to cry. In a last effort to break away, Laura's teeth bit into his lips.

Odell growled, wiping his mouth with the back of his hand.

Laura flinched but prepared herself for the blow she was sure he was going to deliver. When she opened her eyes, she saw that Samuel had returned and was restraining Odell.

"What in the hell do you think you're doing?" he yelled.

"She bit me," Odell barked back.

"And what did you think she was going to do?" Samuel released his hand. But the look in Odell's eyes told Laura that he still wanted revenge. "Get ahold of yourself, Odell. Our time is running out."

"What are we going to do with her anyway?" Odell asked.

Laura looked at Samuel—she, too, wanted to know the answer to that question.

"We can't hurt her. She's valuable," Samuel sneered. "Now

get your stuff. We have a lead. Sonya Walters was spotted this morning on a Marta bus.''

Laura's heart skipped a beat. ''What are you going to do to my sister?'' she asked before thinking.

''Gag her,'' Samuel instructed and left the room.

Odell gagged Laura with a look of contempt. ''I'll tell you what we're going to do with your sister. First, we're going to see if she has our merchandise. Then we're going to kill her.''

Chapter Twenty

Sonya twitched nervously in a small wooden chair and waited patiently for her mother to enter the room. Every so often, she would dart her eyes around, relieved that no one seemed to notice her. She pulled her baseball cap down farther. *Maybe this isn't a good idea. This is a mistake.*

She reached for her purse and stood up from the chair just as the prison door opened. Sonya stopped in her tracks and turned slowly to see her mother enter the room. Dorothy Walters, a heavyset woman, had her massive salt-and-pepper hair pulled into a loose bun. A few strands framed her cinnamon-hued skin. Though her mother appeared older than her years, there were still no wrinkles visible on her face.

A guard directed Dorothy to an empty chair in front of her daughter. It pained Sonya to see her mother in this place, and she prayed for the day of her release.

Dorothy's eyes sparkled the moment she recognized her daughter. "Sonya."

Despite her agonizing depression, Sonya smiled at her mother.

"My God, what did you do to your hair?" Dorothy asked, leaning in for a better look.

Sonya's hand lifted to her head to pull her cap down tighter. "I thought I needed a change," Sonya lied.

"And what is with those shades? There isn't a sun in here. Take those off." Her mother smiled.

If Sonya's nervousness wasn't apparent, it was now as her hands trembled to remove her glasses. "Hello, Mama."

Dorothy's smile dropped at seeing Sonya's red eyes. "What's wrong?"

Sonya clasped her hands together, not knowing where to begin. Her monthly trips to the prison were meant to brighten both their lives. Since Laura's sudden marriage to Curtis, Sonya's role became the bearer of bad news. And today she would have to tell her mother everything that had transpired in the past month. *Where do I begin?*

"I asked you what's wrong. Why are you dressed like that?" Dorothy asked with a twinge of dread in her voice.

"Mama, there's something I have to tell you. It's about Laura." Sonya longed to touch her mother, so she placed her hand against the glass that separated them. Dorothy followed suit. When she looked into her mother's questioning eyes, she prayed for strength to get through this.

As if sensing the news was bad, Dorothy squared her shoulders to prepare herself for the worst.

Sonya took another deep breath, stared down at her hands, and told her mother everything while twisting her gold coin habitually. Her mother's unnerving silence played havoc with her emotions.

"Is she dead?" Dorothy's voice trembled.

Sonya met her mother's steady gaze. "I don't know," she answered. The uncertainty is what hurt so much, Sonya thought.

Dorothy bit her bottom lip to prevent it from trembling. However, there was no mistaking the pain streaked across her face. "But it's a possibility?"

Sonya knew she had let her mother down. Sonya shook her head, not knowing what else to say.

"Maybe it's my fault," Dorothy said, wiping away her tears with the back of her hand. "I let you girls down."

Sonya's hands covered her mouth. *How could she think that after all she'd done?* Sonya shook her head. "No, if it's anyone's fault, it's mine. I was responsible for Laura. I could have taught her not to be like—" Sonya stopped herself, but it was too late.

"Like me?" Dorothy asked as tears glistened in her eyes.

Sonya removed her hand from the glass. She would give anything to hold her mother, to comfort her, to assure her that none of this was her fault. "I didn't mean it like that." When she didn't respond, Sonya called to her, "Please, don't cry."

Dorothy removed her hands, her face drenched with tears. "I have to believe that she's all right," she said, thrusting up her chin. It was her strength talking, strength that Sonya had always admired. "What are the police doing about this?"

"I really don't know. I have to keep moving, someone might recognize me." Sonya glanced around to the other visitors.

"I don't understand why someone would be trying to kill you." Dorothy followed her daughter's gaze.

"I don't understand it, either—but I'm not going to stick around and find out."

Dorothy continued to wipe at the tears flowing down her cheeks. "Surely the police can do something to protect you."

Sonya shook her head. "I don't trust them. I don't trust anybody, really."

"That's a pretty harsh statement," Dorothy said.

"It's a harsh place we live in." Sonya regretted the words immediately. She was speaking out of pain, and she knew it. Her heart had been broken, and she didn't know how to handle it. This is what she had fought so hard to prevent, and now she was confused: confused about her life, and what she wanted.

"Something else is bothering you, Sonya. Do you want to talk about it?"

Sonya smiled. Her mother could always see through her brave facade. "I don't know where to start."

"Start with his name."

Her mother knew her well. Sonya took a deep breath before starting. "His name is Dwayne Hamilton, and I think I'm in love with him."

Dwayne ran through the floors of his office building, wanting to get his hands on Sonya's file. He couldn't remember which detention center her mother was held at. That was the only place he hadn't checked.

He turned on the light in his office.

"What the hell?" Everything was in shambles. Books had been thrown from the shelves, and important documents covered the floor. Dwayne pinched the bridge of his nose. He needed to calm down.

He walked over to his desk and checked all the drawers. Empty. Next he went to his knees and began turning over all the papers on the floor. He had to find that file. He had no doubt whoever shot up Walters' Intercorp trashed his office.

Hearing heavy footsteps enter the room, Dwayne looked up to see Anthony staring down at him. "Don't ask," he instructed, but the question had already fled from Anthony's mouth.

"What happened?"

"You don't want to know." Dwayne continued to search through the scattered papers.

"Mind if I ask what you're looking for?" Anthony asked, taking off his jacket.

"I'm looking for Sonya's file. It has to be around here somewhere. Didn't you leave it in my office?"

Dwayne stood up from the floor and walked out to Carmen's desk. He tossed papers around as he tried to find the missing file. When he couldn't find it, he looked back at Anthony. "How about Laura's folder?"

"I delivered it to Malik."

"Damn!" Dwayne snatched the phone and dialed Malik's office. As he waited for the connection, he tapped his hand impatiently on Carmen's desk.

He hung up the phone after the tenth ring. "I have to find that place!"

"What do you need to know? I prepared the charts."

"I need to know at which facility Dorothy Walters is held."

Anthony looked away, tapping his right index finger against his temples.

"Think, Anthony. Which center?"

"Oh," Anthony kept repeating to an impatient Dwayne.

Dwayne pinched his nose again, this time harder. *How hard could this be?* "Anthony, who did you get your information from?"

"Ah ha!" Anthony shouted. "Atlanta's Correction Detention Center Annex. Quite a mouthful, huh?" Anthony's smile faded behind Dwayne's retreating figure. Anthony raced after him.

Dwayne ignored the curious stares from his office mates as he ran down the hallway with Anthony right behind him. When he reached his Lincoln, parked illegally in front of the building, it had a ticket stuck behind the windshield wiper.

The men jumped into the car and quickly sped down the busy intersection. Anthony reached for his seat belt. He knew Dwayne's driving well.

Dwayne cursed his luck when a pair of flashing blue lights appeared in his rearview mirror.

"You know, for a lawyer, you get more tickets than anyone I know," Anthony commented.

Dwayne gave a scornful look as he pulled over and reached to retrieve his insurance card from the glove compartment. When he reached for his back pocket, he remembered leaving his wallet on his dresser this morning. *Could today get any worse?*

"License, registration, and proof of insurance," the policewoman asked, after reaching the driver's side.

Dwayne looked up and gave his Hollywood smile, as Bridget called it, hoping it would have some effect on her.

She asked again.

Dwayne could only shake his head. The angels were definitely not with him today. "I seem to have left my wallet at home." Dwayne purposely talked slower. Bridget often teased that he sounded like Barry White when he did that.

When the officer pulled out her pad, he knew he was getting a ticket. He made a conscious note to extend Bridget's restriction.

"Hello, Rhonda." Anthony waved.

"Anthony!" she said, waving back at him. "I haven't seen you in a while. How have you been?"

"Great. I just got back from my trip to Bermuda. Beautiful place."

"Really? That's great."

Dwayne looked over at his assistant. He observed his skinny frame and his regular-joe speaking voice. He looked back at the officer, who was obviously smitten by Anthony.

"Is this going to take long? We're kinda in a hurry." Anthony glanced at his watch.

The officer looked back at Dwayne who gave her what he thought was a friendly smile, but she didn't seem to notice. "Is this your boss you were telling me and the girls about?"

The girls? Dwayne looked back at Anthony. Was he aiding and abetting a playboy?

"Yes, we're on a big case, so can we hurry this up?" Anthony asked.

"Well, I guess I can let you go on a warning." She looked back at Anthony. "If you pick up that rain check I've been holding."

Dwayne gave Anthony a pleading look.

"Deal," Anthony agreed.

The officer blew Anthony a kiss, and Dwayne started the car and continued on his way. Just as he rounded the corner, he of course picked up speed.

"Whoa! Where's the fire?" Shock G. commented as a gold Lincoln flew past him and Bridget.

"That was my dad," Bridget said, leaning over the steering wheel. "I wonder what's going on?"

"Someone should tell him that the speed limit is forty-five on this road and not ninety-five."

"Get out."

"What? I was just joking, Bridge," Shock G. replied.

"I know. I'm going to follow him. He would hit the roof if he saw you with me. I'll call you later." Bridget gave him a quick kiss on the cheek and fanned him to get out of the Jeep.

"I don't think that's a good idea." Shock G. reached for the door handle.

"George!"

"I'm going, I'm going." George got out of the car and watched Bridget hang an illegal right to chase after her father.

Bridget fussed at the hard time she had keeping up with her father. But she did learn from the best and was able to remain no more than three cars behind him. *Where is he going in such a hurry? Was something wrong?*

Bridget ran a stop light to stay behind her father, but she was thankful no cop witnessed the dangerous act. Someone else was in the car with him. She couldn't make out who it was, but she had every intention of finding out.

She reached the highway, and it was the battle of the race cars. The car chase soon turned into a game for Bridget as she fought to keep up with the Lincoln.

"So you love him?" Dorothy said, smiling at her daughter.

Sonya didn't see anything worth smiling about. The man she allowed into her private world had made a fool out of her. She had promised herself she would never fall into the same trap that so many women had.

"Sonya, don't look so sad. Love isn't that bad."

"Don't mind me if I don't share your opinion," Sonya retorted.

"Come on. I think it's past time you found a little happiness for yourself."

Sonya could only shake her head. "I don't understand you.

After all you went through, how can you preach about love being this glorious thing to celebrate?''

''All I can do is hope that you could find something I never had. I have to believe in a greater love. Look what I'm forced to endure every day. I have less than a year before I'm up for probation, and I promise you, I'm not going to live in fear of men.''

That statement got Sonya to reflect on the many years her mother had lost, and a deep sense of guilt consumed her. ''I'm so sorry. It's my fault that you're even in here.''

Dorothy's eyes flashed her anger. ''Don't let me ever hear you say that again. I don't regret what I did for you. I would do it all over again. It's worth every day I serve in here to see you make something of yourself. Do you know how much that means to me?''

Sonya turned away from her mother. This was too hard.

''Sonya, I know that I stayed with your father longer than I should have. I suffered all kinds of abuse, but the day I saw him trying to molest my baby . . .''

More tears sprang from Sonya's eyes as she remembered the day well . . .

''Sonya, get me another beer out of the refrigerator.'' Darryl Walters bellowed the order to his daughter from the living room.

Thirteen-year-old Sonya angrily placed her pencil down on the kitchen table. She would never finish her homework at this rate.

She pulled out another beer and tiptoed into the living room. Her father was in a foul mood again. He had lost another job, so Sonya knew to try and stay out of his way. When she entered the living room to hand her father his beer, she noticed him glaring at her.

What did I do? She looked at the bottle and realized that in her haste she forgot to remove the bottle top. She quickly raced back into the kitchen to remedy the problem. When she reentered the room, her father's eyes were still glued to her.

Slowly she walked over to him, extending her arm, hoping that he would just take the bottle from her so she could get back to her homework.

Darryl Walters took the bottle from his daughter, but his penetrating glare never left her.

Sonya backed away, wanting to leave the room.

Her father smiled lazily at her, and Sonya knew then he was drunk. "How old are you now, Sonya?" He shut off the TV with the remote control.

"Th-Thirteen," she answered. She prayed that Laura and her mother would hurry back from the grocery store.

"Thirteen? I bet you're driving the boys wild down at that school of yours, huh?"

Sonya shook her head. She felt her stomach clench in a hard knot. Her father's gaze left her face and traveled down her small frame.

"You have a boyfriend, Sonya?" His words slurred.

Sonya tried to swallow the lump enlarged in her throat. "No, sir."

Her father stood up from his chair, and Sonya took two steps back. She was caught off guard the moment his arms snaked out and grabbed her.

She tried to fight him off. She kicked and bit him as hard as she could, but all she could hear was his sinister laughter echoing in her ears.

He jerked open Sonya's jeans just as the living room door jerked open to reveal her horrified mother.

Sonya blinked away her tears and looked back at her mother, sitting on the opposite side of the Plexiglass. "I can't wait until your release date. You, of course, will stay with me. It will be the three of us."

A prison guard walked up to Dorothy. "Please visit me when there's more news."

"I will," Sonya promised. She continued to watch her mother as she was led out of the room.

When she was gone, Sonya placed her sunglasses back on and left. She walked down the stairs and across the lobby, unaware of Odell following close behind her.

Chapter Twenty-One

Dwayne parked his car outside the Atlanta Detention Center and took a moment to calm down. Maybe he was over-reacting. She may not even want his help.

"Are you all right?" Anthony asked.

Dwayne impulsively shook his head, but then contradicted himself. "Yes, I'm fine. Come on."

The men stepped out of the car and headed toward the building. Dwayne's mind crowded with words he wanted to say to Sonya. There was no doubt in his mind that she wouldn't cooperate in leaving with him. He had to make sure he explained everything to her.

Entering through the glass doors, a petite woman passed them. Anthony's head turned, then he collided into a brawny frame that nearly knocked him to the floor. "Excuse me," Anthony said to the man—who didn't bother to stop.

Dwayne stopped, then turned to ask Anthony a question, when he noticed a familiar-looking man walking down the steps. The man seemed intent on his destination. Dwayne caught a glimpse of a young woman walking only two paces ahead of the stranger. She seemed nervous to him. She kept glancing from side to side but never turned around to check behind her.

Dwayne started back toward the door.

"What's wrong?" Anthony asked as he passed him.

Dwayne's eyes followed the short trim of her hair and down the small slope of her neck. When she made a full turn to face the building, his eyes rested on the gold chain that lay in the crescent valley of her breast. He grabbed Anthony's shoulder. "There she is!"

Both men ran back outside. Dwayne's heart wedged in his throat the moment his eyes saw the gun the stranger pulled from his jacket.

Malik handed the picture of Laura to David. He had used the young boy for information before and found that the fifteen-year-old knew a lot of important information about the streets.

"I've never seen her before," David said.

It was an obvious lie. Malik reached into his pocket and pulled out a wad of money.

David's eyes twinkled as he began to nod his head. "Well, maybe she does look familiar."

"I thought she might." Malik stopped at two hundred dollars before David remembered hearing about a job concerning Mrs. Durden.

"What kind of job?"

David flashed Malik a golden smile (only a few of the boy's teeth didn't have caps on them). "Word has it that she has something really valuable that somebody wants. The job was for somebody to retrieve it."

"And you don't know what it is they're searching for?"

David held out his hand implying he needed more money for that piece of information.

Malik handed him another hundred dollars, only to be disappointed by his answer.

"No."

Malik fought the urge to wring the teenager's neck. His

clients had often criticized him for his expensive rates, but if they knew how much it cost to get people to talk on the streets, they would change their tune. "Do you know who accepted the job?" When the boy didn't answer, Malik's jaw flexed in anger.

"It's cool, it's cool," he said, trying to pacify Malik. "I don't know, but I know who might be able to help you. Go down to William's Place. You know William Gainey?"

"Yeah, I know him."

"Well, he might be able to help you out. He used to do some work for Frank."

"Thanks." Malik shoved the picture back into his jacket and looked toward his destination. This wasn't going to be easy. He and William had fallen out about two years back. He had doubts as to whether William would provide him with the information he needed.

Malik strutted down Henderson Avenue. He locked gazes with the many street thugs that questioned his presence on their turf. Although no one physically approached him, Malik knew he was being watched.

Malik entered the small pool hall, otherwise known as William's Place. The men stopped what they were doing to assess their new visitor. Malik knew the routine. Many just wanted to know whether or not he was five-o. He snatched his shades from his face and scanned the room, looking for William.

One man stood and walked boldly over to him. He was equal to Malik's height and build, but it didn't phase him a bit.

"What can I help you with?" the man asked. His stance said he was ready to rumble anytime.

"I'm here to see William." Malik took the same stance.

"And who the hell are you?" the man challenged.

"Just tell him Malik wants to talk." If the man recognized his name, he didn't show it. He just continued with the interrogation that Malik knew was routine.

"William's busy," he lied.

"You didn't even check," Malik said, losing his patience.

"I don't have to check. He's busy." He gave Malik his back,

and Malik knew it was a sign that he had to fight him in order to see William.

Malik grabbed the man's right shoulder and ducked just in time when the man immediately turned, swinging. Malik delivered a powerful uppercut that sent the man sprawling across a nearby pool table.

The men in the billiards room cheered Malik's attacker toward victory. Malik's opponent pulled himself up and landed some hard punches across Malik's jaw. But that was all he could do before Malik proved why no one messed with him. His attacker was covered with blood from open cuts across his face.

The cheering ceased, and Malik gave a final blow that knocked out his opponent. Malik saw a few men exchange money for bets laid on the short fight.

"Now can someone tell me where I might find William Gainey?" No one said anything. They just turned back to what they were doing. Suddenly there was a lone clapping sound coming from the back of the room. Malik turned to see who it was.

"Bravo," the voice said.

Malik recognized the voice immediately. "William."

"Hello, Malik. I see you're going to just stand there." When Malik didn't respond, he said. "Now come on. Is that any way to greet your younger brother?"

Bridget parked her Jeep outside the detention center just as her father raced down the pavement with Anthony following close behind him. *Something is going on.* She quickly jumped out of the Jeep, momentarily startled to see a woman she was sure looked familiar.

"Sonya?" she called. When Sonya didn't respond, she was convinced she didn't hear her. That must be who her father was running after. "Sonya!" she called again.

This time Sonya did hear her. She took off her sunglasses

and smiled. Just then, a man who was behind Sonya grabbed her roughly by the shoulder. Bridget raced to Sonya's aide.

Sonya struggled to pull herself from the man's grasp. Bridget didn't understand what was going on—she just realized Sonya was in trouble. Bridget reached Sonya's side and was able to successfully pull her protectively behind her.

Bridget heard her father scream her name just as the startled man aimed something toward her. An explosion caused a loud ringing in her ears. She saw Sonya's mouth move but heard no words. The ringing was getting louder. She looked down to see blood everywhere. She looked briefly toward her father, then felt herself falling into a dark cloud.

Chapter Twenty-Two

"Bridget!" Sonya screamed. She tried to kneel beside the young girl but felt herself jerked up by the arm.

"You're going with me," Odell commanded against her ear. Sonya turned—her eyes widened the instant she recognized Richard.

"Where's my sister?" She struck at the sinister-looking man. However, he controlled her hands in an iron-tight grip.

He refused to answer and began to pull her unwilling body along with him. Sonya struggled to break free. She took another glimpse at Bridget's motionless body on the sidewalk.

In horror, a piercing scream erupted from her. She tried desperately to break away.

Odell couldn't drag Sonya far before Dwayne hurled his body against the man's back. When Odell released Sonya, she felt her skin scrape against the cement, yet she ignored her bruises and focused her attention on reaching Bridget. Sonya crawled to Bridget, forgetting the two men behind her.

"I'm going for help. Can you stay with her?" Anthony asked, making his way to her. When he received no response, he spoke louder and succeeded in getting Sonya's attention. "I'm going to get help."

Sonya nodded and pulled Bridget's head into her arms. She pushed a few loose strands of hair from the young girl's face and studied her. *She's so young.* Visions of the vibrant girl projected in Sonya's mind. She remembered how her eyes lit up whenever she talked about her coin collection. *Please, God, don't take her now.*

Sonya looked down to where Bridget's blood covered her shirt. Blinded by her tears, she removed her hand and saw that it, too, was covered with the sticky substance. *What have I done?* Sonya blamed herself for what had happened. The bullet wasn't meant for this innocent child.

Sonya lifted remorseful eyes toward Dwayne, who continued to pound on the man that shot his daughter. *When would this nightmare end?*

Dwayne pulled himself from Odell's limp body. His vision centered on his daughter cradled between Sonya's possessive arms. He wasn't sure whether he walked or crawled over to them. He was only aware of Bridget lying so still.

He pulled her from Sonya and into his arms. He refused to look at Sonya. "Bridget, baby. It's me, Daddy. Wake up. It's time to go home." When she didn't respond, her angelic face blurred from the tears that escaped his eyes. "Bridget, please," he moaned.

Dwayne buried his face in her soft hair. That's when he heard it. She was breathing. Suddenly there were swarms of people surrounding him, trying to coax him to release Bridget into their care. He looked at the police officers and nurses that had scrambled from the detention center to try to help him.

"Sir, please let us take her," a strange woman said to him. But he couldn't let Bridget go. "Sir, please."

It took some coaxing before the officers successfully eased his daughter out of his arms, but Dwayne followed close behind them.

"Where are you taking her?" he asked with his voice thick with emotion.

"We're going to have to take her to Grady," a nurse answered.

"I'm riding with her. I'm her father." Dwayne saw a pair of flashing lights and was relieved that help arrived so soon.

The paramedics arrived and had Bridget secured in the ambulance within a matter of minutes. He climbed aboard the ambulance without a backward glance.

Sonya's hand covered her mouth as she watched Dwayne and Bridget leave. *What have I done?* Guilt consumed her heart. When Sonya felt a heavy hand on her shoulder, she swirled around to face Anthony. Relieved, she sought comfort in Anthony's outstretched arms.

She didn't know how long she remained in his embrace, but she felt grateful that he was patient enough to let her. "Thank you," she finally said, withdrawing from him.

"There's no need to thank me, Miss Walters. Are you all right?"

Sonya nodded. It was a lie, but she refused to seek further comfort from him.

"Excuse me?" a voice asked from behind.

They turned to see an officer.

"I'm sorry to disturb you, but I'm afraid that I'm going to have to ask you some questions."

Sonya glanced toward the heavens. It seemed that talking to policemen was becoming a constant occurrence lately.

"Of course," Anthony said, giving the officer his complete attention.

Sonya, however, glanced to where her attacker had lain. Fear grabbed her heart. "Anthony," she said, tugging on his arm.

"Yes?" he asked, looking down at her.

Sonya pointed to where she had last seen her assailant. "He's gone!"

Malik clasped hands with his brother. Their dark gazes locked. His brother stood at an even six feet. His black skin matched his eyes. It had been a long time. However, he could see that not much had changed with his brother. He was still playing the street game.

"It's good to see you," Malik lied effortlessly.

"It's good to see you, too. You wanna drink?" William said, taking a chair.

Malik watched the men that encircled his brother and assumed they were his bodyguards. "Sure, I have a few minutes to kill."

William smiled. He seemed pleased by Malik's answer. "Robert"—he signaled to the bartender—"bring us two forties."

Malik shook his head at his brother. He knew William would never change. He took years to build a reputation on the streets, and he wasn't about to walk away from it now. But Malik knew that his life on the streets would only lead to one thing. Death.

He knew all too well the life expectancy on Atlanta's hard streets was age twenty-five. His brother had just reached that peak.

"What brings you on my side of town, bro?" William asked.

"Let's just say I heard that you could probably help me with a favor."

William lifted an amused brow. "You're coming to me for help? Well if that don't beat all."

Robert arrived with their two beers.

"Stranger things have been known to happen," Malik replied.

William took a long gulp of beer, then said, "Tell me your problem, and I'll see if I can help you."

Malik reached into his jacket and pulled out the bent picture of Laura. "I'm looking for her," he said, tossing the picture onto the table.

William glanced at the picture, uninterested. "Never seen her."

Malik expelled a long sigh and propped his elbows on the table. "Cut me a break, William. We grew up with her in Techwood. Now tell the truth. Do you know where she is?"

William gave a small smirk and shook his head. "You'll never change, Malik."

"Neither will you. Now, have you seen her?"

William leaned in as if he had a secret to tell. Malik followed suit.

"Maybe," was his soft response.

Malik restrained himself from wrapping his hands around William's neck. He didn't want to play a guessing game with him but knew that this was William's style.

"When do you think you'll be arriving at a decision? Either you have or you haven't."

"Patience, my dear brother, patience. Drink your beer."

Malik grabbed the bottle and took a sip. The last thing he wanted to do was to let William pump him with beer. He placed the bottle down and tried his interrogation again.

"I don't have much time on this case, William. Can you help me?"

William leaned his elbows on the table and formed a temple with his hands. "What makes you think I can help you?"

Malik's patience went out the window. He hated when William would answer a question with another question.

"Word on the street is you pull jobs for Frank."

William's jaw twitched as Malik realized he had hit a nerve. "Who told you that?"

Malik smiled, trying to cover his anger. "I have my contacts. Why are you working for Frank again?"

William held Malik's steady gaze. "Let's just say I owed him a favor."

"William, you know you'll never finish repaying Frank for one of his *favors.*"

"Are you playing the concerned brother?" William asked, with disgust shining in his eyes.

"I'm not here to discuss family problems with you, William. You chose your own destiny," Malik said seriously.

The two men were silent for a moment, then William broke out in a wide grin. "So now you need my help?"

"Enough of the cat chase, William. Have you seen her?"

William took another long sip of his beer and looked around the billiard room, then looked back into Malik's intense gaze. "Yeah, I've seen her."

Sonya and Anthony repeated to the police the events that occurred for the third time. But no one seemed concerned that the attacker had gotten away.

The officer asking the questions put an APB out on the fleeing assailant, but something wasn't right.

Anthony gave her smiles of encouragement, but she felt everything but safe. It seemed strange to sit between police officers and still feel like an open target.

She wasn't too surprised to see Sergeant Freeman arrive on the scene. He pulled up and asked a nearby officer a question. The officer pointed toward her, and the sergeant made his way over to her.

"Ah, Miss Walters. Why is it whenever there is a disturbance in the area, I can almost count on you being in the midst of it?" Sergeant Freeman asked with a stiff grin.

"Probably because you're assigned to every case, no matter where it's located. At least I know this is in your jurisdiction," Sonya answered with razor-sharp sarcasm.

"What happened this time?" he asked, ignoring her contempt.

"Richard."

"Your brother-in-law?" Freeman cocked his eyebrow.

"The impostor." Sonya wrapped her arms around herself as if to protect herself from him.

Freeman walked over to the officer that questioned her earlier, then returned frowning.

"Did you find out where your sister is?"

Sonya shook her head at the ridiculous question. "No, we didn't have time to exchange civil conversation."

Freeman gave her a hard look, which Sonya returned.

"Are you ready to accept police protection now, Miss Walters, or do you want to wait until someone is killed?"

Sonya glanced around at the police that were busy searching the crime scene. When she turned her attention back to Freeman, she noticed Freeman's eyes glued to her neck. Sonya closed her jacket. "I think that I'll stay with Mr. Hamilton," she answered, shocked by her declaration. The truth was, she felt safe with him, and she should have remained under his protection. But the sight of him holding Carmen in his private study still pained her.

"Are we free to go now, Sergeant?" Anthony interrupted.

The sergeant looked from Sonya to Anthony and nodded. "But perhaps, Miss Walters, you should keep in contact with the department."

Sonya looked at him oddly.

"In case we get word on your sister," he offered as an explanation.

Sonya nodded and allowed Anthony to pull her away from Sergeant Freeman.

Much later Sonya arrived at the sixth floor of Grady Hospital. She headed straight to the waiting room with Anthony. She saw Dwayne sitting alone with his hands clasped over his head. She immediately ran over to him. She stopped, however, when he lifted his head and locked gazes with her.

The pain she saw reflected in his eyes tore at her soul as she took a brave step forward. His face, at first, seemed hard. She feared that he would turn her away, but then his expression softened, and he reached out and pulled her closer to him.

Sonya couldn't move. She just stroked the top of his head as it lay flat against her stomach. She kneeled down in front of him to look into his eyes.

"I'm so sorry." Her lower lip trembled from both guilt and heartache.

Dwayne said nothing as he leaned in until their foreheads touched. There, in their secluded space, Sonya watched his silent tears stream down his face. She thought nothing of being there to comfort him.

When Anthony sat two seats down from them, Sonya felt Dwayne grow tense. She reached up and smoothed away his tears. She knew that he would put up a brave facade in front of another man.

Dwayne pulled away from her, but kept both of her hands locked securely in his. She read the look of uncertainty in his eyes. His expression gave him a childlike appearance. She wished she could console that child but didn't know how.

Sonya stood and sat next to him while they continued to hold hands.

"How is she doing?" Anthony asked.

"I don't know yet," Dwayne answered, his voice no more than a trembling whisper.

"Do you want me to call Sharon?" Sonya offered after everyone had fallen silent.

Dwayne gave her a look of appreciation. "Do you have the number?"

"No, but I remember the name of the hotel. I'll call information."

"Thank you." The corners of Dwayne's mouth lifted, but it wasn't a smile.

Sonya leaned in and kissed him. The moment their lips made contact, Sonya felt him drawing on her strength—strength he needed to get through this nightmare.

Sonya pulled away gently to see his gray eyes probe her own. She squeezed his hand, then went to find a pay phone.

She had no trouble finding one. But before she could bring herself to dispense the quarter into its slot, Sonya's head slumped against the phone booth, and she began to cry.

She remained there for quite a while before she felt Dwayne's strong hands caress her shoulders. She turned around, letting the phone dangle from its silver cord. She immediately buried her head in his broad chest.

He held her until the sobs ceased, stroking her short hair. When her tears subsided, she remained in his embrace. He said nothing as he kissed the top of her head.

Sonya squeezed her eyes shut. She wanted so desperately

for this to be a bad dream. She felt one of Dwayne's hands reach to retrieve the phone. He dropped a quarter into its slot and dialed for assistance.

It wasn't long before he had Sharon's hotel and number and was charging the call to his home phone number. All the while Sonya remained submerged in his embrace.

"Hello, Sharon?"

A few hours later, Sonya, Dwayne, and Anthony sat in a half empty cafeteria. Cups of steaming coffee were set before each of them. Dwayne and Sonya continued to hold hands across the table.

Anthony's beeper went off. He looked at the tiny screen and excused himself.

Dwayne watched Anthony leave, then his eyes fell on the clock above the exit door. "She's been in there going on four hours," he commented, looking up at the clock.

"We must be patient," Sonya said, squeezing his hand for emphasis.

Dwayne pulled his hand away and reached for his coffee. The hot liquid warmed him but only briefly. He couldn't shake the thought of Bridget lying in the emergency room—fighting for her life—and he was completely helpless.

He replayed the series of events leading to this moment, and he couldn't come up with any answers. Where had she come from? And why did she jump in front of Sonya?

Anthony returned to the cafeteria and asked to speak with Dwayne in private. Sonya looked at the men strangely as they moved to the far side of the room.

"What is it?" Dwayne asked, observing Anthony's troubled look.

"Malik just paged me. He has some information. I'm going down to meet him now," Anthony said, looking toward Sonya.

Dwayne nodded. He'd forgotten the private investigator. "Did he tell you what he's found?"

"**No**. He sounded like he couldn't really talk then, so I'm **meeting** him where Ray's Barbecue used to be."

"Popular place," Dwayne reflected.

"What?" Anthony asked, not understanding his meaning.

"Nothing. Keep me informed."

Anthony agreed and started to leave. "Anthony," Dwayne called after him.

"Yes?"

Dwayne held his questioning gaze. "Be careful."

Anthony smiled. "Of course." With that he turned and left the cafeteria.

Dwayne returned to the table, his mind traveling in two different directions. He was now concerned for Anthony's safety.

He returned to the table where Sonya sat. He avoided meeting her eyes. Being in this cafeteria gave him a strong sense of déjà vu.

Sonya slid her hand across the table, taking his hand in with hers. "She's going to be all right."

Dwayne shook his head. His last thread of hope snapped in half. "I've been here before," he whispered more to himself than her. He removed his hand from hers and stared at them. A feeling of helplessness settled on his shoulders as he began to prepare for the worst.

"I remember being in this very hospital thirteen years ago. I thought that she could pull through it. She was strong and I . . . I couldn't help her."

Sonya felt a sharp stab of pain pierce her heart. Her mouth trembled as she asked him, "How did it happen?"

"My wife died of breast cancer." Dwayne balled his hand to stop the trembling. "I can't lose her, too." He closed his eyes and willed his tears away.

Sonya left her chair to enclose him in her arms. Dwayne turned and held on to her for dear life. They remained embracing for a long time.

Dwayne finally grabbed hold of his emotions and turned away from Sonya again.

"Do you want to go back into the waiting room?" Sonya asked gently.

Dwayne wanted to show his gratitude for her kindness, but he couldn't muster the strength. "Yeah," he answered, standing up.

Sonya stood and offered him a smile.

Dwayne noticed her smile shed a glimmer of sunlight, but it soon faded. They returned to the waiting room just as a doctor followed them in.

"Mr. Hamilton?"

Dwayne turned and faced the elderly doctor. He instantly saw the worried lines in the doctor's face. "I'm Mr. Hamilton."

The doctor removed his black-framed glasses and wiped at his brow.

Sonya moved behind Dwayne. "How is she?" they asked in unison.

The doctor smiled reassuringly, "She's going to be fine."

Chapter Twenty-Three

Anthony parked in front of Ray's Barbecue. He swallowed the lump of fear enlarged in his throat. The neighborhood looked nearly deserted. The people he saw milling around sent shivers down his spine.

However, the street remained ominously quiet except for the clicking sound of a woman's high heels hitting the pavement. He immediately grew tense. After a pair of fishnet stockings strolled past his car, he relaxed. *What am I doing out here this time of night?*

Anthony looked out the passenger's side window in hopes of seeing Malik. He saw only boarded-up restaurants. *He should've been here by now.*

He glanced back at his watch. Eleven-thirty. Malik said he would be here by eleven. A loud bang echoed in the distance, causing Anthony to jump. *Gunshots!* He fumbled with the keys, trying to turn on the ignition. This meeting wasn't worth the risk.

Shock penetrated through his very being when the engine refused to start. His heart skipped a beat as he tried again. This time, the engine revved up, much to his relief. Yet he nearly let out a startled scream when the passenger door flew open.

"Drive," Malik commanded, stumbling into the car.

Anthony didn't hesitate to do so. He swerved around Henderson Avenue and headed toward downtown. He stole a quick glance at Malik, whose heavy breathing and sweat-drenched face frightened him.

"What's going on?" Anthony asked, trying to ease off the accelerator.

"Let's concentrate on getting out of this area first. I'm not sure that we're not being followed," Malik answered in a harsh tone.

"Followed?" Anthony glanced into his rearview mirror to see a black Bronco trailing him. His foot slammed on the accelerator. "Are those friends of yours?"

Malik shook his head.

Anthony noticed Malik's hand covering his right shoulder. "What happened?"

"It's just a flesh wound," Malik answered calmly.

Anthony's eyes widened. He turned another corner. "I think that you need to tell me what's going on."

"Perhaps you're the one that needs to come up with some answers. This is more than just a missing-person's case." Malik turned to look out the side mirror. "Can't you drive faster than this?"

"I'm doing the best I can," Anthony retaliated. "What do you mean, this is more than a missing-person's case? What kind of trouble are you talking about?"

"Watch out," Malik shouted, pointing to a gray Toyota, which Anthony nearly crashed into.

Anthony swung into the wrong lane to avoid the car.

"Look, just get us out of here. I'll take this up with your boss later," Malik said.

"Who's following us?" Anthony asked, unable to shake the black Bronco.

"Frank's men," Malik replied, laying his head back.

"Who's Frank?"

Malik fell silent. There was only the steady rhythm of his breathing which told Anthony he needed medical assistance. A sense of hopelessness covered Anthony.

He glanced at the gas gauge and cursed violently. It was almost empty. He had to come up with a plan, and soon.

"I want him found," Frank demanded through the phone. "He knows too much, and I want him taken care of. *Now.*"

"We've already put two men on his trail. Consider it taken care of," the nervous man replied.

"Is there a chance he has told anyone else?"

The phone line grew quiet.

"Samuel, has he told anyone else?"

"We're not sure."

Both men were silent again before Frank replied. "I suggest you find out. And don't botch this up. I already have to clean up that mess you made at Walters' Intercorp. You and Odell are getting too clumsy lately."

"We have everything under control. Trust me," Samuel replied nervously.

"Do you have my merchandise?"

Samuel dreaded the question. "No, sir. But we have located it."

"You're running out of time."

"Yes, sir." Samuel was unable to say anything more before the line went dead. He stared at the phone in his hand while he shook his head. They had come so close today. Now they were down to twenty-four hours.

"What did he say?" Odell asked.

"We screwed up," Samuel answered sharply.

"It's not my fault. How in the hell did I know she would interfere?" Odell shouted.

"It's your job to take all precautions. It's a miracle you escaped," Samuel retaliated.

"Everyone's attention was focused on that girl."

"That little girl saved your hide," Samuel said sarcastically.

Odell glared at Samuel. "What do we do now?"

"We find out which hospital that girl was taken to, and we'll find Miss Walters. This time we will succeed in getting our merchandise."

"What if she's not there?"

"Then I suggest that you pull out your last will and testament. The boss won't tolerate any more screwups. We're down to twenty-four hours."

"What about Laura?"

"I don't see why we can't take care of her first thing tomorrow."

Laura continued to rub the ropes of her bound hands against the rugged edge of the wooden chair. She had to get loose, she reasoned. No one could find her here. She would have to escape on her own.

Her wrists felt raw from her constant rubbing, but she ignored the pain. When her door burst open, she stopped. However, Samuel did no more than check on her, then slam the door shut.

Relief flooded through her as she picked up her urgency in escaping the ropes. A small breakage in the rope told her she had made progress. Her awkward position also caused the rope across her legs to cut her cruelly. Laura closed her eyes against the pain, but never stopped working her hands.

Another hour passed, and Laura felt the rope begin loosening. Her wrists stung mercilessly, but she refused to give up. She could no longer ignore the pain. Her shoulders ached in pain from vigorous labor.

When the shack was quiet again, she knew the men had left. This is it, she thought. It was her chance to escape. She opened her eyes and looked around the room. The only illumination filtered through a dingy white sheet that decorated a small window on the opposite wall.

The rope suddenly snapped in half, and Laura slumped exhausted against the chair. She took a moment to gather her strength, before she knelt down to untie her legs. Finally free from the chair, she stood then crept silently toward the door.

She glued her ear against the wooden entrance, listening for sounds. Silence. Laura turned the doorknob. Unlocked, just as she suspected. The men obviously felt confident that she couldn't escape her bonds.

Laura held her breath as the door creaked open. She half-expected the men to jump out at her any moment. Slowly she moved through the door and headed toward the front of the house. She felt freedom with every step she took.

Laura made it out of the house and marveled at the feeling of the cool night air caressing her face. Inhaling the fresh scent, she couldn't help smiling at its meaning.

Deciding not to waste any more time, she scrambled off the porch and headed for trees along the nearby road. She had no idea where the road would lead, but she had no other choice but to follow.

Anthony turned off the headlights and pulled into a dark alley just as his car died. Malik opened his eyes as Anthony gently shook his unwounded shoulder.

"Where are we?" Malik asked, looking around.

"I'm not sure. I've turned down so many alleys and isolated roads that I don't know where we are. How are you feeling?"

"I've had better days," Malik answered, flinching.

"We need to get you a doctor," Anthony observed.

"It's just a flesh wound. Believe me. It's not as bad as it looks. Did we lose them?"

"I think so. Are you able to walk? We're out of gas."

Malik nodded. "Yeah, let's go."

The men climbed out of the car and walked down the dark alley. A loud roar caused them to look up to see a plane hovering overhead.

"We must be close to the airport," Malik reasoned.

"Let's just try to find a phone so we can get some help," Anthony said, glancing over his shoulder. Suddenly a prickly sensation began itching up his spine. Keep walking, he told himself.

Anthony noticed Malik's hand reach inside his jacket and pull out a .45. He must have heard the intruder also.

"We're going to have to make a run for it," Malik said.

Anthony nodded his head nervously as he first started a slow trot, but when a bullet whizzed by his ear, he picked up speed.

Dwayne leaned over his daughter's small frame. The pain that ripped through his heart sent silent tears flowing down his face. He reached for her hand, and noticed how small it seemed within his own. He observed how soft and delicate it felt.

His eyes traveled to her stilled profile. She looked no more than twelve. A silent wish formed from his heart: the wish of taking her place. He would give anything to trade places with her.

Dwayne leaned in farther and placed a kiss on Bridget's forehead. When his lips made contact, a sob sounded from within him. He couldn't stop the violent tremor that shook his body.

Dwayne fought the urge to sweep Bridget's tiny form into his arms. He wanted to comfort her and make her well again. Numerous visions of Bridget as a child flooded his mind. He remembered her first step, her first day of school, and her first ballet recital. To him, there wasn't any difference between then and now. She was still his baby, his little girl.

Dwayne felt a gentle hand touch his shoulder and knew that it was Sonya. He'd forgotten she was in the room. Her touch offered comfort, yet he didn't want to turn to it. He wanted to be alone with his daughter. He turned to face her. He had every intention of telling her that he wanted her to leave, but the pain that reflected in Sonya's eyes prevented him.

Torn between two women, Dwayne finally turned back to Bridget. He couldn't bring himself to accept the solace of Sonya's arms. He wanted to remain with his daughter. He continued to gaze at Bridget as if willing her to open her eyes.

Sonya didn't take Dwayne's indifference as a personal insult. She understood what he was going through. She was experiencing the same emotion. She couldn't explain it, but she felt connected to Bridget. She studied the young girl from over Dwayne's shoulder and knew that she should be lying in this bed.

Slowly the peaceful sight of Bridget turned into Laura. Sonya covered her mouth at that horrifying thought. Had her sister met the same fate? She had no way of knowing. If Richard was trying to kill her, it was very possible that he had killed Laura.

Sonya's temples throbbed mercilessly from the stress she felt. She didn't know what to do. She had placed everyone's lives in jeopardy. She had even entertained the idea of grabbing some money and just disappearing, but she couldn't leave, knowing that her sister could be out there somewhere. She also knew she couldn't just walk out of Dwayne's life.

Just then, Dwayne's hand reached out and grabbed hers. As if he read her fears, he pulled her closer to him and Bridget.

When she looked into his tear-brimmed eyes, a sharp pain stabbed her heart.

She opened her arms, and Dwayne instantly hugged her in a savage embrace. Sonya felt his tears soak her short shirt. She returned his hug with the same intensity.

They remained there in the room with Bridget long into the night, both refusing to leave when the doctor had asked them to go and get some rest. Yet as dawn approached, Dwayne and Sonya found hope that Bridget had won the fight.

Dr. Browning came in around eight o'clock the next morning to check on Bridget. He expressed his surprise and informed Dwayne and Sonya that Bridget's vital signs were stronger.

Sonya gave a prayer of thanks as Dwayne swooped her into his arms out of joy.

"Bridget's going to make it!" he declared.

Sonya laughed at his excitement and believed his claim. Bridget had made it through the worst part, and both felt confident that soon the young teenager would be back to normal.

* * *

Laura woke up feeling something crawling across her leg. She let out a startled scream when she saw a small lizard trot across her. She kicked violently at the tiny intruder. Looking around at her unfamiliar surroundings, Laura shielded her eyes from the morning sun that fell on her face.

She pushed herself up and dusted most of the dirt off her clothes. Her mouth felt dry, and every bone in her body ached. *Where am I?* She had no idea. She didn't know how far she was from Odell and Samuel's hiding place, either, but she didn't doubt that they were looking for her now.

"I see you finally decided to wake up."

Laura turned at the hauntingly familiar voice. She knew it was neither Odell nor Samuel. When she faced her intruder, she let out a paralyzing scream.

Chapter Twenty-Four

Sonya and Dwayne arrived at the Sundial Motel, exhausted. Sonya waited alone in the lobby, while Dwayne walked to the front desk to get the rooms. She glanced around the tiny room and cringed at the sight of dirty wallpaper and ugly brown carpeting. The furniture looked worn while the black-and-white TV's picture rolled constantly.

Sonya contemplated whether to ask Dwayne to pick another motel, but she decided against it. This would be the perfect place for her to keep a low profile. She had to be cautious—however, at times she felt she had reached the point of paranoia. Around every corner was a potential threat. Someone wanted her dead, and that chilling fact terrified her.

Dwayne insisted on paying for the rooms, and Sonya had no choice but to let him. She didn't trust trying to get money from the bank or using her credit cards.

Dwayne returned to the lobby and handed her a set of keys. "You're in room 217, and I'm in room 218."

Sonya nodded, then headed toward the elevators with Dwayne following close behind her. They stepped into the elevator and pressed the button for the second floor. Neither spoke as they rode up.

Sonya felt as if she were sleepwalking. She dreamed of the bed that awaited her in the room. The elevator bell chimed, and the doors opened.

Sonya again noticed the dirty wallpaper and old carpeting as they searched silently for their rooms. If she saw one bug she was out of there, she vowed. Sonya jingled her keys while she tried to unlock room 217. Sleep, her mind echoed. She needed sleep. By the weary look on Dwayne's face, she knew he felt the same way.

When she unlocked the door and stepped inside, she felt disappointed at finding the modest room in the same condition as the rest of the motel. Sonya relaxed the moment she saw the full-sized bed donned in fresh linen.

"Is everything all right?"

Sonya jumped from the sound of Dwayne's voice.

Dwayne's hand shot out to hold her upright. "I'm sorry. I didn't mean to startle you," Dwayne apologized.

The electrical current from his touch did nothing to calm her racing heart.

As if touching her had caused the same effect in him, Dwayne dropped his hands. "Sonya, we need to talk. About Carmen—"

Sonya held up her hand to stop him. "Please, not now."

Dwayne held a look of regret, and Sonya almost relented. He walked to the closet and set down her bags, then he headed toward the door without another word.

Sonya stopped him just before he could walk out. "Dwayne?"

He turned with a lifted brow. "Yes?"

"Did it mean anything to you?" she asked, holding his gaze.

"Did what mean . . . ? Oh." Dwayne gave a passionate look. "What happened between us meant everything."

His sultry tone caused chills to dance along every inch of her being. Sonya swallowed the lump gathered in her throat. She felt her cheeks flush while a sensation tingled through her body. Unaware of walking toward him, Sonya closed the gap between them. Dwayne gave a mind-boggling kiss that melted the rest of her defenses.

She molded her body against his muscled frame. How long had it been since she'd tasted paradise? She couldn't remember. What mattered was that she'd found heaven in his arms again.

Dwayne ran his hands along the length of her back, causing her to shiver uncontrollably against him. All sense of reality fled her mind. She could only give in to the splendor of his kiss.

He removed Sonya's shirt and dropped it to the floor. In one fluid motion, he removed her bra.

Sonya pressed her body closer, trying to fill a deep hunger she knew only he could satisfy.

Sonya sighed. The sensation of his fingers combing through her short hair fueled her with a burst of energy. She clawed at his clothes. When the burden of his shirt slid to the floor, she was rewarded with the feel of his hard physique pressed against her.

The rest of their clothes fell to the floor. Sonya marveled at the sight before her. His long, powerful legs, his flat stomach, and handsome face modeled perfection. Her eyes followed his dark chest, down past his hips to his swollen manhood. When her naked body came against his, she quivered as her flesh tingled. Dwayne scooped her into his arms and in two confident strides, he carried her to the bed.

His exploring hands moved slowly and sensuously down her throat and across her breasts, gently caressing the tanned tips.

She groaned with pleasure. When one hand moved down her stomach to lightly rest against her inner thigh, she couldn't breathe. His gentle touch felt as if he feared Sonya would break.

"You're so beautiful," he said in a husky voice. "I ache for you. Do you ache inside, Sonya?"

She was incapable of answering when his head moved to sprinkle kisses over her stomach. *Yes, I ache inside,* she thought wildly. He had set her body on fire and he knew it. Drawing his face up to her lips, she spoke. "I ache, Dwayne," she admitted at last.

Dwayne's breath caught in his throat the moment he tasted her sweet lips. He wanted to master her tonight, but in truth, she had become the master. His lips deserted hers to circle a firm breast. Her quick intake of breath heightened his arousal.

The sight of her smooth skin reminded him of delicious caramel, and his tongue treated it as such. He tasted every inch of her breast. Her body reacted in violent spasms. Gently he parted her legs and continued to let his tongue explore the valley between her thighs.

Sonya's cheeks flamed from the invasion of his magical tongue. She cried out his name in repetitive abandonment until she felt scorched by an inferno that blazed within.

Dwayne reclaimed her lips in fierce possession. The kiss sent him on a cloud of divine ecstasy. His body reacted from a single stroke of her hand descending his back. His mind tried to focus through the thick cloud of haze but couldn't. He felt a hot tide of passion rage through him.

Dwayne entered her slowly, stroking her budding desire into a turbulent whirlpool. Sonya tore her lips away from his to throw her head back, surrendering to his power. At his steady rhythm, Sonya entombed him with her legs, urging him on to a faster pace.

When his mouth returned to a taut nipple, Sonya automatically slid her arms around him in a lover's embrace. Her breathing became shallow as his hips pumped wildly, but her eager response matched his own.

"Dwayne . . ." she groaned. He seemed to be caressing her inner body, making her drift on an endless sea of pleasure. Soon a familiar sensation ebbed its way from the depths of her soul. Its eruption caused her to soar into a shuddering ecstasy as her body vibrated with liquid fire. She heard Dwayne groan as one shiver after another shook his body.

"My love," he murmured against her ear.

Sonya's eyes flew open at his whispered confession. When

his lips sprayed feathered kisses near her ear, she melted and gave in again to the magic he performed on her body.

Dwayne woke hours later, his body still entwined with Sonya's. A smile caressed his lips as he stared down at her. Somehow she had come to mean life to him. He wasn't sure when or how, but he knew he'd fallen in love with her. He tried to pull away to give her more room to breathe, but she moaned her displeasure, so he stayed put.

He gingerly stroked her face with a finger, teasing her until her eyes fluttered open.

The moment her eyes focused, she smiled. "What are you doing?" she asked in a sweet tone.

"I'm trying to wake you," he said, then gave her a feathery kiss.

"I'm not sure I want to wake up," she moaned as she stretched against him.

Dwayne's expression grew serious. "We have to talk, Sonya. I don't want any questions or doubt lingering between us."

Sonya blinked. She knew what he wanted to talk about, but she wasn't sure she wanted to have this conversation. The thought of rejection scared her. She looked at him, unable to hide her heart that shined brightly in her eyes.

"First, I wish that you had given me the chance to tell you about me and Carmen."

Sonya's body tensed. Dwayne stroked her face tenderly, forcing her to relax against him.

"There is nothing between us. She means nothing to me," he said in a serious tone.

Sonya lowered her gaze to study his chin. Tears gathered in her eyes, but she willed them not to fall. "Has there ever been anything between you two?"

Dwayne waited a moment before answering. "There was one night over two years ago. I was lonely and feeling depressed about some things and . . ."

Sonya tried to pull away, but Dwayne refused to let her. "It was a long time ago, Sonya. It was before I met you."

Sonya looked back into his eyes. This time her tears succeeded in escaping. "Please, let me go. I can't talk about this right now."

"No. You're not going to run from me. We will talk about this now," he said in a gentle tone.

Sonya wiped her tears with the back of her hand. "What do you want me to say? That it doesn't matter? That it doesn't hurt? Well, I can't say that. I'm not angry. I'm just confused about what's happening between us. I'm confused by my own thoughts and my own feelings. For a brief moment, I forgot that."

"What can I do to help you with this?" he asked, his own insecurity reflected in his voice.

"Be patient," she answered in a whisper.

Dwayne studied her for a long moment before climbing from the bed. He retrieved his clothes and dressed in silence. She watched helplessly as he tucked his shirt in his trousers.

Without a backward glance, he left the room, shutting the door quietly behind him. She had the strongest urge to run after him and beg him not to go. She hated herself for causing the hurt she had seen in his eyes.

Lying back in bed, Sonya pulled the covers over her. She cried tears of despair when she realized what she had done to Dwayne tonight. Why was she so determined to throw happiness away? And that was what Dwayne could offer her—her heart kept telling her this and now she was forced to listen. In the next moment, she had cried herself back to sleep.

Sonya sat in the corner near the exit door of Shoney's. She kept her head low and her eyes constantly wandered about to see if anyone was watching her.

When Dwayne returned to their table with a huge second helping from the breakfast bar, Sonya could only shake her head.

"What? I'm a growing boy." He chuckled.

"Growing in which direction?"

Dwayne laughed as he shoved a strip of bacon into his mouth. Then an uncomfortable silence grew between them. The events of last night were posed like a brick wall between the couple.

Sonya took another sip of her coffee, desperately wanting to say or explain herself more clearly to Dwayne. She appreciated the fact that he hadn't brought up what happened, but she knew that she could no longer avoid it.

"Dwayne."

"Sonya." They said each other's name in unison.

Sonya blushed. "Go ahead."

"No, you go." Dwayne passed the buck.

Sonya took a deep breath and squared her shoulders. "I guess I want to talk to you about last night. I believe I owe you an apology."

Dwayne picked up his napkin and dabbed at the corners of his mouth.

Sonya continued. "I mean, what I'm trying to say is, I know that Carmen is someone from your past. I'm not upset or angry about that. I'm more confused than anything about what I'm feeling."

Dwayne reached out and touched her hand. The small gesture comforted Sonya somewhat.

"I've never felt this way, and I'm not pretending that the situation sits right with me. I mean . . . I never depended on anyone in my life. I never needed or wanted that burden. I've come from an abusive family. And I've seen only abusive relationships between men and women. Well, except for Sharon and James."

Dwayne smiled but remained quiet.

"The strange part is, now I want to give us a chance."

Dwayne squeezed her hand as both of their eyes began to glaze over.

"Dwayne, I'm scared."

"I know. So am I." Dwayne moved his plate aside and took

both of her hands into his. "I never thought I could find anyone after Theresa. No one ever compared or came close in my heart, until I met you. Now all I do is think about you. I want to give us a try, too."

"I need us to go slow, Dwayne. I want us to become friends first. Is that too much to ask?"

Dwayne gave her a handsome smile. "I'll give you all the time you need."

Chapter Twenty-Five

Two days later . . .

Dwayne knocked on Sonya's door and waited.

"Who is it?" Sonya asked in a hushed voice.

"Dwayne."

He heard the lock click, then turned to watch Sonya pull open the creaking door. He snickered at the vision of her short hair sprouted across her head and sleep-filled eyes that squinted to see him.

"Good morning, sleepyhead," he greeted cheerfully.

Sonya rubbed her eyes, unsure if she was seeing him at the door. "Is it morning so soon?" she asked in a hoarse voice.

"Can I come in?"

Sonya stepped back and allowed him to enter. "Why didn't you call before you came over?"

"My room is just next door. I figured you wouldn't mind."

"What time is it?" she asked, looking toward the small alarm clock beside her bed.

"It's five A.M."

Sonya frowned. "You're kidding, right?"

"I'm afraid not. Get dressed. We're going to the hospital. Dr. Browning just called—Bridget's awake."

Sonya combed her fingers through her hair, briefly forgetting the new short style. "Oh, great," she perked up. Her mouth still felt like it had been stuffed with cotton. She headed toward her bags by the closet and pulled out a pastel baby-doll dress that she had bought with Bridget.

"You don't mind us going so early, do you? I can go alone." Sonya bumped into a wall, trying to find the bathroom.

Dwayne hid a smile.

"No, of course not. I'll be out in a moment." She made it to the bathroom without another incident and closed the door behind her.

Once he heard the shower turn on, he took a seat in a vacant chair. After he'd received the news on Bridget's condition, he quickly showered and brushed his teeth before rushing to Sonya's room.

He was glad he chose to stay here near Grady Hospital. Sonya also wanted to stay so she could keep a low profile. She seemed obsessed with that idea lately. She constantly looked over her shoulder to make sure no one was watching her. Dwayne struggled with her paranoia as well with his concerns for Bridget.

He understood Sonya's reasoning. It was obvious someone wanted her dead, but he had no idea why. Richard—or whatever his name was—recognized her when he didn't. He did know one thing and that was as long as Sonya's life was in danger, he was going to protect her. Every time he looked at her, he felt that familiar dance in the pit of his stomach. He found himself constantly staring at her, hanging on every word she spoke. And whenever she wasn't around, he would dream about her.

All finances came out of his pocket, as Sonya refused to use the bank. She also avoided credit cards. He had to admit all her precautions made sense. At least until they found out who was looking for her. Fortunately she felt safe at Grady. She believed no one would look for her there. Dwayne didn't agree with that reasoning, but promised to never leave her side just in case.

Sharon and James were arriving back in town today. When they told him they'd cut their trip short, he felt relieved. He needed Sharon's comforting ways now more than ever. His thoughts reflected on Sonya's strength. She'd been there for him the past few days, and he was grateful. He couldn't have asked for a better friend.

The shower stopped, and Dwayne anticipated her presence like a kid in a candy store. He strummed his fingers patiently on his knee and waited for her. The bathroom door cracked open, and Sonya dashed into the room as she brushed her damp hair.

Her short dress gave a beautiful view of her long legs, and Dwayne lifted an interested brow. She said nothing as she went through her bags and pulled out the blow dryer that Dwayne had bought yesterday for her. She rushed silently back into the bathroom and closed the door.

Dwayne frowned as he stood and went toward the bathroom. At the sound of the blow dryer's loud hum, Dwayne gently pushed open the door so he could see her primp in front of the mirror. She sang their song, Killing Me Softly, while she styled her hair.

Dwayne smiled as she struggled to get her hair to lie flat. It had a natural wave since she'd had it cut. She became frustrated as she couldn't do much about it snapping back into its curly position. Nevertheless, he found the short style bewitching. Her hazel eyes seemed wider, brighter than before; her face even appeared younger.

Sonya turned off the blow dryer and reached for her makeup bag. She applied a small amount of mascara and a light coat of lip gloss, then she was ready.

Dwayne quickly raced back to his chair. He barely made it back before the bathroom door swung fully open. Sonya looked at him quizzically as if she suspected him of foul play, but Dwayne just smiled and gave her an innocent look.

"What are you doing?" she asked suspiciously.

"Nothing. I'm just waiting for you." Dwayne felt like his hands were caught in a cookie jar.

Sonya shook her head and went to retrieve her purse. "I don't know about you, Dwayne."

Dwayne grinned. "Are you ready?"

"All set. Are you sure we'll be able to see her this early?" Sonya asked, heading for the door.

Dwayne stood and followed her. "Dr. Browning assured me that we can see her."

Sonya snapped her fingers as if she forgot something. When she turned suddenly, she bumped solidly into Dwayne's brawny chest.

Dwayne's nostrils picked up the fresh smell of her hair immediately. He looked down to stare into her beautiful eyes and felt a strong magnetic force pull him closer to her. By the look in her eyes, he knew that she was feeling the same blistering emotion that scorched him.

Dwayne cupped her small face in his hands, then kissed her tenderly. The kiss slowly turned into something more urgent. His hands slid to the back of her neck to press her head even closer.

Deliberately Sonya shifted her head, nestling her face in the naked hollow of his throat. "Dwayne, please . . ."

Dwayne knew what she was asking him, but the mere thought of stopping tore him up inside.

"Sonya," he begged in an agonized voice.

Sonya waited, listening to the powerful beating of his heart. She felt the tensely coiled muscles of his body as he held her. It took everything she had to break from his passionate kiss, but there were too many problems she had to sort out. Still, his nearness caused her to shiver uncontrollably. She couldn't hide the feelings that ached in the pit of her stomach and the breathless tightness of her own throat.

She lifted her head again and saw he was fighting the same emotions.

"I miss you." His voice had thickened, and without him being aware of it, he gripped her chin, then slowly let his fingers spread lightly over the warm, silky texture of her cheek, stroking it soothingly.

His eyes and voice seduced Sonya as they caressed her gently, like only a lover could do.

Dwayne leaned in again but paused only inches away from her face. Her breath was warm and sweet against his face, while her fingers had curled into his shirt. Even that brief touch speared him with desire; need coursed through his body, making him feel hot.

Cautiously, hardly daring to breathe, she raised her hand to his face, letting her fingertips brush the hard edge of his throat. She couldn't help herself as she continued to touch his mouth, his beautiful, sensuous mouth.

Her touch drove him mad as his lips crashed hard on hers. He listened to her moan. Or was it him?

Reacting to Dwayne's unleashed passion, Sonya sighed and wrapped her arms around Dwayne's neck, losing herself in the dark magic of his lips. She returned his kiss almost desperately with all the frustrated yearning he had aroused in her body. She strained against him, the swollen tips of her breasts pressing against his hard chest.

By the time Dwayne broke off the kiss and drew away, her breath was coming in soft pants, and so was his. The pause was long enough for Sonya to come to her senses. With wobbly knees, Sonya stepped around him to retrieve her key from the nightstand. She also picked up a small pearl drop necklace and slipped it around her neck.

"You're not wearing Bridget's favorite coin necklace?" Dwayne asked. It was apparent he wanted to lighten the mood between them.

"No, it wouldn't go with the outfit. You don't like this?" She tried to act as if nothing had passed between them.

"I think you're beautiful, no matter what you put on," he commented seriously.

Sonya averted her eyes to avoid meeting his. She stepped around him and headed out the door. Once outside the small motel, they flagged down a cab.

They arrived at the hospital by six o'clock and hurried to see Bridget.

When they reached Bridget's room, Dwayne eased his head in first, then walked slowly into the room with Sonya following close behind him. Sonya didn't notice a difference in Bridget's appearance, not until Bridget slowly turned her head toward them. When she smiled, tears instantly sprang into Sonya's eyes.

Dwayne leaned down and kissed her forehead. Sonya saw pride shining in his eyes as he gazed down at his daughter.

"How's my little girl?" he asked as he lifted a loose curl from her face.

"I've been better," Bridget joked.

Sonya felt like an intruder on their private moment, but Bridget soon turned to face her and smiled. "Hello," Bridget greeted.

Sonya walked closer and clasped the young girl's hand into her own. "Welcome back."

"It's great to be back." With innocent eyes, she looked back toward her father. "Are you angry with me?"

Dwayne laughed at the absurd question. "How could I be mad with you?"

"Because I left the house while I was on restriction. I raced at eighty-five miles an hour to catch up with you, then foolishly jumped in the way of a bullet." The twinkle in her eyes made Dwayne laugh, but Bridget only laughed briefly before pain flashed across her face.

"What's wrong, Bridget?" Dwayne asked, instantly concerned.

"It hurts when I laugh."

"Then, I forbid you to laugh," Dwayne said seriously.

Bridget had to laugh at his ridiculous order.

"Don't you know by now that she doesn't do what she's told?" Sonya added.

"I'm not that bad," Bridget answered.

Both Sonya and Dwayne gave each other comical looks.

"Okay, okay. I'm a little hardheaded," Bridget agreed, smiling. She kept closing her eyes as if they were too heavy for her.

Dwayne stood and gave her another kiss. "You get some sleep, Bridget. We'll be here when you wake up."

Bridget nodded weakly and quickly drifted off to sleep.

Hours later, Sonya and Dwayne sat in the cafeteria. Sonya hated to admit to herself that she was beginning to like hospital food. She was almost through with her meal when she looked up and saw Sergeant Freeman stroll into the room.

"I don't believe it," she said, placing her fork back on her tray.

Dwayne followed her gaze and saw the sergeant headed toward them.

"Good evening," Freeman greeted. He rudely took a seat next to Sonya.

"Please, have a seat," Dwayne offered sarcastically.

Sergeant Freeman ignored Dwayne as he looked directly at Sonya. She noticed Freeman's odd expression as he stared at her. Her hands flew to the small opening of her cleavage as she gave him a disgusted look.

"Actually I came to deliver some disturbing news." Freeman brought his eyes level with Sonya's.

Sonya lifted a curious brow. "How did you know where to find me?"

"I didn't. I was here on another case when I saw you sitting here. Lucky me, huh?"

Sonya gave Freeman a sour look. "So what's your disturbing news?"

"We've found the body of an Odell Hill." He received no reaction from her. "He also had a fake ID with the name of Richard Durden on him."

Sonya's eyes fluttered rapidly as she tried to understand what he was saying. "He's dead?"

Dwayne shifted in his chair. "Your men are sure that this is the same guy?"

Freeman reached into a folder he was carrying and pulled out a photocopy of the ID. Dwayne accepted the photocopy and looked at it. "That's him."

Sonya reached for the paper. When she looked at it and recognized the man staring back at her, she was confused by what this all meant. "What about Laura?"

Freeman shook his head. "No trace of her. We found him with an unidentified body last night. Your sister is still at large."

"At large?" Sonya asked and then remembered Freeman's theory. "You still believe that my sister has skipped town?"

"Do you want to offer a better explanation? You claimed that this man took her. So where is she?"

It took a great deal of Sonya's willpower not to leap across the table and wrap her hands around the sergeant's neck. Dwayne reached over and took her hand.

"Do you need us to come down now?" Dwayne asked. He gave Sonya's hand a firm squeeze.

"Yes, I do."

Sonya stood up from her chair. Her jaw clenched in anger. Sergeant Freeman's constant doubt of her sister was taking its toll on her. She knew that had it not been for Dwayne, she would have given him an earful.

"I'm coming with you," Dwayne offered.

Sonya shook her head as she turned to face him. "No, you stay here. I'm sure this won't take long."

Dwayne glanced up at her. He didn't like the idea of her being out of his sight. "I'm coming with you," he told her instead of asking.

"Dwayne, that's insane. You have to pick Sharon up from the airport in less than an hour. I'm sure that Sergeant Freeman will bring me safely back to the hospital when this is through." She turned back to see Freeman nod in compliance. "You stay here, and I'll see you in a few hours," she assured. Sonya watched Dwayne struggle with his decision. She gave him a tight smile and turned to face the sergeant. "Shall we go?"

Freeman's dull brown eyes seemed to lighten as he offered

her his arm. Sonya whirled away, ignoring his arm, and strode out of the room.

Dwayne smiled at his self-assured businesswoman, who left Freeman to trail after her. One thing he couldn't shake was the fact that he didn't like her leaving with Freeman. He looked down at their half-eaten food and let his mind focus on what was the right thing to do.

Bridget heard the door to her room open. She fluttered her eyes open to see her George tiptoe into the room. He looked unsure, and Bridget was moved by his shyness.

"Hello, stranger," she whispered.

Shock G. nearly dropped the flowers he held. "Hey," he answered. He continued to look around the room, seemingly rooted to the spot by the door.

"Are those for me?" she asked, trying to loosen him up.

"Uh, yeah," he answered after realizing he was still holding them. He walked closer to the bed with the flowers in his outstretched hands. Only when he arrived at her bedside did he comprehend that she was unable to take the flowers from him. "Oh, I'm sorry, I'll put them"—he looked around the room and saw a cleared spot in a chair beside her bed—"over here."

Bridget continued smiling. "Thank you."

George nodded his head in response. Then his face grew serious. "I couldn't believe the news when your father called."

"My father called you?" Bridget asked, surprised.

"Yeah. He was pretty cool, really. He told me all that happened and how you really fought to hang in there." George looked up and held her gaze. "I'm really happy you decided to come back to us."

Bridget slowly moved her hand to touch his. "I'm happy to be back." She watched George's eyes glaze over, and she decided to change the subject.

"George, I've been thinking a lot lately."

"So have I," he said with sincerity.

"What have you been thinking about?"

"You remember what you said about college and all that?" George cupped her delicate hands into his.

"Yes."

"Well, I've been thinking. There's a lot to be said for what you were talking about. I mean, what happened to you got me thinking how short life really is. You can be here today and gone tomorrow," he said, looking away from her.

"I've been thinking the same thing. I want to do so much more with my life. I know it sounds lame, but I remember all those speeches my dad gave me, and suddenly everything seems crystal clear."

"I know what you mean. I keep asking myself what do I want to do. And I'll tell you something. I'm not exactly looking forward to taking over Uncle Tyrone's business—"

"That's a relief," Bridget interrupted. She saw his confused expression and apologized.

George laughed, then returned to his speech. "But seriously, Bridge, I dug what you said, and I want to go to college, too. Maybe I can be a big-time lawyer like your father. Maybe then he'll approve of me."

With the rest of her strength, Bridget reached up and wiped away a few tears that trickled down his face. "Is that what you want—my father's approval?"

"More than anything."

Dwayne closed the door to his daughter's room and shook his head. Maybe he'd been wrong about George. He was seeing a different side of him around his daughter, and he wasn't sure how he felt about it. He glanced at his watch and knew he should get down to the airport if he was going to pick up Sharon and James on time.

No sooner had he turned around, did he see his sister and James heading down the hallway.

"Dwayne, we came as soon as we could," she said half-way down the hall with her arms outstretched.

Dwayne accepted her in a strong hug. Seeing Sharon brought all his emotions back to the surface. Sharon began to sob softly on his shoulder. Dwayne pulled her away and gazed down at her.

"She's awake," he told her confidently.

Sharon broke away from him and stared at him. "Where is she?"

"Right here in room 718—"

That was all he could get out before Sharon raced toward Bridget's room. Dwayne turned back to James and smiled.

"I'm happy everything is all right," James said.

"Thank you for cutting your trip short to bring her home."

"Are you kidding? We're family. That's my little niece in there, so if you don't mind, I think I want to check on her."

Dwayne smiled and offered James his hand. The men exchanged a firm handshake, then suddenly gave each other a brief hug. They strolled together toward Bridget's room.

"Excuse me, Mr. Hamilton?" a nurse called to Dwayne from the nurses' station.

"Yes?"

"I have a call for you on line two. He says it's urgent," the nurse said, holding out the phone for him to take.

"Excuse me," Dwayne said to James, who continued to head toward Bridget's room.

"Hello?"

"Dwayne?"

Dwayne recognized the powerful voice immediately. "Malik?"

"Yeah, man. I need your help," Malik said in hushed rapid words.

"Of course, man. Where are you? Where's Anthony?" Dwayne felt uneasy.

"I've found Laura and she needs our help *now.*"

"Okay, okay. Where are you and Anthony?"

There was an unnerving silence on the phone.

"Malik?"

"I'm sorry, Dwayne, but . . . Anthony's dead."

Chapter Twenty-Six

Sonya waited patiently for Sergeant Freeman to return to his office. She had answered pointless questions for over an hour. She didn't know anything about this Odell Hill. When the sergeant pulled out a four-inch-thick police file on the man, Sonya felt faint.

Odell Hill was wanted in Alabama, Florida, Mississippi, and Georgia. There were pages of reports of burglary, car-jacking, and bank robberies. All this information had caused her temples to throb mercilessly.

She had allowed a murderer to stay in her house. How could she have been so gullible? Her concern for Laura's welfare heightened. Did all this mean that Laura was dead?

Sonya shook her head, not allowing herself to think the unthinkable. She had to believe Laura was still alive, despite how things looked right now. She relished this time alone while Sergeant Freeman went to find some aspirin for her. His tough interrogation played havoc with her emotions, and she sorely wished that Dwayne were here. She hated to admit the fact she had come to depend on Dwayne in ways she had never thought she would.

Even when she had seen Dwayne in his weakest state, he seemed to carry a strength she couldn't help but lean on. She allowed her mind to wander back to their short time in his home. She smiled at the vision of them singing in the kitchen, and having dinner with him and his daughter. Even watching *Gone with the Wind* with Bridget and Sharon had been fun. Somehow they'd made her feel part of the family.

Sonya embraced herself as she stood up from the chair and looked at the many pictures that hung from Freeman's wall. She had to get her mind off Dwayne and back to what was happening around her. After staring at the sergeant's pictures and medals, she found herself impressed by Sergeant Freeman.

She laughed at the younger pictures of him sporting an Afro in the seventies. When she noticed his full name inscribed on the plaques, her laughter increased.

"Find something humorous?" Freeman asked, entering the room. He handed her the aspirin and water she had requested.

Sonya quickly swallowed the pills and handed back the half-emptied glass.

Freeman removed his hat and walked behind his desk. "You didn't answer me. What was so funny?"

Sonya smiled again. "Nothing, Francis."

Freeman scowled as he accepted the glass. "I'm glad you got such a kick out of my name." He turned his attention back to the file he was holding. "I think that will be all for today, Miss Walters. If you like, I can take you back to wherever you're staying. Are you staying at Mr. Hamilton's residence?"

Sonya sobered as she eyed him suspiciously. "What makes you think I'm not staying at my place?"

Freeman's speech altered momentarily as he looked at Sonya, surprised. "I've tried to reach you on occasion."

Sonya couldn't help the feeling of uneasiness settling in the pit of her stomach. "No, I think I should return to the hospital."

Freeman nodded, but Sonya noticed the angry expression surfacing his usually calm demeanor. She retrieved her purse and walked toward the door.

"Miss Walters?" Freeman called out just before she was able to slip out.

Sonya turned around slowly trying to hide her anxiety.

"Where are you staying, Miss Walters?"

Sonya's eyes widened in alarm.

"Just in case there's news of your sister," he added.

Sonya edged closer to the door. "I'll call you," she answered with as much aloofness as she could muster.

"Miss Walters?" he called again.

Sonya turned and eyed him nervously.

"Don't you still need a ride to the hospital?"

"I can manage," she replied, then slipped out the door before he could stop her. *Something isn't right,* her inner voice seemed to shout through her headache. She couldn't quite put her finger on it, but she could feel that something wasn't right.

As she marched through a swarm of police officers, she felt like open prey near a den of lions. She couldn't explain that feeling. Making a quick glance over her shoulder, she wanted to make sure that Freeman wasn't behind her, but instead she slammed in the back of another officer.

"Oh, excuse me," she apologized.

The officer held her arm too tight and too long, it seemed, as he peered quizzically into her eyes.

"Are you all right, ma'am?"

Sonya instinctively jerked her arm from his grip. "I'm just fine," she snapped then turned her back to the officer. *I have to get out of this place.*

She made it out of the police department without another incident, but now her anxiousness was replaced with the feeling of urgency. She needed to get back to the hospital—back to Dwayne. Sonya glanced from side to side, wondering how she was to make it back without any money. Her headache intensified. When were those damn pills going to kick in?

Riffling through her purse, Sonya tried to dig out enough change to at least take the bus. No such luck. She couldn't even find enough to make a phone call. Nevertheless, she did have plastic. *How did I get in this predicament?* Looking up through the crowded streets of Atlanta, she saw Nationsbank about two blocks down. She knew she didn't have a choice, so she headed in that direction

When Sonya emerged from the bank, she clutched her head then shook it to clear the foggy haze. She turned to look for a pay phone.

Carmen stopped at a red light across the street from Nationsbank. She removed her sunglasses and squinted at the woman in front of her. *Is that Sonya?*

Bridget felt her spirits soar when Sharon entered her room. "Auntie," she whispered with her fading strength.

Sharon smiled through tear-brimmed eyes and went to kiss Bridget warmly. "Oh, Bridget," she gushed.

George stepped back to allow Sharon access to her niece. Bridget saw George's uneasiness as her uncle soon came into the room.

"Auntie, I'd like for you to meet my friend, George Whitfield."

Sharon turned and gave him a brilliant smile that instantly put George at ease. "How are you?" she asked, holding out her hand.

George accepted her hand and shook it. "Just fine, ma'am," he answered, then looked surprised to see her uncle's hand suddenly appear. He released Sharon's and accepted James's.

It pleased Bridget to see that her aunt and uncle tried to be congenial toward George, despite his appearance. George loved wearing the baggy look, and he made no apologies for it. His clothes made him look like a gangster, but underneath he was as harmless as a fly.

Everyone's attention returned to Bridget, and she tried to remain awake as long as she possibly could before allowing her exhaustion to settle in. They soon made their excuses and left her to get some rest. Although she was tired, Bridget wondered where her father disappeared to.

Dwayne arrived at Malik's office earlier than agreed upon. But what he saw shocked him. Someone had already been here and left the place in shambles. He peered around the door and called Malik's name yet remained cautious. Glass was everywhere and books were thrown on the floor. When he finally found the phone, the line was dead.

He couldn't decide whether he should go and call for help or wait to see if Malik showed up. There was still the chance that Malik hadn't seen his office, and that whoever had done this, did it as a warning.

Deciding to give Malik a few more minutes, Dwayne paced nervously across the small office. He thought heavily on their last words together.

Malik told him that Anthony was killed in an alley shootout. Nothing Malik told him made any sense. Malik felt like he was being followed and wanted to meet Dwayne. There had to be some kind of mistake. How could a simple meeting lead to Anthony's death?

No matter how many times he reflected on Malik's words, he was sure he had misunderstood him. But his inner voice told him it was true. It had been two days since he'd seen Anthony. It was unlike Anthony not to check in with him.

"Damn!" he cursed. What in the hell was going on? Nothing was what it seemed. This case kept going from one extreme to another, and he had no answers to any of it. Malik told him that he found Laura. Dwayne recalled his first meeting with Laura and remembered his strong sense of protectiveness, but he hadn't been able to protect her.

Now, with Richard, or rather Odell's, death, he wondered if

they would find Laura alive. He also knew if anything had happened to Laura, Sonya would break down mentally at the news. No matter what happened, he would be there for her, the same way she had been there for him.

Dwayne found a new level of respect for her as he remembered her strength. She had said nothing when he cried on her shoulder. She'd only whispered encouraging words and promised him that Bridget would survive, and she had.

Dwayne's thoughts were interrupted by a loud squeak. *Someone's coming in the front door.* Dwayne hid behind Malik's door and waited patiently for the intruder to come into the office.

Sonya had trouble focusing on the sidewalk in front of her as it seemed to spin beneath her. Someone grabbed her by the arm, she was sure of that. The problem was, she didn't know who.

"My head," she moaned, but whoever it was ignored her complaint.

"Get in," a loud voice commanded.

Sonya didn't have the energy to fight against whoever was guiding her into a red car.

"I don't feel so good," Sonya whined as she continued to hold her head.

The person beside her mumbled something she couldn't understand, and she didn't care. She just wished that the dull ache in her head would disappear. Suddenly she felt hot, and it was hard for her to breathe.

"Get me to the hospital," she whimpered, but somehow she knew her words were muddled. "Please," she tried to say, but it was useless—she was slipping into a dark cloud. It was becoming harder and harder for her to keep her eyes open.

"Dwayne," she called quietly, then slipped into her own dark and private world.

* * *

The minute the mysterious intruder had stepped into Malik's office, Dwayne jumped from behind the door and tackled the figure.

"Get off me, man," a young voice screamed.

Dwayne could hardly contain his shock as he rolled off the crouched form. When the boy pulled himself off the floor, Dwayne realized that the boy could not be more than fifteen.

"Who are you?" Dwayne asked, getting up from the floor.

The teenager instantly copped an attitude. "That's not important. What's important is who are you, and what are you doing in my man's office?"

Dwayne restrained himself from strangling the smart-lipped boy. What he did, instead, was stroll closer to the boy and give him a hard look. "I'll ask you again—who are you?"

The boy crossed his arms and tried to give Dwayne a look of indifference, but it didn't work.

"David," he finally answered. "My name is David."

Dwayne gave him a satisfied look. "Nice to met you David. I'm Dwayne." He offered his hand as a truce, and David took his time in accepting it.

"Now what are you doing here?" Dwayne asked.

"I was looking for Malik," he said shrugging his shoulders.

Dwayne could tell that the teenager didn't like his harsh tone, but Dwayne refused to let a child talk to him any kind of way. "When was the last time you saw Malik?" Dwayne continued to ask.

The teenager sighed as if bored from his questioning. "Most people pay to get information from me. That's my business," he answered sarcastically.

Dwayne took a threatening step forward, and David instantly threw his hands up in surrender.

"All right, all right, man. Calm down. I kind of help my man, Malik, out every once in a while. I just came by to see if everything was cool, that's all."

Dwayne eyed him suspiciously.

"Honestly," David added.

Dwayne turned his attention back to the ransacked office. He walked over to the desk and began searching for clues. "You wouldn't happen to know who's responsible for this?" Dwayne asked. When he received no response, he looked up to see that he was alone in the office.

He quickly raced out of the office after the teenager, but no sooner had he stepped out of the office, something hard crashed onto the back of his head. Dwayne dropped to the floor, out cold.

Chapter Twenty-Seven

A steady rhythm of water dripped into a metal pail. Its constant pinging sound echoed loudly throughout the otherwise quiet room to penetrate through Dwayne's unconsciousness.

Dwayne's eyes blinked behind his closed lids in time with the falling water until they finally fluttered open, but only darkness greeted him. His nostrils immediately protested from the musky mildew stench around him. His labored breathing seemed boisterously loud, which made his throbbing headache strengthen in power. *What happened?*

He couldn't remember what happened, so he felt unsure of his memory. When he tried to move, he found his hands were restrained behind his back. Sitting uncomfortably on a hard floor, he waited for something or someone to explain this predicament.

A rattling sound coming from the opposite direction drew his attention just as the door was flung back and a flood of light hurt his eyes.

"Welcome back among the living, Mr. Hamilton," a deep voice said.

Dwayne forced himself to squint against the light to see who had entered the room. He could make out only a large shadow that dominated the doorway. Nothing he saw or heard seemed familiar.

The man stepped farther into the room. His heavy footsteps drummed against the cement floor. Dwayne immediately prepared himself for the worst.

The stranger reached above his head and pulled a silver chain. A bright light bulb clicked on, causing Dwayne to turn away. The man's sinister laughter forced Dwayne's attention back to the stranger.

Dwayne found his captor's dark features hauntingly familiar. His black skin looked as rich as coal, but his eyes seemed darker than that. His haggard-looking beard looked awkward as well as his short hair. *Where have I seen this man before?*

Dwayne searched his memory but couldn't come up with any answers. The man's wicked smile drew the most attention. He possessed the brightest set of white teeth.

Dwayne wished he could pull himself up from the floor to confront this man one-on-one, but his bound legs prevented that simple liberty.

"You seem to have me at a disadvantage," Dwayne replied, never wavering his piercing gaze.

"And I plan to keep it that way," his captor retorted. "Don't worry, you're not in any danger as of yet. I guess that will all depend on your girlfriend."

Anger replaced Dwayne's anxieties. His concern for his safety shifted to Sonya's. He lunged at the man unexpectedly, pushing himself with his knees.

The man made a surprised yelp when Dwayne's body slammed against him. It didn't take long before his captor recovered from his attack and began throwing punches solidly across Dwayne's unprotected face and body. Dwayne grunted in pain when one punch after another landed on him. He could taste his blood trickling from his busted lip.

Only when Dwayne felt himself hanging on the brink of unconsciousness did the stranger end his violent assault.

Dwayne rolled away and began coughing and sputtering blood. *That was a foolish thing to do.*

His attacker spoke in a heavy tone, trying to catch his breath. "I suggest you try to be more cooperative, Mr. Hamilton. It will be much easier on yourself if you do."

Dwayne squeezed his eyes shut against the persistent throbbing in every inch of his body.

The stranger turned and left the room, slamming the door behind him. Dwayne wallowed in silent misery.

A few minutes later, the door was flung open again, and two men rushed into the room, grabbing him from the floor. Dwayne tried to fight against the awkward position they held him in. His struggles proved to be useless, as the men carried him from one room and into another.

In the next motion, he felt his body hurtling through the air like a paper sack. When he hit the floor, he fought to suppress the urge to cry out in pain. The door slammed behind him, yet this time he wasn't left alone.

"What do you mean, you lost her?" Frank yelled into the phone. He could feel his temperature rising again. He couldn't believe the level of incompetence of his men.

"Some lady picked her up in front of the bank," Samuel stuttered.

Frank couldn't help the full minute of offensive curses he shouted into the phone. This latest screwup could very well blow his cover. For every apology Samuel offered, his anger rose.

Frank pulled open the top drawer of his desk and pulled out a brown prescription bottle: his blood pressure pills. What would he do without them? He took a quick moment to calm himself down before returning to his conversation with Samuel.

"Who picked her up?" he asked in a calm voice that camouflaged his rage.

"She drove a red Toyota Camry. I got the license number."

Frank scrambled to retrieve paper and pen. "Give me the

number." Frank nodded as he scribbled down the number. "JRT477, got it. I'll call you back with the name and address."

"Yes, boss."

"Samuel?"

"Yes?"

"Don't screw up." The threat was his final warning.

"Yes, boss," Samuel responded with a shaky, fear-filled voice.

Frank slammed down the phone, muttering more curses. He swore he wouldn't tolerate another foul-up from his men.

Samuel received the call from Frank within ten minutes. He knew from the directness in his boss's voice that if he didn't succeed, it would cost him his life.

He arrived at Royal Walk Luxury Apartments in Decatur in thirty minutes. He drove slowly, trying to locate the familiar red Camry. When he saw it, he parked in the parking lot across from his targeted building. *This is it.* He switched off the engine and retrieved his gun from the glove compartment. *This shouldn't take long.*

Carmen paced across the champagne-colored carpet. Now and then she would glance at the unconscious Sonya with frustration. *What's wrong with her?* She had tried for more than an hour to wake her, but Sonya would only roll her head from side to side.

She had tried for the past hour to reach Dwayne to let him know what was going on. He wasn't at home or in the car. When she tried the hospital, Sharon said that he received an urgent call and had left.

Frustrated, she slammed the phone down. *Maybe I should try to get her to a doctor.* She didn't know. So far it seemed that Sonya was only sleeping. As much as she wanted to hate Sonya right now, she knew she needed to help her. But this whole situation had her on edge.

Just then, a loud knock sounded at her door. She jumped. She dashed for her purse and removed her gun.

The knock sounded again.

I need to get her out of sight.

Placing the gun on a nearby coffee table, Carmen tried to pull Sonya from the sofa but her dead weight made her to stumble. Carmen dropped Sonya on the floor. The knock sounded again, this time more persistent.

"Coming," she called out. She suddenly wished she could cut out her own tongue. *Why on earth did I say that?* Filled with a sense of urgency, she scooped up Sonya from underneath her arms and pulled her into the back bedroom.

Sonya moaned.

"Please be quiet, Sonya."

When Sonya fell silent again, Carmen felt certain that she would remain in her condition long enough for her to get rid of whoever was at the door.

Samuel heard footsteps approaching the door. He gave a quick glance around the empty hallway. When the lock clicked, Samuel pulled out the gun from his jacket and waited patiently for the door to open.

Chapter Twenty-Eight

Dwayne shifted his weight, then pressed his body upright to see who occupied the room with him. Shock riveted across his features the moment he recognized Laura. He looked beside her to see Malik. Both were strapped securely in separate chairs.

"I don't believe it," he whispered.

Dwayne met Laura's unblinking gaze with curiosity. He searched her face for any sign of recognition. She gave none. Her expression remained void of emotion. She appeared older, perhaps jaded, he thought. He tried to imagine the horror she must have experienced the past few weeks, but he just couldn't.

"Laura?" He hoped to draw her out of her deep trance.

Laura glanced at the door, then shook her head. He understood her meaning. Someone was listening.

Dwayne looked to Malik. He must have encountered the same abusive punishment. His face had numerous cuts and bruises—some still bleeding. But behind his bruised face, Dwayne saw life flickering in his eyes. Dwayne knew whoever tangled with Malik endured far worse treatment. Dwayne nodded toward him, and Malik returned the gesture.

Dwayne tried to understand what was going on. The stranger

wanted Sonya. But why? Apparently this wild case wasn't over Laura. They already had her. Nothing made sense anymore. Why did they want Sonya? At times she could be a little rough around the edges, but he refused to believe that she could have such vicious enemies. He looked around anxiously, trying to figure out a way to escape. He had to get to Sonya. Her life was in danger.

"I want her found. I have everyone here except the one I want!"

The men watched C.J. roar. The men looked among themselves as if searching for someone to place the blame on. Time was running out, and they all knew it. They all had as much at stake as their boss.

The door to their small meeting room burst open. C.J. looked at Matt, his anxious employee who entered the room. C.J. signaled him over.

"Samuel's moving," Matt said in a rushed voice.

C.J. turned and motioned for two men, Jack and Benjamin, to follow him. Once outside the room, he spoke in a harsh whisper. "I want you two on Samuel's trail like white on rice. You understand me?"

The men nodded.

"I want to know what Frank knows and if he has what I want. I want you to make sure his plans are destroyed. Do I make myself clear?"

Again the men nodded.

"Good. Now get on it. And don't report back to me unless you have good news," C.J. warned.

C.J. watched them leave with troubled eyes. He couldn't afford another screwup. A buyer wanted the merchandise in two weeks. It meant his life if he couldn't deliver this time. The way he saw it, if he went down, he was taking everyone down with him, including Miss Walters and everyone she held dear.

* * *

Sharon sat next to Bridget's bed, thumbing through one of the books Shock-something-or-another had brought over for her niece to read. The more she read, the more interested Sharon became. The pictures of rare coins fascinated her. She read page after page of intriguing information of lost cities and unique histories.

Finally she turned to a page Bridget had marked off. Sharon stared at the eight-by-eleven picture of a beautiful Aztec coin. Her eyes widened at one beautiful coin called the Amaceo; it had an estimated value of . . . "Twenty million dollars!" she exclaimed, standing up from the chair.

Bridget's eyes fluttered open.

"Oh, I'm sorry, Bridget. I didn't mean to wake you. I guess I had gotten caught up in these books."

"What are you reading?" Bridget asked, rubbing her sleep-filled eyes.

"A book on lost coins and their histories."

Bridget smiled. "Fascinating, aren't they?"

Sharon returned her smile. "I believe I owe you an apology. I was wrong to criticize your dream of being a coin dealer. This stuff is great." Sharon continued to shake her head.

"Did you see the one that looks like Sonya's?" Bridget asked excitedly.

"Sonya's?" Sharon opened the book again. This time she looked closer, and a slow smile creased her lips. "Well, I'll be damned."

"If it's the same coin, it's worth a fortune," Bridget continued saying.

"I see. Do you think this is Sonya's coin?"

"I'm almost positive."

"Sonya wouldn't casually wear a twenty-million-dollar coin around her neck." Sharon's lips twisted into a half frown. "I wonder . . ."

James entered the room, carrying two Cokes. Sharon grabbed her purse and kissed Bridget's forehead.

"I'll be back," she said, heading toward the door.

"Where are you going?" James asked in bewilderment.

"Down to the police station to find Sonya," she answered and slipped out the door.

James turned and looked at Bridget who simply shrugged her shoulders.

Sharon jumped into her silver Mercedes and started the engine. Something felt out of place. During the drive to the police department, Sharon tried to remember when Sonya received that coin necklace.

It took a while before the memory of Sonya's last birthday came to mind. Three months ago, Laura gave her a necklace. Was it the same necklace? She couldn't remember. Sonya owned plenty of jewelry. She couldn't be sure of when she received anything. But twenty million was a hefty price tag. Too big a price tag for Sonya to casually wear around her neck daily.

Sharon parked her car outside of the police station and rushed into the building. She hoped she hadn't missed Sonya. Once inside, an officer pointed her in the direction of Sergeant Freeman's office. She couldn't believe the difference in the police station between night and day. Today there were so many officers crowding the hallway, she hardly recognized the place.

When she approached Freeman's office, she heard the sergeant apologizing profusely to someone. She paused before knocking on the cracked door.

"I'm sorry for the delay," he was saying. "I'll have that coin for you by this afternoon as promised."

Sharon felt as if she'd been punched in the stomach. She prayed she wasn't hearing the sergeant clearly.

"Yes, sir," she heard him say. "Will do. I guarantee you there will be no more problems. The Amaceo coin will be in your hands tonight."

Sharon backed away from the door in horror. The expression

on her face must have conveyed her thoughts as an officer tapped her on her shoulder. She squealed as she jumped.

"Are you all right, ma'am?" a young officer asked with concern.

"Yes, I'm fine, thank you," she lied, backing up from the officer as if he'd burned her. She turned and bumped solidly into another officer. "Excuse me," she said, then stepped around him and rushed out of the station as fast as she could.

Dear God, what should I do? She made it to her car, visibly shaken from what she had discovered. This whole thing was over the Amaceo coin—and the police department was involved. Sharon fumbled through her purse, trying to retrieve her keys. She finally clutched them, then tried to unlock her car door, but her shaking hands caused her to drop them. She quickly scooped them up, then stood again only to come face-to-face with Sergeant Freeman.

Sonya moaned and clutched her head. Its heavy pounding held her at its mercy. She struggled to open her eyes despite the pain. She felt ill. Her stomach threatened to heave its contents. She quickly covered her mouth to prevent the inevitable.

Her stomach delivered on its promise. Once done, she felt better. She tilted her head up toward the ceiling, thankful for the welcome relief.

Sonya pulled herself up on her wobbly legs and felt another wave of nausea threaten. A loud thud drew her attention toward the closed door. *What was that?* Until that moment, Sonya hadn't wondered about her surroundings. She looked around, puzzled. She reached for the door, but something warned her against it. She heard someone searching through nearby rooms.

Sonya turned toward the window and contemplated an exit route. Suddenly a man's voice rang out in the apartment.

"Who in the hell are you?" she heard the man ask in a thunderous voice.

"Friends of C.J.'s," another voice answered.

Sonya covered her mouth when she heard what sounded like muffled shots.

"Is he dead?" Jack asked, waiting for Benjamin to check the body.

"As a doornail," Benjamin replied, shaking his head. "So is the chick. It's a shame, though—she's some looker."

"It's a shame that he tried to work with both C.J. and Frank. He should have known that was dangerous. Search the apartment. That broad has to be here somewhere."

Both men split up and went to search every room.

"She's not here," Benjamin yelled.

"Damn! The boss isn't going to like this one bit," he said, shaking his head.

"He said not to call him unless we have good news. I suggest we try to find her. I'm not about to call him and tell him we came up empty-handed."

"Good point. Let's go. She can't be far."

Malik grew restless, sitting in the wooden chair. No one spoke as they waited in anticipation. He noticed Dwayne trying to loosen his tied hands. Malik watched Laura drift off to sleep. He had watched her saddened expression for most of the day. He read the mistrust in her eyes. She refused to speak to him or Dwayne.

As she slept, she looked much like a lost angel. He remembered her from the old neighborhood. She was a scrawny little thing, just a shadow of her sister's beauty. He remembered her being a quiet girl, never having too many friends surrounding her. Who knew she would turn out to be such a beauty?

Of course her face was smudged with dirt, and her clothes were filthy, but there was more there. He could see it, feel it. He continued to watch her soft breathing pattern in pure fascination.

The door rattled, and everyone became alert, including Laura. Two men entered the room and headed for Laura.

Laura's eyes widened as she pushed her chair away from them, a futile act that didn't prevent them from grabbing her shoulder painfully. Laura cried out.

Malik tried to come out of his chair in an attempt to protect her. The two men jumped away from Malik, fear visible in their expressions. One of the men tried to reach for Laura again but was cut off by Malik thrusting his chair between them.

"Come on, man. I don't want to have to hurt you," one of the men dared to threaten.

"Give it your best shot," Malik challenged. Out of the corner of his eye, he saw that Dwayne had finally snapped his hands free from the ropes. A wicked grin covered his lips as Dwayne jumped to his feet and landed an elbow punch to the back of one man's head.

Malik rocked to his feet and swung around to hit the other man with his chair. He then proceeded to kick the man solidly in his chest and back. He also dealt a quick blow to the man's head, knocking him out cold. He turned back to Laura and saw Dwayne untying her hands.

When he finished, Dwayne proceeded to untie him, too. But when he looked at Laura, she seemed to cower away from him as if she feared him.

"Come on. We have to get out of here," Dwayne commanded.

Laura raced behind Dwayne while Malik took up the rear. When they stepped out of the small room and into a dark hallway, Malik heard Laura gasp. He reached out and took her hand, trying to calm her down, but she snatched her hand away almost in fear.

"Shh . . ." Dwayne whispered.

Malik didn't press the issue. Laura was afraid of him, that much he was sure of.

A light switch clicked on, and the threesome turned toward the source.

"Hey!" a man cried from behind them.

"Go!" Malik shouted, pointing down the opposite hallway.

"The prisoners are getting away!" the man shouted.

Malik raced behind them, glancing over his shoulder. More men filtered through the hallway for the chase. Laura stumbled, but Malik grabbed her before she hit the floor.

"Keep moving, sweetheart," he urged her on.

Dwayne stopped.

"What's wrong?" Laura asked frantically.

"It's a dead end," Dwayne said, looking around.

"What are we going to do now?" she asked when she saw the men gaining on them.

"This way." Malik pointed down another hallway.

Dwayne and Laura wasted no time, but that hallway was another dead end. Laura spotted a small window about seven feet up. Malik followed her gaze.

"Do you think you can fit through there?" Malik asked.

Laura nodded. In the next moment, Malik and Dwayne propelled her up to reach the window. She struggled to pry it open.

"You can do it, sweetheart," Malik encouraged.

The footsteps drew closer just as Laura pushed open the window and pulled herself through.

Chapter Twenty-Nine

Sonya hid behind an old, blue, sixty-seven Monte Carlo trembling. She tried to calm her racing heart but couldn't.

Two men stepped from the apartment building. As they looked from one direction to another, an eerie feeling told her they were looking for her. *Who are they?*

The men shook their heads, then walked to an old Chevy Citation and got in. She inched away from their view. She listened in fear as the Citation's engine revved up and pulled from the parking lot. Sonya sighed in relief, then slumped against the Monte Carlo.

Her mind drew a blank. She placed her fingers along her temples and tried to remember how she ended up in that strange bedroom.

Sonya forced the bits of information from her memory. She remembered the hospital, remembered seeing Bridget. Then Sergeant Freeman wanted her for questioning.

When she stopped rubbing her temples, her eyes widened in alarm. A vision of her accepting aspirin from Sergeant Freeman filtered through her mind.

"He drugged me," she whispered. She stared back at the

apartment building. *This doesn't make sense. Why would he want to drug me?*

She glanced around the complex and contemplated returning to the apartment. She felt nauseated at the thought. *Maybe it's best that I don't know what happened.* However, her curiosity wouldn't let it go at that. She had to know.

Sonya took a step toward the building, still feeling weak and light-headed. She waited, then gathered her courage to proceed toward the building. She made it back to the building, but the moment she stepped into the hallway, an overpowering sense of fear engulfed her. Sonya changed her mind momentarily, but she couldn't stop her feet from carrying her to the unknown.

She rounded a corner and noticed an apartment door opened slightly. *This is the apartment.* This time her feet stopped. She stared at the door. Seconds turned into minutes, and she was unsure of how many passed before she finally pushed open the door.

There, only inches inside the door, lay Carmen's body. Another wave of nausea hit her. This time she was unable to release anything from her empty stomach.

I have to get out of here. She turned to leave the apartment, when out of the corner of her eye she spotted her purse sitting near the coffee table. She quickly retrieved it while trying to avoid Carmen's body.

Just before she picked up her purse, she noticed a gun lying next to it. With shaky hands, she reached for the gun. She was barely able to hold it, her hands shook so bad. She hated guns, always had. This was the first time she had ever contemplated having one. *Protection,* her mind shouted. *I'll just take it for protection.*

Unwillingly she looked back at Carmen's dead body. How many close calls had she suffered in the past few weeks? How many more could she survive? She opened her purse and slipped in the gun.

Sonya knew she couldn't just walk away from the crime scene. She had to do something. Looking around, she found the phone. She pulled a handkerchief from her purse and used it to pick up the phone. With the tip of her nail, she dialed 911.

"Nine-one-one?" the operator responded.

Sonya placed the receiver on the table and let the operator repeat her question to the tabletop. They'll send someone over, she reasoned. All 911 calls were recorded, and she didn't want to be placed at this murder scene.

Without a backward glance, Sonya left the apartment and raced from the complex, while glancing over her shoulder every few feet. Her hand absently touched her purse. She had been caught off guard one too many times. It wouldn't happen again.

Twenty minutes later, Sonya reached a gas station. This time she had money to make a phone call. She dialed Grady Hospital and asked for room 718. Hopefully Dwayne would still be in with Bridget.

"Hello?"

Sonya recognized the voice.

"James, this is Sonya. Is Dwayne there?" she asked in one long sentence.

"Oh, hello, Sonya. No, I'm sorry, Dwayne isn't here. He left a few hours ago."

Sonya shook her head. Just her luck. "Do you know where he went?"

"No, I'm sorry. Is something wrong? Is Sharon all right?" he asked with concern in his voice.

"Sharon?"

"Isn't Sharon with you? She said she was going to the police station to see you."

Sonya's mind reeled. "When did she go?"

"What's wrong? Is Sharon in trouble?"

"I have to go. I'll call back later." Sonya slammed the phone down, then quickly searched through her purse for another quarter. She ignored the gun as she found her coin to place a call to Sharon's car phone.

*   *   *

"Sergeant Freeman, you scared me." Sharon placed a hand over her heart.

"I didn't mean to, Mrs. Ellis." He took a dangerous step forward. "You seem to be in a hurry. Is anything wrong?"

Sharon forced a smile. "Wrong?"

"One of the officers said you were looking for me. You never came to my office. Is there something I can help you with?"

Sharon averted his hard look, afraid that he would see straight through her. He's testing me, she realized.

"Actually, I was looking for Sonya. I was told she came down here for questioning. But one of the officers told me she had already left." She hoped he wouldn't read through her lie.

"Really?" he answered, sounding unconvinced.

Sharon jumped at the sound of her car phone ringing. "Excuse me," she said, trying to open her car door again.

Sergeant Freeman smiled, then waited. He remained standing outside her car while she answered.

"Hello?" her voice quivered slightly.

"Sharon?" Sonya asked.

Sharon fought the urge to shout for joy when she recognized the voice.

"Sharon, are you there? It's me, Sonya."

"Hello, James," Sharon greeted.

"James? Sharon, it's Sonya. Is everything all right?"

"Oh, everything is fine. I made it safely down here to the police station."

Sonya hesitated. "Is Freeman there?"

"Yes, dear. I'm talking with Sergeant Freeman now. It seems I've just missed Sonya."

"Damn," Sonya cursed. "Sharon, you have to leave right now. The man is dangerous. I believe he drugged me. You have to get away from him."

Sharon reached for her door while responding to Sonya over the phone. "Yes, honey, I'm on my way back to the hospital now." She quickly started the car, then smiled prettily at the sergeant while she pulled away.

"Sonya, that was too close. Where are you?"

"I don't know really. Hold on. The address printed on this pay phone is 5455 Memorial Drive. How fast can you get here?"

"Memorial Drive? I guess I can be there in twenty minutes. Don't move."

"I won't. Do hurry, Sharon." Sonya hung up the phone and looked around the station. She had to hide. Those men could show up here looking for her. She spotted the public bathroom by the gas station's convenience store and decided it would be the best place for her to hide.

She ignored the cool breeze that cut across her exposed legs as she hurried toward the bathroom. She slipped in just as that familiar old Citation pulled into the lot. Her heart tripled its pace.

Dear God, what if they saw me? She backed away from the door and waited for the men to barge in at any moment. She looked around but there was no other avenue of escape. Her breathing became shallow when a familiar voice thundered outside the door.

"I'll be right back, Benjamin. I just have to use the john."

Sonya quickly reached out and locked the door. The door-knob turned. Sonya trembled in fear.

"Damn!" she heard him say. Then there was a loud banging on the door.

"Hey, you in there, hurry up!" he shouted.

A lump enlarged in Sonya's throat. *What am I going to do?*

A car horn blared. "Come on, man, do that later. We have to find that broad, pronto!"

Sonya heard the footsteps drawing away from the door. A few seconds later, she heard a car pull off. Was it the Citation? She refused to move toward the door. She didn't want to take the chance of being wrong. She leaned against the small porcelain sink and waited.

After a long period of time passed, she felt confident to look out the door. She peered around the small station just as Sharon's car turned in. "Oh, thank God." She raced from her hiding place and headed straight for Sharon.

In one fluid motion, she opened the car door and jumped in. "Let's go."

Sharon wasted no time in doing as Sonya asked. "What is going on?" Sharon asked.

Sonya kept looking around to see if there was any sign of the Citation. "I'm not sure what is going on anymore," she answered just above a whisper.

"Well, let me tell you what I know. That coin necklace of yours is the reason for all of this!"

Sonya turned and looked at her. "What?"

"Reach to the backseat and grab that book," Sharon instructed.

Sonya grabbed the book and gave Sharon a puzzled look.

"Open it to the marked page."

Sonya complied and found the page Sharon was referring to. She immediately recognized her coin. Hurriedly she read the caption beneath the photograph. *The Amaceo Coin: dated back to early Aztecs, many believe to as far as 15 B.C. Estimated worth:*

"Twenty million dollars?" Sonya nearly shouted.

"That's exactly what I said."

"But . . . I don't understand. How . . ? Laura gave me . . . This doesn't make sense."

"I know. But whatever is going on, your Sergeant Freeman is knee deep into it. I overheard him talking on the phone. He was promising someone that he would have that Amaceo coin to him by tonight."

Sonya reach for her necklace. "I don't have it. It's back at the motel."

"Which motel?"

"The Sundial. It's down by Grady Hospital."

Sharon made a sudden U-turn and headed for the Sundial Motel.

Within minutes, Sharon screeched her car to a halt in front

of the motel. The women jumped out and headed toward the elevator. Sonya pressed the button for the second floor.

The women rode up in silence. Both women hoped their anxieties were in vain. The moment they stepped from the elevator, Sonya's eyes darted toward her room. She quickly grabbed Sharon by the arm and pulled her back.

"What's wrong?" Sharon whispered, looking at Sonya.

"The door is open."

Sonya tiptoed toward her door. She listened briefly, then pushed the door open farther. She eased into the room with Sharon following close behind her. Sonya reached inside her purse and pulled out her gun. This time she would be prepared.

Before Sonya or Sharon could react, someone grabbed Sonya's gun, and they were surrounded by giant men who appeared from nowhere.

"Come in, ladies," a male voice instructed.

Sharon passed Sonya a worried look, but both women did as they were instructed. Sonya became nervous as she heard the door click behind them.

A muscular giant sat on the edge of the bed. Sonya squinted at the familar-looking man and forced her memory to come up with a name. "William? William Gainey?"

William smiled as he stood up from the bed and walked closer to Sonya. "I see you haven't forgotten me."

"You know this clown?" Sharon asked, relaxing.

Sonya nodded, but her guard remained intact. "You're Malik Moyers's brother. What are you doing in my motel room?"

"Let's just say I need your help."

"My help?" Sonya asked, looking around, only to see the angry faces of the men surrounding them. "What on earth can I do for you?"

"Well, you see, my brother was in my pool hall a couple of days ago. He was asking questions about your sister," William began.

"Laura?" Sonya asked with wide eyes.

"Yeah. Malik was hired to find her."

Sonya's face clearly showed her confusion. "Who hired him?"

"You know how tight-lipped Malik is. He wouldn't tell me, but he was rather persistent on finding information on her—"

"I fail to see how all this has to do with anything," Sharon cut in but quickly fell silent under William's hard glare.

"Let's just say that I was able to give him the information he needed," William answered, shifting his attention to Sharon.

"You know where Laura is?" Sonya nearly shouted, gaining his attention.

"No, I simply told him who had her. I don't know where they're keeping her, but it's gotten a little more complicated than that. I sent two of my men to keep an eye on Malik. I mean, we've had our problems in the past, but it doesn't mean I don't care for my brother."

Sonya refrained from rolling her eyes. She just wished he would hurry with the story. "Yes, I understand what you mean."

"Well, anyway, there was some trouble, and they weren't able to keep up with Malik. Now he's missing."

"Do you think the same men who have Laura have Malik?"

"I don't know."

Sonya thought for a minute before directing her next question to him. "I still don't understand how I can help. I still haven't found my sister."

William crossed his arms over his chest and gave Sonya a curious stare. "I was hoping you could tell me who this Anthony Payne was."

"Was?" Sharon asked in a rushed whisper.

William purposely didn't answer her question. He lifted his eyebrow slightly as an answer, and instinctively both women caught on to his meaning: Anthony was dead.

"What happened?" Sonya heard herself ask.

"Let's just say there was a shootout between C.J.'s men,

Malik, and Anthony. That's the night that we lost Malik. However, we did discover Anthony's body."

"How did you know who he was?" Sharon butted in.

"One of my men checked his wallet," William answered nonchalantly. "Now, your turn. Who was Anthony Payne?"

The women exchanged looks before Sharon answered, "He was my brother's assistant."

Everyone in the room settled into an uncomfortable silence. Sonya glanced over at Sharon and noticed her in deep thought.

"What is it, Sharon?" she asked, gently taking Sharon by the arm.

"That name. I couldn't place it before, but now I seem to remember Dwayne leaving the hospital to meet with a Malik. Yes, I'm almost certain that's the name he said."

William stood at attention.

Sonya felt her heart skip a beat. "When?"

"Just as I was arriving at the hospital today."

A teenaged boy stepped from behind the towering bodyguards and whispered into William's ear.

"Describe this Dwayne," William commanded.

Sonya replied before Sharon could. "He's about six-foot-three, with broad shoulders, strong chiseled features but with a clean-cut image, no beard or mustache, a small but noticeable cleft in his chin, dark gray eyes almost almond shaped. He has . . ."

William held a curious expression.

Sonya clamped her jaws shut. After seeing Sharon's astonished look, she felt an embarrassing heat rise in her cheeks.

"David?" William turned his attention back to the boy.

"That's him," the boy confirmed.

William's shoulders slumped. He turned away from Sonya and Sharon. "I'm afraid Dwayne is being held by C.J.'s men. This must mean that C.J. also has my brother."

"Who in the hell is C.J.?" Sharon and Sonya shouted in unison.

"A gangster lord controlling the East Side." William ignored their shocked gasps.

Sonya looked at the other men assembled in her small room before she asked her next question. "Tell me, William, are you in the same business as this gangster lord?"

William smiled. "It's a dirty job, but someone has to do it."

"So what now? This man may have my sister and my . . . and Dwayne." Sonya caught herself, but it was too late. By the look on Sharon's face, she knew she had some explaining to do later.

"If C.J. does have Malik, it could mean only one thing," William answered in a cool voice that sent chills running down Sonya's back. "War."

Laura marveled from the feeling that a fresh bath and hot food could do for one's soul. The hell she had been living the past few weeks had come to a close, or so she hoped. Those men were still out there looking for her, but she wouldn't allow herself to think for one moment that they would find her.

Bishop Spencer had taken her in, and she felt safer here in the small church but right now she had to find Sonya. She was in danger, especially as long as she had that necklace. How did she ever make such a terrible mistake? Somehow the coin she bought for Sonya had gotten replaced by a priceless coin. She shook her head, not understanding how she could make such a drastic mistake.

When she finished with her bath and was dressed in clean clothes, Bishop Spencer came back into the room to show her to his office. Once there, he left her alone to make her phone calls. First, she tried Sonya's house; however, she became disappointed when the answering machine picked up. She left a quick message but refused to say where she was on the machine. Next she tried Sonya's office. Tina answered the phone.

"Hello, Tina? This is Laura. Is my sister in?"

"Laura? Dear God, where have you been?" Tina shouted.

"It's a long story. Is Sonya in?"

"No, she's on a leave of absence. Mr. Harrison is in charge

of the office right now. Both Sharon and Sonya are out. Laura, are you all right? Where are you?''

"I'm fine, but I'd rather not discuss anything in detail on the phone. Would you happen to have Sharon's home number?''

"Yes, I have it somewhere on my desk.'' Laura heard Tina shuffle through papers before she came back on line with a number. "I found it.''

Laura wrote down the number. "Thanks, Tina, you're a life saver.'' Laura hung up the phone and quickly dialed the number. The answering machine picked up. "Damn!'' She patiently listened so she could leave a message.

"Sorry we're not in right now, but if you could leave a brief detailed message, and the time you called, we'll get back with you as soon as possible. If this is an emergency, you can reach me at 770–555–3640, or if you need James, call 555-2193.''

Laura scribbled down the numbers on a scratch piece of paper lying on the desk before her, then quickly dialed the emergency number.

Sonya and Sharon watched the men file out of her motel room like military men marching toward battle. One man handed back her gun. "Thanks,'' she said sarcastically. She wasn't sure exactly what was going on, but she knew that this whole situation had gotten out of control, and she felt powerless to stop it.

Sonya couldn't talk William out of this war he'd declared on the man named C.J. The whole thing seemed too surreal for her to take seriously. What on earth would a gangster lord want with her sister, or Dwayne?

All the men left, but not before William passed her a number to call if she heard anything concerning his brother.

Sharon plopped down on the corner of the bed and shook her head in dismay. "What on earth have we gotten ourselves into?''

"I don't know.'' Sonya went to her closet and rummaged through her bags to find her necklace. Apparently William didn't know about the coin, or he would have looked for it, she thought to herself.

A piercing beep filled the room.

"What's that?" Sonya asked from the closet.

"It's my pager. Do you mind if I use the phone?"

"Girl, you know better than to ask me that. Of course I don't mind." Sonya found the necklace, and a sense of relief washed over her.

"Laura!" Sharon shouted from the bedroom.

Sonya jumped, then raced from the closet to stare at Sharon.

Sharon waved Sonya over to the bed as she asked, "Where are you? Yes, she's right here." Sharon handed the phone to Sonya, who accepted it with trembling hands.

"Laura?" she asked with fresh tears forming in her eyes.

"Oh, Sonya, you're there." Laura's voice trembled.

"Laura, where are you?"

"I'd rather not say over the phone, but come to where we were both baptized as children."

Sonya nodded her head, knowing exactly where Laura was located.

"Don't move, Laura. We're on our way."

"Maybe we should see if one of these two could lure Sonya here," one of C.J.'s men suggested to him.

C.J. turned around to face Dwayne and Malik. His expression told Dwayne that he was considering the idea.

"Take them back to the holding room, and this time make sure they don't escape."

Suddenly another crowd of men rushed into the room, panting hard from their obvious run. Dwayne smiled once he saw that no one had Laura in their possession.

"Where is Laura?" C.J. roared. The men took a step backward after seeing the vicious look creased in their boss's face.

"I guess if you want something done, you have to do it yourself. Ron and Tony, follow me. I'll find her."

And with that, he was gone.

* * *

Laura continued to look out the church's door, anxious to see Sharon's car pull into the parking lot. It felt like hours since she had hung up when in fact it had been only ten minutes. She paced back and forth to calm her nerves while reciting "Come on, Sonya" to herself.

Peeping out the door once again, a flare of excitement raced through her at the sight of Sharon's silver Mercedes pulling into the parking lot. Stepping out of the church, Laura couldn't conceal the bright smile on her face at seeing Sonya in the car.

"There she is!" Sonya shouted, pointing toward Laura.

Sharon started to say something just as a long, black El Dorado jumped the church's sidewalk and tried to block the pathway between Laura and the Mercedes.

"What the hell—?" Sharon shouted, swerving to miss the other car, then slammed on her brakes. A man jumped from the car and grabbed Laura.

Sonya instantly sprang from the car and screamed, "Laura!"

The stranger lost his grip on Laura and turned to face Sonya.

Laura raced toward Sharon's car. Another man tried to stop her, but Laura easily dodged him and made it to Sharon's car where she jumped into the backseat.

"Let's go!" Laura shouted, but Sonya didn't move. She couldn't. Time had stopped as Sonya stared into the face of a ghost. The ghost of Curtis Durden.

Chapter Thirty

"Sonya!" Sharon and Laura screamed.

When Curtis pointed to Sonya, she remembered the danger she was in. Her hand instantly clutched at the necklace draped around her neck. Curtis and his men raced toward her as she jumped back into the car.

"Let's get the hell out of here," Sonya shouted, slamming her door shut.

"You got it." Sharon floored the accelerator, laying a wheelie any race car driver would be proud of. Laura and Sonya found their seat belts. Within five minutes, Sharon lost the El Dorado.

"They're gone," Laura announced.

Sharon and Sonya sighed in relief. Sonya could still feel the adrenaline pumping through her veins. *When was this nightmare going to end?* She marveled at the fact that they had survived one close call after another.

Sonya unbuckled her seat belt and turned to face Laura. Tears shined brightly in their eyes as Laura also unfastened her seat belt so they could give the comforting hugs they needed.

Sonya's arms locked behind her sister. "I'm so happy to see **you**," Sonya whispered.

"I'm so sorry for this mess. It's all my fault," Laura cried into her sister's ear.

"Shh, it's all right now. You're safe." Sonya spoke the words but had difficulty believing it.

Laura's body vibrated as her grip tightened around Sonya's back. "I'm sorry," she kept saying.

Sonya patted Laura's head in hopes to comfort her.

"Was that who I think it was?" Sharon finally asked.

Sonya pulled away from Laura, wanting to know the answer, too.

Laura nodded.

"But how?" Sonya asked.

"Oh, Sonya, I don't know where to begin. I mean, so much has happened," Laura moaned.

"First, I think we need to ditch this car," Sharon said, checking her mirrors.

"How? A rental car could still be traced to us," Sonya stated, turning back in her seat.

"Maybe we can borrow one?" Laura suggested.

"From whom?" Sharon and Sonya asked.

"How about Tina?" Laura suggested.

"Good idea," Sharon agreed.

A few minutes later, the women pulled into a restaurant's parking lot to use the pay phone.

They decided Sharon would make the call. Forty-five minutes later, Tina pulled up in an old, beat-up, red Celica.

Sonya and Laura hid inside the restaurant while Sharon and Tina exchanged cars. After Tina drove off, the two women rushed outside.

"What did you tell her?" Sonya asked.

"I just told her that I was back in town, and I didn't want my husband to know."

"She bought that?" Laura asked.

"Tina is always willing to be part of the lastest gossip. I

don't doubt half the office will think I'm cheating on James by the time she gets back."

Later Sharon pulled up in front of the Sundial Motel.

"Where are we?" Laura asked.

"My new home," Sonya answered in absent humor.

The women got out of the car and headed up to Sonya's room.

Laura inspected her surroundings, then glanced at her sister in total amazement. "You're staying here?"

"It's a long story," Sonya said, pulling out her key.

"I guess you'll also tell me what happened to your hair?" Laura asked, shaking her head.

"That's a long story, too."

"I think we also need to change motels," Sharon suggested.

"Good idea," Sonya agreed. "Let's exchange information first, then find another place."

Once inside, the three women sat on the bed and positioned themselves so they could share information.

"I want to know what's going on. Start from the beginning, and please don't leave anything out," Sonya told Laura, crossing her legs Indian style.

Laura took a deep breath, then struggled with exactly where she wanted to start her story.

"First, Richard is a fraud," Laura began.

"We know. The same day you turned up missing, Dwayne's office discovered that Curtis was an only child."

"Dwayne?" Laura asked. She glanced at Sharon, who looked toward the ceiling like a cat with a secret.

"Anyway . . ." Sonya rolled her hand along, trying to get Laura to continue with her story.

"Anyway, I was held captive for I don't know how long in some small shack with Rich . . . I mean, Odell and Samuel—"

"Who is Samuel?" Sonya cut in.

"I don't know. I never saw the man until then, and to tell you the truth I haven't seen him since. Anyway, I escaped. Only I left one hostage situation to land in another."

At Sonya and Sharon's puzzled looks, she explained further.

"I made it through only one night. The next morning, I woke to see my husband standing over me."

"Curtis," Sonya said softly.

"I don't get how all this is connected," Sharon said, rubbing her head.

"Let me finish," Laura continued. "For Sonya's birthday this past April, I went to a coin collector, out in Kennesaw, to find a nice coin necklace for Sonya. After I purchased the coin, I just kept it in the closet. From what I can figure, Curtis got his hand on an authentic Aztec coin and also hid it in the closet. When it was time for me to have my coin encased in a gold band and made into a necklace, I took the wrong one."

Small beacons of light lit both Sonya and Sharon's eyes.

"Curtis sold the wrong coin to this big-time Mafia-type guy. I believe Curtis said his name was Gae ... Gaetano, or something like that. When the guy found out that Curtis sold him the wrong coin, he gave Curtis a certain amount of time to come up with the real one or return his money. But Curtis had already invested that money into something else dirty and didn't have the cash—"

"So he faked his own death?" Sonya broke in on the story.

"Surely this Mafia guy would find that too coincidental," Sharon reasoned.

"The death thing was only to buy himself some more time," Laura added.

"So that whole night was staged?" Sonya asked in amazement.

"I don't know. Maybe after I passed out, the idea came to him. I'm not sure."

"This all makes perfect sense," Sonya reflected.

"I'm glad you think so," Sharon replied. "I don't understand where Sergeant Freeman fits into all this."

"Maybe he works for this Mafia guy," Sonya suggested, shrugging her shoulders.

"The police are in on this?" Laura asked with a look of astonishment.

"I'm afraid so," Sonya answered, shaking her head.

"So what are we going to do? We can't go to the police," Laura half-whispered.

"I know." Sonya crossed her arms, then tried to think of a solution to their situation.

"We could go to the district attorney's office. Don't they investigate the police?"

"I don't know, but it's worth a try." Sonya leaned over and picked up the phone while Sharon began to relay the events that had happened while Laura was away.

Sonya hung up the phone the same moment Laura squealed, "Twenty million dollars?"

"Can you believe the district attorney's office doesn't work past five o'clock?" Sonya asked with a disgusted look.

"They're not there?" Laura asked.

"No one answered the phone."

"So what now?" Sharon moaned.

"We need to find help to free Mr. Hamilton,"—Laura looked toward her sister, "—or Dwayne . . . from that building."

"You know where Dwayne is being held?" Sonya leaned in and grabbed Laura by the arm.

"They're in the same building I just escaped from. In fact, he helped me get out," Laura replied, turning her attention to Sharon.

"They?" Sharon asked.

"Yes, he and Malik." Laura looked back at Sonya. "Do you remember Malik Moyers from Techwood?"

"So Curtis is this 'C.J.' William is spouting out about." Sonya's hand absently went to her necklace. Out of habit, she rolled the thin chain between her fingers as she digested this new information.

"William?" Laura asked.

"Malik's brother," Sonya answered.

"Little Billy? Is he involved in this whole thing, too?"

"No, he's just looking for his brother," Sonya said.

"We have to call him and let him know where his brother is," Sharon reminded Sonya.

"And start a war?" Sonya retaliated, shaking her head. "Too

many people have been hurt already. No, we're going to have to do this on our own.''

''Are you crazy? I don't know about you, but I have had more than my share of *Cagney and Lacey* to last me for the rest of my life. I think we need to wait until tomorrow and talk to the D.A's office,'' Sharon responded.

''They could kill your brother tonight,'' Sonya snapped.

Sharon and Laura were silent. Sonya stood and paced the floor. ''There has to be some way we can help Dwayne and Malik,'' Sonya mumbled.

''Then maybe our best hope is to go to William. At least he has an army of men behind him,'' Sharon insisted.

Sonya gave her a disapproving look.

''Sonya, where else can we go? We are three women. What can we possibly do?'' Sharon continued to reason.

Sonya knew Sharon was right. Her mind was a blank—there wasn't a thing the three of them could do.

''All right, we'll call William.''

Dwayne and Malik had been imprisoned in their rooms only an hour before Dwayne freed his hands from the tight ropes.

''How did you learn to do that?'' Malik asked while Dwayne began untying his hands.

''I wanted to be the next Houdini when I was a child,'' Dwayne replied.

''A handy trade,'' Malik joked as he stood up from the chair. ''Now how do we get ourselves out of this joint?''

''The ceiling.''

Malik glanced up. ''The ceiling?''

''Yeah, you're not still afraid of heights, are you?'' Dwayne started stacking the chairs on top of one another.

When Malik didn't answer, Dwayne shook his head. ''I can't get over a big ox like you afraid of heights,'' Dwayne joked.

''Let's just get this over with,'' Malik said with a brave voice.

Dwayne hid a smirk. ''After you.''

Malik climbed the first chair with no problem. But when it came to the next chair, his body froze with one knee on the second chair and the other leg still glued to the first chair.

Dwayne shook his head. "Come on, Malik, you can do it," Dwayne tried to reassure.

Malik moved to the second chair and stood on his wobbly legs. Dwayne coaxed him into lifting up his arms and pushing up the cardboard ceiling panel with his hands.

Fifteen minutes later, Dwayne had finally gotten Malik through the top of the ceiling. He quickly climbed up after him. They balanced their weight along the wooden panel strips between the cardboard. As they moved along, Malik could no longer see he was actually on a ceiling, which caused him to relax.

Dwayne and Malik made it to the roof, and as expected Malik took one look over the side of the building and froze.

"Please don't do this. We're almost free," Dwayne pleaded.

Malik didn't respond.

Dwayne threw his hands in the air. He knew what he had to do. He pulled Malik away from the edge of the roof and like magic, Malik came out of his coma.

"I hate to do this to you, buddy." Without another word, Dwayne swung his fist across the giant's jaw, and he instantly sank to the ground.

Dwayne waved his hand in the air, trying to ease the stinging pain. *He has to be made out of stone.* Taking off both their shirts, he tied and looped shirts so he could strap Malik to his back and drag him down the platform fire escape.

After he placed Malik on the ground, he tried to revive him. Unfortunately Malik woke up swinging. One punch landed firmly across Dwayne's jaw, knocking him back a few feet.

"Man, calm down. It's me," Dwayne hissed, rubbing his chin.

Malik glanced around anxiously. "Where are we?"

Dwayne blinked to clear the stars that danced before his eyes. *What did he hit me with? A ton of bricks?*

"We're off the roof, if that's what you're concerned about."

Malik's shoulders slumped slightly. "Thanks, man."

"You sure have a funny way of showing your gratitude." Dwayne chuckled. "Here put your shirt back on." Dwayne put his on also.

Malik stood up and dusted off his leather pants with his hands. "Let's get the hell out of here." Malik started walking.

"You know where we are?" Dwayne asked.

"I know the streets of Atlanta like the back of my hand. Of course I know where we are."

Dwayne stayed close behind, but the paranoia of someone following them kept him turning around every few seconds.

Suddenly there were voices filtering down the small alley. Dwayne turned to tell Malik, but he had already heard them and had placed a silencing finger before his lips. Then he pointed toward a large Dumpster located a few feet down the alley.

Dwayne's first instincts were to shake his head, but as the voices grew louder, he agreed and followed Malik into the Dumpster.

Curtis stormed down the alley with his men. "Where in the hell are they?" he barked at no one in particular. His men searched the alley but came up empty.

"Maybe they've already made it to the main road," someone suggested.

"Do you think?" came Curtis's sharp reply. The man fell silent.

"I want them found. I can't lose everything in one day. I can't afford for him to make it back to town. I won't have any bargaining power to get that necklace. As long as Sonya thinks I have the lawyer, I have a better chance of her handing over that damn coin," Curtis shouted.

More men scattered down the alley to search for Dwayne and Malik.

"If you find them, this time I want them dead. That's less trouble for me to deal with."

"But what about the necklace?" someone asked.

Dwayne listened as Curtis stood outside the dumpster.

"Sonya will never need to know. Just as long as she thinks I have him. Do I make myself clear? If you find them, kill them."

Francis Freeman sat in his office tapping his fingers nervously against his desk. Beads of perspiration formed along his brow. The last few hours were spent agonizing over his next move. A thousand excuses ran through his head. What was he going to tell Mr. Gaetano? He'd promised to deliver the Amaceo coin. He studied the medals and plaques that hung on his walls, then a deep sense of dread crept into his bones. How could he have sacrificed his career for this?

His subconscious knew the answer to that question. It was his chance to retire with more than a gold watch from the department. It was his chance to go out with a bang. He deserved this break for all the years of putting his life on the line. But nothing had worked out as planned. There was too much attention being drawn to Miss Walters and her sister. Now, Internal Affairs had started asking questions.

Freeman opened his top drawer and pulled out his blood pressure medicine. It wouldn't be long before a connection between Officer Samuel Coleman and himself was made. His only hope was to get his hands on that damn coin and get out of Atlanta. The problem now was locating Sonya.

Freeman's eyes darted to his clock. Time was running out. Cradling his head between his hands, he tried to come up with a solution. *There has to be something that I'm overlooking.*

The sudden ringing of the phone scaled ten years off Freeman's life. He felt an immediate acceleration of his heart while his temples throbbed. He reached to answer the phone.

"Freeman." He failed to conceal the tension in his voice.

"We need to meet," came the familiar voice of Mr. Gaetano.

"I've asked you not to call me on this line." Freeman stood up from his chair.

"We need to talk," Gaetano repeated.

Freeman shook his head against the phone. He recognized the dangerous tone in Gaetano's voice.

"I'm . . . um . . . busy right now. I can call you with an available time and place," Freeman reasoned.

"I will be in your office in twenty minutes. I suggest that you don't leave."

The line went dead. Freeman continued to hold the phone. *What am I going to do?* He glanced up to his clock. Seven o'clock. He had twenty minutes to come up with a plan, and time was of the essence.

Sonya, Laura, and Sharon sat across the table at the busy pool hall and talked to William. The deadly look in his eyes warned them not to leave anything out.

William listened. A dark expression covered his face. Occasionally he would nod his head, but it was apparent to each of the women that he was not happy about what he was hearing.

"C.J. is your husband?" William finally asked while signaling men from behind them.

Laura nodded, then looked to Sonya, who in turn, tried to give an encouraging smile. But Sonya's hackles stood at full attention. She didn't like this place. Everyone's eyes were glued to William's table. She couldn't help but catch every movement of William's men out of the corner of her eye.

"Do you think you can find the building you were held in?" William interrogated.

"Yes—"

Sonya cut into the conversation. "I don't want my sister going back down there. She told me the location. I will be more than happy to show you, but I don't want Laura going back there."

William's gaze shifted to Sonya with a curious brow lifted. "That's fine with me. I just want to find my brother."

"Then what?" Sharon asked.

William's stone-chiseled face broke into a slow smile. "Now

don't you go worrying your pretty head about it. If your brother is with Malik, I will return him safely to you."

"I don't like the sound of that. What exactly are you planning to do?" Sharon insisted.

William's demeanor visibly didn't change, but his voice reflected his impatience. "The less you know, Mrs. Ellis, the better off you'll be. Don't you agree?"

Sharon held his dark gaze for a brief moment before nodding in agreement.

William looked to the bodyguards that stood behind the women and barked out orders. "Take the women back to the Sundial Motel, and meet me back here in an hour."

The women stood up from their small table.

"Except for her," William pointed to Sonya. "She stays."

Sonya's stomach lurched, but she held her brave facade. Laura clutched Sonya's arm, her concern mirrored in her face.

"It's all right," Sonya assured her.

Laura refused to move until Sonya gently pried her fingers from her arm.

"Trust me, Laura." Sonya leaned in and hugged Laura while whispering into her ear, "I'll be back."

Sharon touched Sonya's shoulder. Sonya turned to her.

"I think I should be the one that goes. Dwayne is my brother."

Sonya was silent for a moment, then answered, "I know, but I love him. He wouldn't be in this mess had it not been for me. Let me do this."

Sharon gave a weak smile while her eyes glossed over. "Are you sure?"

"I'm positive."

"I hate to break up the soap opera," William interrupted, "but it's time to move."

Sonya gave Laura her motel key, then leaned in to whisper, "There is a gun in one of my bags at the motel. Keep it for protection."

Laura nodded. "I will."

Sonya then watched as Laura and Sharon were led out of

the pool hall without a chance for either of them to change their minds. She was putting her trust in William. But it was the only way to help Dwayne.

James paced the lobby of the Sundial Motel. He stopped in midstride, the moment his wife and Laura walked through the door. In two angry steps, he stood before Sharon. "Where on earth have you been?"

Sharon looked over her shoulder to see William's men backing out the lobby. She turned to her husband with a bright smile. "Everything is fine, honey."

James's face sagged the moment he recognized Sonya's sister. "Laura?" He looked from Sharon to Laura, waiting for at least one of them to tell him what was going on. "Where have you been? Everybody has been looking for you." He continued after neither of them volunteered any information.

"James, calm down," Sharon said in an sugary tone. "Let's go up to Sonya's room, and we'll talk there. Laura is tired and needs her rest."

James allowed his wife to lead him toward the elevator. Laura walked silently ahead of them.

"Sharon, this time I don't want you to leave anything out," James warned.

The threesome made it the second floor as James persisted on getting answers.

Laura unlocked the door, blocking out James and Sharon's conversation. Her mind was occupied with thoughts of Sonya. *If William is successful in rescuing Dwayne and Malik, will that mean the end of this madness?* She doubted it. *What we need is to get that coin to the right people. But who?* She pushed open the door just when the bedside lamp clicked on.

Laura jumped back, hitting Sharon, who stood directly behind her.

"Come in," a stranger's voice instructed them.

"Who are you?" James thundered, stepping in front of the two women in a protective gesture.

Sharon released a startled scream when six men suddenly appeared behind them.

"Please," the stranger said, signaling for them to enter the room.

The threesome looked among themselves before following the man's instructions. The door was shut firmly by the last man entering the room.

"I knew we should have changed motels," Sharon moaned.

Laura propelled a brave chin forward and watched each man cautiously. All seven were dressed in identical black suits.

"Let me introduce myself. I'm Lieutenant Stephen Rayford with the Federal Bureau of Investigation."

"The FBI?" Sharon and James asked in unison.

The lieutenant nodded.

"May we see some sort of proof?" Laura asked sarcastically.

As if on cue, all seven men pulled out wallets that displayed their badges.

Laura inspected Lieutenant Rayford's badge, then crossed her arms. "That could be fake."

Rayford gave a tight grin. "Ma'am, we are only here to help."

"Who said we needed help?" Laura continued.

Rayford held up his hands as if to ward off the abusive tone. "The FBI has been on this case for well over a year now, Mrs. Durden. That coin your husband stole has landed you into nothing but trouble."

"What coin?" James asked, looking at Sharon.

"Shh, not now, honey. I'll tell you later," Sharon responded.

"The Amaceo coin," Rayford answered.

Laura clenched her jaws. "So what do you want from us?"

Rayford stood, showing his complete six-foot frame. His dark brooding eyes pierced her as much as his next statement. "We want you to help us hunt down your husband."

The room's silence thickened before James asked his next question. "Isn't her husband dead?"

Rayford lifted a curious brow in James's direction just as Sharon elbowed him to remain quiet.

"Why would I want to help you?" Laura finally asked.

"Come on now, Mrs. Durden. I'm sure you want this nightmare to end for both you and your sister."

"You mean to tell me that the FBI knew what was going on this entire time?" Sharon asked incredulously.

"We were about to close in on Curtis Durden about a month back. But his staged death threw us off track."

"How was he able to stage his death?" James asked, trying to keep up with the conversation. "Wouldn't the police know that wasn't his body?"

"Unless the police are in on it," Sharon said, looking to Rayford for confirmation.

"I see you've put a lot together," Rayford acknowledged. "Yes, the Bureau has connected Sergeant Freeman with Mr. Durden—that is until Curtis decided to cut him out of the deal."

Sharon tried to understand everything. "So Freeman helped stage his death, then when Curtis refused to cut him in . . ."

"He made a deal with Mr. Gaetano himself," Rayford finished for her.

"Who is Gaetano?" James asked.

"Mafia."

The threesome became deathly quiet. Laura held the lieutenant's gaze for a long time before saying, "So what do you need for me to do?"

Chapter Thirty-One

Dwayne and Malik climbed from the Dumpster after hours of waiting for the coast to clear.

"I can't believe I got in there," Dwayne mumbled.

"You're alive, so it served its purpose." Malik wiped the trash from his clothes.

"Where do we go now?"

"My brother owns a billiards joint not too far from here. We can at least get a bath and something decent to wear."

"Lead the way." Dwayne followed Malik down a dark alley while the moonlight served as their only guide. "Are you sure you know where you're going?"

"We're almost there," Malik whispered over his shoulder. "There it is."

Dwayne spotted the small building across the street. "Your brother owns that place?"

"Trust me. It may not look like much, but William is definitely making loot."

Dwayne shrugged. "Whatever, as long as I can get a bath and fresh clothes, he's all right by me."

"Well then, follow me."

Malik entered the small pool hall, surprised to find it empty.

"Yeah, business is really booming," Dwayne observed.

"Something's wrong."

Dwayne followed Malik to the back. When they opened a door, an army of men turned and pointed automatic weapons at them. "Friendly business your brother has here," Dwayne whispered, drawing his hands above his head.

"Dwayne!"

Dwayne recognized Sonya's voice seconds before she raced from the back of the room with outstretched arms. He opened his arms and embraced her. He leaned his head down against hers as she continued to squeeze him.

Catching a good whiff of his clothes, Sonya pulled back to pinch her nose. "Oh, my. Where have you been?"

"It's a long story." Dwayne tried to fold her back into his arms, but she gently pulled away.

"Well, if it isn't my big bro'," William greeted, walking into the room. All weapons descended. William approached his brother; however, he walked only as far as Sonya when their scent hit him. "Damn, man, where have you been?"

"Can we talk about that later? I would really like to take a bath and get some clean clothes, if you don't mind."

"You'll get no argument from me," William answered, taking a step back. "Follow me." He waved to both Malik and Dwayne.

Sonya followed. She didn't want to be alone with William's men. She was ecstatic to see Dwayne.

William led them to the rooms located above the pool hall. "You'll find everything you need in these rooms. Malik, I'll have to send someone to get you something to wear. None of the clothes I have will fit you."

Dwayne smiled and slapped Malik on the back. William entered one room, but quickly returned with a stack of clothes for Dwayne.

"I'm sure you can find something here that will fit you."

"Thanks." Dwayne accepted the clothes, then walked to a vacant room. Sonya followed two steps behind.

"Dwayne, there's so much I have to tell you," she began.

Dwayne closed the door, and before Sonya could say anything else, he crushed her body to his. He gave her an overpowering kiss that sent her mind reeling. His arms moved around her waist, drawing her even closer. "I've missed you," he whispered, pulling his lips away to nibble on her ear.

Sonya drew in a ragged breath as she tried to hang on to her deteriorating composure. Her head felt light, and she was once again floating on a familiar cloud. When Dwayne stepped away from her, Sonya's body screamed in protest.

"I'll be right back." Dwayne went into the bathroom where Sonya heard him turn on the water. She waited patiently as he took his shower. There was so much she needed to tell him.

Later after Sonya had shower and changed, Dwayne emerged from the bathroom, wearing a pair of black jeans and matching Tee-shirt.

"Dwayne, how did you escape from Curtis's men?"

"So Laura did make it back to you?"

Sonya nodded. "She's back at the motel. Hopefully by now Sharon has moved everything to a safer spot."

"Safer? Did something else happen while I was away?"

"What didn't happen? I was drugged, chased—"

"Drugged? Chased?" Dwayne walked over to her. "Are you hurt?"

Sonya turned from him, determined to finish telling him everything. "Sergeant Freeman is in this up to here." She leveled her hand over her head for emphasis.

"What?" Dwayne thundered.

"Oh, Dwayne, that's what I've been trying to tell you. This whole thing has gotten out of control."

"Wait a minute." Dwayne pinched the bridge of his nose. "Sergeant Freeman and Curtis Durden are in this together?"

Sonya calmed down so she could explain everything clearly to him. She watched the look of disbelief cover his features as she filled him in. When she finished, Dwayne leaned against a desk deep in thought.

"You mean to tell me, all this has been over your coin necklace?" Dwayne shook his head.

"It is estimated at twenty million dollars."

Dwayne stood at hearing that. "We need to call the authorities."

"But the police are in on it."

"Then we'll call the FBI. Somebody has to be looking for that coin."

Sonya paced the room.

"What do you think we should do?" He wasn't sure what Sonya was thinking.

Sonya turned toward him. "I don't know what we should do. I don't even know who we should trust. Nobody is who they appear to be." Sonya held up her hand and began counting. "Richard, Freeman, Carmen . . . "

Dwayne cocked an eyebrow. "Carmen?"

Sonya wanted to kick herself. She forgot to tell him about Carmen. "I'm not sure about all the details just yet, but Carmen . . . Carmen is dead."

Dwayne blinked, then stared at her. "Dead?"

"After Freeman drugged me, I woke up in an apartment. I found Carmen's body there."

"I see."

Sonya waited while Dwayne turned his back to her.

After a long, deathly silence, he spoke. "Do you know who's responsible?"

When he faced her again, Sonya squared her shoulders, to prepare for more bad news.

"Anthony's dead also."

Sonya's eyes widened. "Oh, my God."

Sonya closed her eyes as a wave of anger and helplessness washed over her. With every discovery, she felt overwhelmed.

Dwayne closed the gap between them and enclosed Sonya in his arms. She laid her head against his shoulder and sought comfort in his embrace.

"We'll get through this together," he promised.

Sonya felt his head lying against her own. She inhaled his

fresh scent. Gently Dwayne tipped her head back to capture her lips in a sweet, tantalizing kiss.

A sharp knock at the door jolted them back to reality.

"Who is it?" Dwayne called out.

Sonya stepped out of his arms.

"It's me, Malik."

"Come in," Dwayne instructed.

Malik entered the small room. "I think you two need to come downstairs."

Within minutes, Malik, Sonya, and Dwayne descended the stairs. She was shocked to find the number of people had increased by at least a dozen.

"Miss Walters?" a man dressed in a black suit asked as he stepped into the center of the floor.

Sonya looked around and saw Laura, Sharon, and James. "What's going on?"

"Miss Walters, I'm Special Agent Stephen Rayford." The man flashed a badge. "I'm with the Federal Bureau of Investigation. I was hoping I could ask you a couple of questions."

Sonya watched the man with mixed emotions. *Why am I not happy to see this man?* After a month of deceitful people, she wasn't about to blindly trust this man without proof. "What kind of questions?" she asked with both hands on her hips.

"First of all, I need you to hand over the coin."

Sonya kept her eyes leveled with Agent Rayford's. "And what coin is that?"

"The Amaceo coin. It was stolen from the Chansler Museum in New York. It's my job to retrieve it." He edged closer to the staircase. "You can make this a lot easier on everyone if you just hand it over."

Dwayne shook his head. "We need more proof than a possibly fake badge."

Sonya nodded in agreement.

Agent Rayford glared at Sonya. She glared back. His eyes resembled jet-black marbles. He was tall, very muscular and working-man hard—then suddenly his face broke into a smile, a warm, contagious smile. He reached into his jacket and pulled out his badge again. This time, he walked over and handed it to her.

Sonya inspected Rayford's badge, then handed it back. She didn't know whether it was a real badge or not, but she had no other choice than to play along.

"I don't have the coin," she confessed. "I hid it."

"Where?"

Sonya stepped from the last stair and walked to a nearby pool table. She hid the coin a few moments before Dwayne and Malik had showed up. She reached inside a corner pocket and pulled it out. Before she could turn around, Rayford reached out and took the coin.

"I'm glad it's over," Dwayne said as Sonya slid back into his arms. She ignored the heightened eyebrows from Laura and Sharon.

"Not quite," Agent Rayford announced. "We need you to help us capture Curtis Durden."

"Help you? How?" Sonya asked with a sinking feeling.

"We need you to help lure Curtis with this coin—"

"Come again?" Dwayne interrupted.

"Durden needs the coin back. We need Durden. We'll set up a meeting to make him think he's getting the coin. Then we'll catch him. It's that simple."

"I don't see anything simple about it," Sonya protested. "How do you suppose we get this meeting with Curtis? Just call him on the phone? Invite him over for tea?"

Rayford smiled at her sarcasm. "I'm sure we can get a message delivered." Rayford singled William out from the crowd with a hard, penetrating look.

"It could be arranged," William replied.

"Tell him that Miss Walters wants to exchange the coin for her freedom. He'll believe that. It's important that he thinks that you just want him off your back. He'll meet you. He's a desperate man."

Sonya looked at Dwayne.

"What do you want to do?" he asked, touching her shoulders gently.

Sonya debated on her next move. Curtis would continue to haunt her and Laura until he had what he wanted. With that in mind, she had no choice but to go along with Agent Rayford's plan. "All right, I'll do it."

Twenty-four hours later, Dwayne sat in Sonya's bathroom, running her a hot bath. "I think it's ready," he called out.

Sonya appeared in front of the bathroom door. "I can't begin to tell you what a relief it is to be home."

"You look tired."

"I'm nervous. What if something goes wrong?"

"Nothing will go wrong. The FBI is taking care of everything."

Sonya shook her head. "I don't know."

"Come on. You need to take a long hot bath to relax. Everyone will be here in a couple of hours. There are two agents posted on the grounds now. You're safe."

Sonya wanted to believe him. "Maybe you're right."

Dwayne stood and walked over to her. "I know I'm right." He leaned down and gave her a long, intoxicating kiss. When he pulled away, Sonya smiled up at him.

Dwayne returned to the edge of the marble and granite tub. His eyes brimmed with passion as Sonya held his gaze. Slowly she moved in front of him, feeling her own passion mounting. When she lifted her cotton T-shirt, she displayed to Dwayne a beautiful, black-laced bra. Her hardened nipples told of her body's excitement. Dwayne reached up and ran his thumbs along the lacy texture.

Her body exploded with tingling sensations as she unfastened her bra.

Dwayne turned off the water and stood before Sonya. With a smile, she held up his shirt and tossed it into the air. His upper torso was exposed to the warmth of her gaze. She slid her hands to his belt buckle.

"Let me," he offered.

"This is part of my pleasure," she protested.

"You mean part of my torment."

Sonya continued to undress him while feeling his body's muscles flex and relax beneath her touch. When she finished, she allowed him to undress her.

His movements were slow and deliberate, causing her to take in sharp breaths of air.

Dwayne stepped into the steaming hot water, then offered his hand to Sonya.

She entered the water, ignoring the first sting surrounding her legs. Her eyes watched Dwayne as he sat in the tub.

"We're in luck. This tub seems long enough for the two of us," he whispered.

Sonya nodded and took a seat facing him on his right leg. She reached for the bar of soap lying in its dish and gently began rubbing his body until he was covered with white suds. Their eyes remained locked together. Neither spoke. Both just enjoyed the feel of one another.

Slowly Sonya brought the soap lower. She listened as Dwayne's breathing became shallow and his eyes closed in anticipation of her next move. Her fingers curled around his shaft as she proceeded to stroke and caress him.

She felt her own wave of desire at knowing she had aroused Dwayne to such a state. She studied the whole man—the broad shoulders, the firmly muscled midriff, and slim hips—while her hand explored the silk and steel of his heavy arousal.

Sonya watched his intriguing expressions, then leaned in and kissed him hungrily. Dwayne returned her kiss. The fresh smell of soap enticed Sonya's senses.

In a flash, Dwayne switched positions with Sonya, sending a wave of water to cover the bathroom floor. "Try to tease me, will you?"

Sonya's fingers massaged his hair as he brought his mouth down to her breast and lightly touched the swollen tip with rhythmic, flicking motions of his tongue.

He drew her into his mouth, gradually expanding the circle his tongue made until Sonya closed her eyes against the exquisite sensations. Flashes of light played against her eyelids, and her heartbeat seemed to pulse whenever Dwayne moved his tongue.

"Love me, Dwayne," she pleaded in a voice she hardly recognized.

His fingers raked gently over her abdomen, then lower to take her in a slow, intimate possession. She tightened her muscles at the pleasurable feeling. He relaxed his movements only to begin again. The tip of his tongue caught the edge of her mouth to outline the fullness of her lips before plunging inside.

Sonya released a deep moan and felt her body being lifted from the water. The next thing she knew, Dwayne had placed her on the bed. The silk sheets felt cool, but Dwayne's skin scorched her own.

"Please," she whispered, reaching for him. She was full of sensations, but she felt empty without him.

Dwayne didn't know where he found the strength to be gentle, but with infinite care, he drew Sonya beneath him and entered her.

The first velvet thrust brought her hips upward and pulled him deeper. Again she moaned, surrendering to the fluid pulsing inside her body, the damp rush of hunger for him. Every nerve quivered to life, every impulse centered on the need to absorb him, to deliver herself to him. His hips surged, pressed, invaded, and conquered her body. Sonya's legs twined around his, resisting him every time he drew back. His pace increased, driving her to a pinnacle, pushing her to a moment of perfect unity with him.

Dwayne paid homage to her perfection with his hands and mouth. He whispered words in the hollow of her throat. He closed his eyes and sank into the euphoria of ecstasy. Every inch of her body molded itself with his. He couldn't get enough of her. She was addictive as any drug, and Dwayne was in danger of an overdose.

The familiar wave of pleasure rippled through his body as he clutched her closer. He felt her body vibrate against him, then relax. Soon after, Sonya surrendered into a deep sleep.

* * *

Hours later, Sonya stood before her full-length mirror. She reached above her right breast to feel the tiny microphone. She was nervous. *Can I pull this off?* A tight ball of tension attacked her stomach. A soft comforting hand from Dwayne appeared and gently rubbed her shoulders. She smiled and admired their reflection in the mirror.

"Are you nervous?" he asked.

"That's an understatement." She attempted to laugh. She relaxed and enjoyed the magic his hands performed on her shoulders.

"It will be over soon," he assured her. He placed a light kiss on the back of her head.

"I wish I could believe that."

Dwayne turned her around to face him. "Believe it."

Sonya smiled. "How's Bridget doing?"

"She's a little sore, but she's recovering nicely."

"I'm sure she's happy to be home after a week of being in the hospital."

Dwayne placed another kiss against her forehead. "I am, too." When Dwayne pulled back, he stared in the soft glowing pools of her hazel eyes. There he saw exactly what he had been waiting to see when she looked at him: love. She had never said the words to him, but her actions spoke volumes. He kissed her again.

Sonya wished that she could remain in Dwayne's arms forever. How did this happen to her? She didn't need anybody. She had spent a great deal of her life convincing herself of that. Now she had this big, strong man that would do anything for her, including love her for the rest of her life.

She wanted to say the words to him, she needed to say it, but she was afraid. Afraid that suddenly he would turn into what she experienced all men to be like; dominating, demanding, and violent. No, her heart screamed, he could never be that.

Sonya pulled away to look at him, "Did you get in contact with Anthony's family?"

"Yeah. The funeral is tomorrow. Carmen's is Wednesday," he said solemnly.

"Dwayne, I'm so sorry."

"You have nothing to be sorry for. It's not your fault. Tonight we're going to get the one who is responsible for all of this."

A knock sounded at the door. "Sonya," Laura called out. Sonya rushed to answer it. "What's wrong?"

"You have to come see this." Laura grabbed her hand and practically dragged her into the guest room where the news was on.

"This just in. The body of Sergeant Francis M. Freeman, from the Atlanta Police Department, was found late last night in College Park. The police department has issued no official statement but is said to be baffled by the execution-style killing of one of their top men."

"Dear God," Sonya whispered. Suddenly she felt her knees weaken. "You don't think that Curtis killed Sergeant Freeman?"

"We doubt it," Agent Rayford answered from the door's entrance. "Mr. Gaetano has been spotted in town."

"How would you know that?" Dwayne asked with a frown.

"It's my job to know, Mr. Hamilton."

"Mr. Gaetano?" Sonya asked Rayford.

"He's no one to tangle with. He claims his profession is a jack-of-all-trades, and none of them is legal."

"Then why would he kill Freeman if he was working for him?" Laura asked.

Rayford's expression became serious. "Freeman couldn't deliver what Gaetano wanted—the Amaceo coin."

Sonya shook her head. *Will this ever end?*

"It's almost time. Are you ready, Miss Walters?"

"Do you think that he'll show up?" Sonya asked the agent.

"William's man said that he was more than willing to meet with you," Rayford replied with an encouraging smile.

"But how safe will she be?" Dwayne asked, looping a protective arm around Sonya's shoulders.

"We have men placed all around the designated place. She'll be safe, Mr. Hamilton. You can trust me on this."

"Well, let's get this over with," Sonya said with fake enthusiasm.

Rayford smiled. "Let's go."

Curtis smelled a rat. Something wasn't right. This was too easy, but what other choice did he have? He had to get his hands on that coin. Word of Mr. Gaetano's arrival had spread like wildfire on the streets. He knew that Gaetano had something to do with Frank's death—it was probably a warning to him. He needed that damn coin before he was next on Gaetano's hit list.

Frank had made the same mistake he had. He should have never dealt with an untouchable Mafia godfather.

Curtis went over his plan in his mind. He couldn't afford to allow anything else to go wrong. His men had already taken their places. He didn't believe in taking any chances. This could be a setup.

Underground Atlanta flowed with its usual crowd on a Saturday night. Couples passed Sonya while they held hands and laughed at the night's festivities. The crowd was exactly what Sonya had hoped for. She felt safer to do 'the exchange' here.

She inhaled the fresh air, wanting desperately for the night to be over. She spotted Dwayne across the street. He wore a pair of baggy blue jeans with an oversized Falcon jersey. His matching cap was pointed backward to complete his disguise as he blended with the crowd perfectly.

Having him as a protector relaxed her even more. Nothing could go wrong.

"Hello, Sonya," Curtis's familiar voice said from behind her.

He's early. Sonya's eyes widened in horror, but before she could turn around he stopped her.

"Not so fast. Act normal," he commanded.

A large crowd of people obstructed her view of Dwayne. *He can't see me.*

"A nice ensemble of people you showed up with."

"I don't know what you're talking about," Sonya lied.

"I'm sure you don't. Walk."

Doesn't anybody see him? Where is everybody?

Sonya did as she was told. The moment she walked around a corner, everything went black.

Chapter Thirty-Two

Back at the FBI building . . .

"Your plan failed," Dwayne roared, sending an empty glass to shatter against the office wall.

Rayford's men flinched from Dwayne's venomous tone.

The office grew quiet as Rayford stood up from his desk to glare at Dwayne. "You need to calm down, Mr. Hamilton. My men are on top of the situation right now."

"Do your men know where Curtis took her?"

Rayford was silent.

"What happens to her when he discovers he has a fake coin? Have your men thought of that?"

"Fake? The coin was a fake?" Rayford shouted. His anger flared in his eyes.

"You don't think she was stupid enough to trust any of you idiots with the real thing, did you?"

"Then where in the hell is the real coin?"

Dwayne leaned over Rayford's desk with a balled fist. "I have it. I am the only one she trusts."

Rayford came around his desk to stand in front of Dwayne. "Give me the coin, Mr. Hamilton."

"Nobody gets anything until Sonya is found and returned safely to me."

As Rayford glared, Dwayne watched the muscles along the agent's jaw twitch.

"I could have you arrested," he finally retaliated.

"Then you will never find that coin."

"Mr. Hamilton, it's my job—"

"Your job was to protect Sonya. Why in the hell couldn't you do your job then?"

The steady hum of an incoherent operator over Rayford's walkie-talkie filled the room. Dwayne fought for control. This man had guaranteed him Sonya's safety, and now she was gone. "I want her back."

"We're doing all we can, Mr. Hamilton."

Dwayne turned his back to the incompetent agent. He didn't want him to see the fear creeping into his eyes. He couldn't lose Sonya like this. Curtis Durden was a smart man—he proved that tonight—but he was also a desperate man, and that made him dangerous.

"You are making a big mistake by not handing over that coin. Perhaps I should give you some time alone to really think it over," Rayford replied before he and his men left the office.

Dwayne heard the soft click of the door. *Is that it? We're doing the best we can. Sonya's life depends on these agents.*

Dwayne sat in the empty office and listened to the agents buzz outside the door. There had to be more he could do. The doorknob turned, and Dwayne jumped to his feet. Slowly a small head peeked in.

"Bridget," he whispered with outstretched arms.

She entered the room, then raced to him. They embraced. Dwayne was careful not to crush her bandaged shoulder. They held each other for a long moment as they both sought comfort from one another.

"I was so worried about you." Bridget pulled away.

Dwayne touched her cheek gently. "Thank you." He withdrew his hand, but she grabbed and held it in her own.

"I care about her, too."

Dwayne stared at his daughter, who had fresh tears trailing down her face. "We're going to find her."

Bridget nodded and forced a weak smile. "I hope so."

Her simple statement touched Dwayne's heart. He squeezed Bridget's hand for added comfort. "Maybe this is a good time to talk. There is something I want to discuss with you. It's about Sonya."

Bridget remained silent.

"I know that this might come as a shock to you, or you may have a lot of questions—"

"Do you love her?" Bridget interrupted.

Dwayne's thumb gently massaged the knuckles of her hand. "More than anything."

She smiled. "I do, too."

Dwayne clutched his daughter again. "I'm so happy to hear you say that."

"Dwayne?" Malik rushed into the room.

Dwayne and Bridget released their embrace.

"I have a lead," Malik announced "We gotta move. One of William's men spotted Curtis's crew out in Marietta. We better go if we want to catch them."

"I'm coming." Dwayne turned to his daughter. "You stay right here. Go stay with your aunt Sharon and uncle James downstairs until I get back."

Bridget grabbed his arm. "Shouldn't we tell Agent Rayford?"

Dwayne looked at Malik, who in turn shook his head. "I think we ought to go alone on this one, sweetheart."

"But Daddy . . . "

"Bridget, trust me."

"Daddy, I'm scared. What if something happens to you?"

"I'll be all right, honey." Dwayne tried to reassure her, but her grip tightened.

"Why can't we inform Agent Rayford?"

"They've already botched one job," Malik answered for Dwayne.

"Look, sweetheart, I'll make you a deal. If we're not back here in three hours, you can tell Rayford where we've gone. Deal?"

Bridget looked from her Dad to Malik, then nodded in agreement.

"Malik, where in Marietta are we headed?"

"The Cambridge Apartments off Atlanta Road."

"You got that, Bridget?"

Bridget nodded again, then grabbed her father for another hug.

"I'll be back," Dwayne whispered, kissing her forehead.

The two men left the office building and headed toward Malik's car.

"What are you planning to do with me?" Sonya asked, masking the fear in her voice.

"Stop it with all the questions," Curtis shouted. He looked out the window for the millionth time.

"Are you nervous?" Sonya taunted.

"I'm not the one that needs to be nervous." Curtis gave her a dangerous look, but Sonya forced a cool smile.

"I bet Gaetano's men are looking *mighty* hard for you. This is the second time you've cheated him out of his merchandise."

"Shut up!"

Sonya's head reeled backward from Curtis' powerful backhand. She tasted the blood oozing into her mouth.

"He probably has men stationed at the airport and every bus station in the Metro area," she continued to taunt.

Curtis grabbed her arm and roughly lifted her out of the chair.

Sonya ignored the sharp stab of pain ricocheting throughout her body. She tilted her head up a notch.

"I'm warning you, Sonya. One more peep out of you, and I'll give you something to control that mouth of yours."

Sonya gave him a hard glare. "I'm not afraid of you."

Curtis's grip tightened. "You should. You should be terrified."

Sonya clenched her teeth in anger and resentment. Why was she pushing her luck?

Deep lines of aggravation penetrated his profile. Sonya felt proud to know the source of his frustration. Curtis was on the edge. He released her arm, letting Sonya fall back into her chair.

"I have to find another place," he mumbled.

Sonya's heart skipped a beat. She didn't like the sound of Curtis moving around so much. Her chances of a rescue decreased with every move they made.

"We'll leave in an hour," he said more to himself than to her.

Sonya held back her tears. She would not show him any weakness. She gave him a disgusted look. "They'll find you," she said in a low venomous voice.

"Who? That lawyer boyfriend of yours? I'm shaking in my boots."

Sonya's eyes pierced him to the wall. "He *will* find me," she answered confidently. In her heart, she knew that to be true. Dwayne would find her.

Curtis leaned into her profile until she could feel his breath against her cheek. "I can make it very easy for him, you know. It's up to you. Do you want him to find you dead or alive?"

Laura stood up from her chair in the break room and dropped two quarters in the drink machine. She silently wished she had something stronger than a Coke. They'd been sitting in the FBI's building, waiting to hear something about Sonya. She couldn't stand this waiting. *What will Curtis do with Sonya?*

"Laura, please sit down," Sharon pleaded.

"I can't. I'm too nervous."

"Dwayne is talking to Agent Rayford right now. He'll be back to tell us what's going on," Sharon reasoned.

"He's been up there for a while. Do you think we should go upstairs to make sure everything is all right?"

"He wanted us to stay down here in the break room until he returns."

"She's *my* sister. I have every right to know what's going on."

Sharon held up her hands. "I didn't mean to start up an argument. Let's wait until James comes back from the bathroom, and we'll walk upstairs with you."

Laura ignored her plea. "I'm going up."

Sharon stood up from her chair. "Well, wait for me."

They made it to the bay and waited for an elevator to arrive. Laura smiled at Sharon as she tried to relax. Maybe she was nervous about nothing. Then Laura thought she saw a familar face walk past the other end of the bay.

She walked around Sharon.

"What's wrong?"

"Nothing. I just thought I saw someone I know." A nagging feeling wouldn't let her dismiss what she saw.

"Where are you going?" Sharon asked as she followed Laura.

"I just want to see who that man is."

"What man?"

Laura ignored her question and continued along the hallway, searching for the familar face. Soon she came upon hushed, yet angry voices.

"How in the hell was I to know that she gave me a fake coin? I'm no coin expert," Rayford's voice boomed.

"Gaetano is not going to like this."

"What are we going to do? Without that coin, we are two dead men."

Laura gasped at what she heard.

"Oh, my God," Sharon whispered.

Laura placed a silencing finger over her lips, then continued to listen in on Rayford's conversation.

"You mean to tell me you replaced a fake with another fake?" the other man's voice boomed.

"Keep your damn voice down. You want the whole building to know what's going on?"

"What difference does it make? We're dead anyway."

"We have to get that damn coin from Hamilton," Rayford mumbled.

"And how do we do that?"

"Hell, we could take his daughter or sister. Take some damn body. All I know is, I didn't risk my job for this sh—"

Laura leaned against the door too hard. Before she knew it, she and Sharon tumbled into the room.

"What in the hell?" Rayford shouted, going around the women to shut the door.

Laura and Sharon quickly jumped to their feet.

"What in the hell do we do now?" the man Laura recognized as Benjamin said.

Rayford drew his gun. "You get back down to the Cambridge Apartments before Durden discovers you're missing. I'll handle everything here. Maybe we still have a chance of getting that coin."

Laura remembered the gun she had found in Sonya's motel room and hid in her purse.

"Are you sure, man?"

"Yeah, I can handle these two with no problem."

Benjamin looked to the women a final time, then slipped out of the door.

When it was just the three of them, Sharon spoke first. "So what's the real story here?"

Rayford shook his head. "I'm real sorry you've learned about this."

"Spare me," Laura said, crossing her arms. Hoping her movement wouldn't cause attention, she tried to snap open her purse.

"Since you're going to kill us, suppose you tell us the truth. Who are you?"

"I'm who I said I was. Special Agent Stephen Rayford."

"So you really do work for the FBI?"

"If you must know, yes. I work for the FBI. I also work for Mr. Gaetano."

"Damn. This man must have one hell of a payroll," Laura sneered. She pulled open her purse then slowly reached inside. Rayford didn't seem to notice.

"Mr. Gaetano is a very powerful man. His eyes are everywhere."

"Did he really kill Freeman?" Sharon wanted to know.

"Gaetano never dirties his hands."

"So what happens now?" Sharon leveled her eyes with his.

"Now I get that coin from your brother, Mrs. Ellis. That's all. He hands over the coin, and everything will be all right."

"What makes you think he has the coin?"

"He told me himself, Mrs. Durden."

"And you believed him?"

Rayford's smile dropped. "What do you mean?"

"I mean just that. He doesn't have the coin."

Rayford blinked, then shook his head. "I don't believe you."

"Suit yourself."

Rayford lowered his gun slightly to contemplate whether or not to believe her. That was just the break Laura needed. She shouted, *"Duck"* to Sharon while helping to push the woman's head down.

Laura extended her arm with the gun pointed to Rayford and fired.

Rayford had no time to react as he slammed back into the door, dropping his weapon.

Blood poured out of his shoulder as he stared blankly at her.

Sharon retrieved his gun just as the room was swamped with agents.

James pushed his way through the agents, then gathered his wife in his arms. "What happened?"

"He works for Gaetano. He was going to kill us." Sharon buried her face in James's chest.

Agents quickly grabbed both women and tried to handcuff them.

"No. You don't understand," Laura screamed.

"Stand aside," a voice thundered, coming into the room.

The women looked up to see a towering man with jet-black eyes and distorted features enter.

"Who are you?" Laura asked first.

Rayford moaned as a look of defeat shrouded his face.

"I'm Wade Harrison, the agent-in-charge. Suppose someone tells me what the hell is going on in here?"

Chapter Thirty-Three

Malik and Dwayne arrived at the Cambridge Apartments.

"Do you know which apartment?" Dwayne asked. His adrenaline pumped wildly through his veins.

"William has a man stationed in the back."

"How many men work for your brother?"

Malik gave him a you-don't-want-to-know look.

"Hey, isn't that one of Curtis's men?" Dwayne nodded to a man standing nonchalantly in front of an apartment building. It was hard to see the face clearly in the dark, but Dwayne was certain the man worked for Curtis.

In that instant, they were recognized. Curtis's guard wasted no time to draw his weapon and fire at the approaching vehicle. Malik and Dwayne ducked just as two bullets penetrated the windshield.

"Reach inside the glove compartment and get that gun," Malik shouted.

Dwayne did as he was told. "Can you see where you're going?" Dwayne asked, knowing Malik could crash at any second. And he did.

* * *

"We still don't have the real coin," Jack yelled, looking at Curtis.

Curtis's men agreed, shaking their heads in agreement. Curtis eyed every man with contempt. "Don't you think I know we don't have the coin?"

"Do you have a plan to get it back?" someone shouted from the back of the room.

"The FBI must have it. How do you suppose we get it from them," Curtis sneered.

"So we're dead men?" Benjamin asked. Every man in the room knew that Gaetano was in town, and he knew every man working for Curtis. They were in just as much danger as their boss.

"Not necessarily. We still have the girl."

"Mr. Gaetano wants the coin, not the girl," Jack said, shaking his head.

"But she's bargaining power for the FBI," Curtis defended.

"We have company," one man announced, rushing in the door.

"Damn!" Curtis hissed as his men filed out of the small apartment.

Within seconds, the Cambridge Apartments was turned into a battle zone. Dwayne climbed out of Malik's late-model Thunderbird and was instantly encircled by William's men.

"Where is she?" Dwayne yelled to a nearby man.

"She's in that building over there, downstairs."

A bullet whizzed by Dwayne's ear. He ducked lower then tried to calculate a plan to rescue Sonya.

Sonya listened to the gunfire outside of the apartment. *They found me.* She ran to the door of her small room. She knew before she reached the knob that it would be locked. She banged on the door. "Let me out," she screamed. But of course no one heard her cries.

She listened as the battle continued. *What's going on? Who's out there? Is Dwayne here?* She raced to the barred window in hopes of seeing what was happening.

When the door burst open, Sonya jumped. By the angry expression on Curtis's face, she, for the first time in her life, feared him.

"This is all your fault," Curtis accused.

Sonya backed away.

"Come here. You're going to be my ticket out of here."

Sonya took another step. *He's going to hurt me.* Curtis walked farther into the room. Sonya's eyes stayed glued to the opened door. She had to get past him, but how? He edged closer. Sonya felt trapped. There was no way she was going to get past his towering frame, not without a fight—a fight she knew she would lose.

A bullet pierced through the window and hit Curtis directly in his shoulder. He fell to the floor, howling and clutching his wounded shoulder.

Sonya wasted no time racing for the door. She dodged past two surprised men and made it out the front door. Three shots nearly missed her as she made it outside.

"It's Sonya!" Dwayne grabbed Malik's arm. "I have to get to her."

Malik jerked him back. "You can't just waltz through there, you'll get shot."

Sonya crawled to a nearby car and hid. Violent tremors shook her body along with the night's cool air. She searched frantically around her, looking for an avenue of escape. The streetlights were out, making it almost impossible for Sonya to make out her surroundings.

The shooting stopped. Sonya held her breath until a dull ache forced her to expel it. *What happened?* Time seemed to have stopped as Sonya tried to gather the courage to peek around the car. She couldn't see anything. She didn't hear anything. She crept back until her foot hit something solid. Swiftly she turned. She released a startled scream the moment she saw Curtis crouched behind the car with her.

Curtis reached for her, but she sent a powerful kick to his wounded shoulder. Curtis reared back with a thud, giving her plenty of time to jump from behind the car and race down the parking lot. Gunfire immediately erupted.

"I have to go after her!" Dwayne jumped from his secluded spot, giving Malik no time to stop him.

"Dwayne!" he heard Malik call from behind him.

Sonya made it to a gate behind the complex. She made a leaping effort to climb the fence, but her foot was snatched from underneath her. *How did he catch up with me so fast?*

"Come here you little bi . . . ahhh." Sonya again attacked his injured shoulder. By the time Curtis recovered himself, Sonya was halfway over the fence. He leaped to catch her and was again successful in grabbing her foot.

Sonya screamed the moment her body was slammed back into the fence. He had a strong grip on her foot. She swirled to free her foot. Finally her foot slid from her tennis shoe, causing her to fall to the ground, but she had made it over the fence. She forced herself up and disappeared into the woods.

Dwayne made it to the fence just in time to see Curtis disappear into the woods after Sonya. At the sound of approaching footsteps, he sprang around to see Malik coming up behind him.

"What happened?"

"They're in there," Dwayne answered, already climbing the fence.

Malik followed.

The woods became increasingly dense as Sonya struggled to race through them. The low-hanging branches clawed at her arm, leaving long scratches. Curtis had to be coming after her now—she could feel it.

Sonya settled into a jerky rhythm of running and stumbling forward. The ground felt soft beneath her feet.

Then she heard him crashing about behind her. *Faster,* her mind screamed, and she fumbled trying to do just that. There was a clearing just ahead. She made it. But when she took one look around, she realized that she had made it only to an isolated street. She continued running. She knew she couldn't afford for time to become her enemy.

Dwayne made it through the woods, suffering from minor scratches. He looked around the quiet street, not sure which way he should go from here.

"Where did they go?" Malik said, appearing at his side.

"I don't know," Dwayne answered between breaths.

"Let's split up then. You go that way and I'll go this way. Whoever finds Curtis, beat the hell out of him."

"Deal," Dwayne yelled, already running in his pointed direction.

Sonya ran as fast as she could down a dark street. She could feel her heart making loud whumping sounds as she sweated profusely in spite of the nasty, steady, cool night air. Blood pounded furiously in her head, while every muscle and tendon in her body strained. She ran like the wind, crying inside, holding back the tears as she tried to escape.

She passed ghost store after ghost store that were boarded up with dark, rotting plywood and decorated with graffiti.

Faster, faster, her mind screamed. Her neck and arms were on fire and she could feel her stomach clutching hard.

Sonya raced onto a new street just a car screeched to a halt to avoid hitting her.

The driver wore an Atlanta Braves cap pulled to the side, and loud rap music boomed from inside.

"Help me, please," Sonya begged, running toward the driver's side. The man shook his head and screamed that he didn't want to get involved. He then slammed on the accelerator and sped away.

"No! Come back!" Sonya watched the car's taillights fade

into the distance. What was left of her heart sank to the pit of her stomach. Then she heard it: footsteps. He was getting closer.

Sonya turned and continued running down the empty street. She was covered in sweat and her breathing was labored. Her tears were flowing now, blinding her with every step. *Help me,* her mind yelled. *Somebody help me.*

Dwayne sped down another dark street. His blood roared and echoed in his ears. He could feel his heart throbbing hard as his adrenaline pumped furiously. He didn't want to think what could happen to Sonya if Curtis ever caught up with her again.

Dwayne turned down another dark alley. Dead End. Dwayne panicked. *Where are they?*

"No! Come back!" Sonya's voice echoed down the isolated streets. Dwayne followed the direction of her voice. *I'm coming, Sonya. I'm coming.*

Curtis jogged behind Sonya with a sinister smile in place. "I'm going to get you!" he taunted.

Sonya turned abruptly, causing her to fall. Excruciating pain shot through her legs, but she pushed herself up. *Ignore the pain. Keep going.* She ran faster, trying to conquer a steep paved hill. She heard him pounding behind her. He was close, very close.

"Hey, Sonya. I'm right behind you. Here I am."

Sonya turned around. Curiosity and terror got the best of her.

He was gaining easily and laughing at her.

The pain in Sonya's legs slowed her down. All hope of escape fled her. She experienced a jolting moment of shock and disbelief as she cried out in anguish. She was going to die right here.

Out of nowhere, Dwayne flew into the air, tackling Curtis. Their bodies hit the cement with a thud, then rolled down the hill. When they stopped, Dwayne won the top position and delivered a powerful punch across Curtis's jaw.

Curtis bucked, trying to throw Dwayne off him. But Dwayne was obviously the stronger man as another punch made a cracking sound when it connected.

Sonya slumped to the ground, feeling relief when Curtis's body finally went limp beneath Dwayne. It was over. Loud sirens filled the air as Malik trotted up the hill.

Dwayne stood above Curtis's unconscious body. His eyes leveled with Sonya's. She lifted her arms in invitation. Dwayne rushed to her side and encased her in his embrace.

"You came for me," Sonya sobbed between the kisses she showered upon him.

"Of course I came for you, my love."

His words warmed her body. He truly loved her.

She managed to pull away and smile at him. "I love you."

Dwayne's heart burst with joy and love at hearing her accept his love. He gave her a kiss that made them oblivious to the swarming blue lights that now surrounded them. They were lost in world where only they existed.

Epilogue

One year later . . .

Sonya turned from her left profile to her right, to assess her figure in the pearl-colored wedding gown. She took a deep breath to calm her racing heart, but it seemed to pick up its pace with every tick of the clock. In a few minutes, she would be Mrs. Dwayne Hamilton. The sound of the name made her smile as she reflected on the past year.

She glanced at the four-carat diamond ring that sparkled on her left hand, then back to her reflection in the mirror. *This is it.* Hearing a light tap at the door, Sonya bid her guest to enter.

"Are you about ready?" Sharon asked, peering into the room.

"I feel as if I swallowed a jar of butterflies," Sonya answered honestly.

Sharon entered the room with Bridget right behind her. Their strapless turquoise gowns were beautiful, Sonya thought, as they gathered around her.

"That's only normal. You'll be fine," Sharon encouraged.

Bridget nodded in agreement. "I felt the same way last week

at graduation. I kept thinking that I was either going to trip or forget something.''

Sharon looped her arm around Bridget's shoulder. ''We're all so proud of you,'' she said, kissing her niece's forehead.

''So are you ready for college?'' Sonya asked, taking the young girl's hand into her own.

''I guess so. Spelman, ready or not, here I come.''

''Well, we'd better take our places. The music should be starting soon. Is there anything we can do for you?'' Sharon offered.

Sonya inhaled then exhaled slowly. ''No. I think I'm going to be all right.''

''Okay, see you downstairs.''

''Break a leg.'' Bridget placed a kiss on Sonya's cheek.

Sonya turned back toward the mirror. Her nerves were still on edge. Another tap sounded at the door. ''Come in.''

Laura pushed open the door and stepped inside. ''Are you nervous?''

''My knees are about to give out on me,'' Sonya confessed.

Laura's eyes glistened. ''You look beautiful.''

Sonya opened her arms. ''Come here, you.''

Laura rushed and embraced her sister. When they pulled away, they realized they were in danger of losing their makeup.

Sonya turned and grabbed two Kleenex from the table. ''Who would have ever believed that I would be getting married?'' she said as they blotted their eyes.

''I always had hope,'' Dorothy answered from the door.

''Mama.'' Sonya raced to hug her mother.

They remained locked in each other's arms for a brief period of time. Everyone heard the music begin to play.

''I think that's your cue,'' Dorothy said, easing Sonya from her arms. ''We'll see you downstairs.''

The two women left Sonya alone to finish getting ready. When she heard the sound of the organ, her heart seemed to enlarge in her throat. She gathered her courage and smiled one last time in the mirror, then turned to meet her future husband downstairs.

*   *   *

Dwayne straightened his tie for the millionth time. *Why is it so hot in here?* He looked at James, his best man, and noticed his calmness. *Maybe it's just me.* He glanced at the large crowd of people sitting in the pews and shook his head. There, sitting in six rows, were William Gainey and half his gang. He smiled at the sight of William's men arranging and rearranging their suits.

The music started. Soon after the flower girls made their way down the aisle. He watched as Bridget, Sharon, then Laura glided down. Then he became oblivious to everything else as he waited patiently for Sonya to appear.

Sonya looped her arm through Malik's and gave him a nervous smile.

"Are you ready?" he whispered.

Sonya's body trembled as she nodded her head.

"Okay, here we go," Malik said, turning her down the aisle.

All eyes were on her, but Sonya noticed only Dwayne's smoldering gaze. She missed a step, so she pulled her eyes away from Dwayne's to concentrate on what she was doing.

As she neared the first pew, her eyes sought the loving gaze of her mother's. This was the happiest day of her life.

The music blared from the reception room of the Sundial Motel. Sonya stood in the center of the motel and closed her eyes. In one quick swoop, she tossed her bridal bouquet into the crowd of anxious women. When the crowd made an audible gasp, Sonya turned to see Bridget holding the bouquet.

George—dressed in a fine, black tuxedo—stood and applauded. Dwayne elbowed the teenager into silence. The guests roared with laughter.

"Sonya," Sharon whispered, rolling her finger to instruct Sonya to come closer.

"What's wrong?" Sonya asked the obviously excited Sharon.

"I have to tell someone," she whispered, looking around.

"What?" Sonya felt her own excitement mount.

"I wasn't sure until this morning, and I'm waiting until tonight to tell James."

"What?" Sonya grabbed her hand excitedly.

"I'm pregnant."

"No," Sonya and Bridget said in unison.

Sharon and Sonya turned. They didn't realized that Bridget had walked up behind them.

"That's great, Auntie," Bridget said, leaning in to hug Sharon.

"What's great?" James asked, handing a glass of punch to Sharon.

"Oh, I'll tell you later, dear." Sharon winked.

The women laughed at James's puzzled expression. The lights dimmed, and Sonya turned to see her husband.

"I believe this is our dance."

The soft music of "Here and Now" began to play over the PA system. The crowd backed away from the newlyweds just as Malik picked up the microphone to sing their song.

Sonya leaned against Dwayne's frame while she moved in time with his.

"So, Mrs. Hamilton, I guess you're stuck with me for life."

"I have experienced worse," she teased.

Dwayne laughed but then grew serious as he gazed into her eyes. "Are you happy?"

"More than I ever thought possible."

Laura squeezed her mother's hand as she watched her sister glide across the floor. "They make a beautiful couple."

Dorothy patted her youngest daughter's hand. "They sure do. How are you holding up?"

Laura glanced over to Malik and felt a heat evolve in the pit of her stomach. "I'm doing much better."

Dorothy followed the direction of Laura's eyes and smiled. "He seems nice."

Laura squeezed her mother's hand again. "He is nice."

"Do I hear more wedding bells?" Dorothy cocked an eyebrow.

Laura turned back to her mother. "I'm not ready. Malik hasn't pushed the subject, but who knows what the future will bring?"

George handed Bridget a glass of punch. "So you're the next bride."

Bridget shook her head. "Don't count on it being anytime soon. Are you ready for school?"

"I can't believe we are going to spend the next four years apart. I'll be in Washington at Howard University, and you'll be here at Spelman."

"We'll see each other on holidays and some weekends." Bridget promised.

"It still won't be the same."

"Come on, don't look so sad. This is a wedding. We're suppose to be happy." Bridget leaned against him.

George smiled despite himself and gave Bridget a quick kiss.

"I can't believe Sonya bought this motel." Tina glanced around her. "She said this place held some kind of sentimental value."

"It does." Sharon said.

Tina smiled. "Well, you would never recognize the place. The money she spent in remodeling has made this place a beautiful motel."

"Excuse me, will you?" Sharon walked over to James and leaned against him. She couldn't wait until tonight.

"Enjoying yourself?" James smiled.

"I'm having a wonderful time."

James eyed her suspiciously.

"What?" Sharon smiled.

"You're just acting a little strange."

"Well, I do have something I want to tell you."

A loud shout filled the room. Sonya and Dwayne turned toward Sharon and James.

"I guess Sharon told James the good news," Sonya observed.

"Yeah, I guess so."

Sonya looked at him. "You knew?"

"Yeah, Sharon never could keep a secret."

Their song ended while other couples drifted to the dance floor as the next song began to play.

Sonya raced to change her clothes.

"It's about that time." William came and pounded on Dwayne's back.

"Yeah." Dwayne smiled.

"So where're you guys going?" Malik joined the conversation.

"Puerto Rico."

A few of William's men nodded their approval as they gathered around Dwayne.

"Are you going to continue your practice here when you get back?"

Dwayne became curious. "Yes."

William draped his arm around Dwayne's shoulder. "Well, we were wondering if you could handle a few of our cases."

Dwayne laughed while shaking his head. "We'll talk about it when I get back."

"Cool." William smiled.

When Sonya appeared from the elevator, dressed in a pearl-colored pantsuit, Dwayne rushed over to her to take her things. A crowd gathered once again to throw more rice at them. They rushed from the Sundial Motel arm in arm and into the waiting limousine.

Once inside they turned and waved goodbye to the fading crowd.

"I'm glad that's over," Sonya said, slumping against Dwayne.

Dwayne hugged her closer to him. "Now it's just you and me for the next two weeks."

"Mmm, two weeks of fun in the sun."

"Sun?" Dwayne asked shocked. "I don't think so, Mrs. Hamilton. I don't plan on letting you out of that bed."

"Oh? Don't I have a say in this?"

"No."

"Can't I plead my case."

"You don't have a case, Mrs. Hamilton. I plan to leave you totally defenseless."

"Oh," Sonya moaned as he captured her lips in a passionate kiss that promised her more to come.

The use of the Aztec coin in *Defenseless* is purely fictional. To the best of my knowledge there is no such coin in existence or estimated at such a value.

ABOUT THE AUTHOR

Adrianne Byrd resides between her homes in Memphis, TN, Sunnyvale, CA and Marietta, GA. This former entertainer has loved romance novels half her life and had started writing professionally before finishing high school. Her goals are to continue to write novels and start a budding career at screen-writing.

Special Thanks

This book would never have been written had it not been for the list of the following. God bless many of us with friends to love us along the way. I was blessed with angels: My family, Deloris, Channon, Charla, Lawerance and Charles Byrd and Alice Coleman. For support and encouragement: Loretha Lipscomb, Beverly, Kevin and Carnelia Hunt. Raymond Johnson, Lori Moore, Patty Moeller, Charlotte Harris, Sharon Freeman, Tonya Payne, Sonya Ellis, Rhonda Walters, Jeanette McClung, Ron Bower, Curtis Smith, Sonia Durden, Francesca Washington, The Mahoney boys, Patricia and Robert Barrett, GRW Chapter, Bridget Anderson, Angela Benson, Carla Fredd, Carmen Greene, Francis Ray, Joyce Dutton, Charlene Berry, Sandra Chastain. To the best critique group in the world: Shirley Harrison, Adrianne Thompson, and Marcia Kelley.

Look for these upcoming Arabesque titles:

December 1997
VOWS by Rochelle Alers
TENDER TOUCH by Lynn Emery
MIDNIGHT SKIES by Crystal Barouche
TEMPTATION by Donna Hill

January 1998
WITH THIS KISS by Candice Poarch
NIGHT SECRETS by Doris Johnson
SIMPLY IRRESISTIBLE by Geri Guillaume
A NIGHT TO REMEMBER by Niqui Stanhope

February 1998
HEART OF THE FALCON by Francis Ray
A PRIVATE AFFAIR by Donna Hill
RENDEZVOUS by Bridget Anderson
I DO! A Valentine's Day Collection